At

iol

D0567103

A DEADLY HABIT

A PENELOPE SANTUCCI MYSTERY

A DEADLY HABIT

ANDREA SISCO

FIVE STAR
A part of Gale, Cengage Learning

Nobles County Library
407 12th Street, PO Box 1049
Worthington, MN 56187
31315002118425

GALE
CENGAGE Learning™

Detroit • New York • San Francisco • New Haven, Conn • Waterville, Maine • London

GALE
CENGAGE Learning

Copyright © 2009 by Andrea J. Sisco.
Five Star Publishing, a part of Gale, Cengage Learning.

ALL RIGHTS RESERVED
This novel is a work of fiction. Names, characters, places and incidents are either the product of the author's imagination, or, if real, used fictiously.
No part of this work covered by the copyright herein may be reproduced, transmitted, stored, or used in any form or by any means graphic, electronic, or mechanical, including but not limited to photocopying, recording, scanning, digitizing, taping, Web distribution, information networks, or information storage and retrieval systems, except as permitted under Section 107 or 108 of the 1976 United States Copyright Act, without the prior written permission of the publisher.
The publisher bears no responsibility for the quality of information provided through author or third-party Web sites and does not have any control over, nor assume any responsibility for, information contained in these sites. Providing these sites should not be construed as an endorsement or approval by the publisher of these organizations or of the positions they may take on various issues.
Set in 11 pt. Plantin.
Printed on permanent paper.

LIBRARY OF CONGRESS CATALOGING-IN-PUBLICATION DATA

Sisco, Andrea.
    A deadly habit : a Penelope Santucci mystery / by Andrea
Sisco. — 1st ed.
      p. cm.
    ISBN-13: 978-1-59414-795-1 (hardcover : alk. paper)
    ISBN-10: 1-59414-795-7 (hardcover : alk. paper)
    1. Probation officers—Fiction. I. Title.
PS3619.I79D43 2009
813'.6—dc22   2009010447

Published in 2009 in conjunction with Tekno Books and Ed Gorman.

Printed in the United States of America
2 3 4 5 6 7 13 12 11 10 09

To Connie Anderson, my best friend for over thirty years. You have supported and encouraged me from the very beginning. Thank you!

ACKNOWLEDGMENTS

A book does not just happen. There are many people involved in its birth. Thank you to Gordon Aalborg for his patience, encouragement, wit and wisdom during the editing process. He's the editor this book needed. Jeanne Fredricks, agent extraordinaire, was introduced to an orphan author and in her kindness, gave me a home. My husband Bob Pike encouraged me to persevere, believing good things would happen. He was right. My son Guy Wegener was a valued reader whose laughter and encouragement kept me going. Karen Saunders and Rosemary Heim were among the first readers and their input is greatly appreciated. Kathleen Baldwin was "spot on" in all her suggestions that made Pen come alive and really live her "take-no-hostages" attitude. Her suggestions made Pen's story so much better. My mother, Shirley Christensen, deserves all the credit for my love of reading and writing and for my deep faith in God. Thank you, everyone.

CHAPTER ONE

"It's been seventeen years since my last confession, Father." I didn't bother to add "and seven months and thirteen days." It didn't make a difference since I'm not Catholic.

"May the Lord be on your lips and on your mind and in your heart." The priest's blessing implied that it was my turn to speak.

"Ah, since I haven't done this in such a long time, do I have to go all the way back, Father? Because that's a *whole* lot of sinning to cover."

Seventeen plus years of my sins could keep us both in this teensy confessional long into my next paycheck. I didn't have the time.

"Yes, I imagine it could be," the priest's voice held a tinge of resignation. I'd bet his gut told him that this confession would take awhile.

With a sigh I said, "I don't think I can remember everything. Would hitting the high points do?"

"Just do the best you can," he replied.

"Perhaps I could lump some of the sins together, you know, organize them into categories."

My pesky obsessive compulsive tendencies were relentless, even in the midst of a crisis.

"However you want to do it, my child." I could almost hear his unspoken order, "just do it."

"Well, I haven't kept the Sabbath in years; I've disobeyed my parents on a regular basis, had impure thoughts—and still do."

I had a rapid-fire rhythm going, so I hung with it. "I gossip. You could call me the queen of gossip. I don't do it to be nasty; I just like to be in the know. So maybe that doesn't count, do you think?"

I took a deep breath and didn't wait for his answer. "Oh, and I've always had a garbage mouth. I used to take the name of the Lord in vain, daily. Except for those rare occasions when I didn't actually interact with other people. I don't curse anymore, at least, I try not to."

I'd read somewhere that cursing reflects a speaker's limited vocabulary. In order to express themselves, they resort to foul language. Translation: people who swear are common. I am a lot of things, but I emphatically reject common.

My left eye twitched. I'd run out of trivial offenses and would have to move on to sins that couldn't be overlooked quite so easily. There were transgressions in my history that even saying the rosary as penance wouldn't cover, not in this lifetime.

I continued, "Umm, I've had sex with a man I wasn't married to. At least, not at the time. The marrying came later. I don't want you to get the idea I'm a slut, excuse me, Father, a loose woman. But I promise, I won't do that anymore either. The sex I mean."

"That's unbecoming too?" he asked.

Ah, a priest with an attitude. Since I didn't have a ready reply, or at least one that resembled respectful, I let it go. For all my sins and lapses of sound judgment, I didn't want this particular priest to think poorly of me. Not now.

"Bed hopping could lead to killer diseases." And I had too many things left on my to-do list to mess with premature death.

And then there was Ma. If my mother ever found out I had premarital sex . . . well let's just say, Ma's wrath trumped God's any day of the week.

The confessional became eerily quiet.

"Continue, my child," the priest urged.

Sheer determination mixed with desperation propelled me to the real reason I found myself packed in this tiny box, sweating like a pig. And I hate to sweat. Not only do I hate to sweat; I don't even like to glisten.

The cramped confessional increased my anxiety, so I blurted, "I committed a felony. A burglary. And during the burglary I found a dead man. He'd been murdered. But you have to believe me, Father, I didn't kill him."

I heard the priest's sharp intake of breath through the thin partition. A murder always adds excitement to a confession. It must have been his first murder of the day.

Suddenly, the seriousness of my situation overwhelmed me. My head dipped toward my chest ever so slightly. "Father, I can't say his death made me unhappy. But like I said, all I did was find the body. I didn't kill him. But it's a safe bet that the cops are looking for me." As an afterthought I added, "Father, just because I committed that other felony, the burglary, it doesn't mean I'm a criminal."

The silence hung, suspended in the confessional, like a bad note. I sucked in my breath and waited. And waited.

Astonishment echoed through the grill from the priest's side of the partition. "Oh, my goodness! Is that you, Penelope?"

My breath erupted from deep in my throat like an asthmatic wheeze. Father Daniel Kopecky couldn't possibly remember that gawky little kid from the neighborhood after all these years!

Beads of perspiration formed on my forehead and rolled down my cheeks.

I hadn't counted on Father Daniel recognizing me. The way I saw it, I could do one of two things: stay and talk, or bolt. Somehow *my* best interest didn't seem well served by randomly discussing my current predicament with anyone, including a

11

priest. Especially a priest. Anonymity is always the safer choice. Running was the reasonable alternative. Unfortunately, I'm rarely reasonable.

Since my options were limited, I went with the truth. "Yeah, it's me, Father Daniel."

Father Daniel's hands beat together in a happy clap. "Penelope. You've come to play your old game of 'I want to be a Catholic' with me?" His laugh started low in his throat and rose in pitch until it sounded like a drunken cackle.

It was then I realized Father Daniel thought my visit, after years of absence, was a form of greeting. Like the old days, when I would sneak into his church and play the good and faithful Roman Catholic confessing made-up sins.

How did I get myself into this mess? I'd never intended to become a criminal, never thought I'd be a suspect in a murder. I'd been raised in a blue-collar enclave of northeast Minneapolis (we call it Nordeast.) We had career day in high school, but no one from the criminal underworld was invited to the festivities.

No, my headlong dive into crime was born out of necessity. Or so I rationalized.

"Now you talk to me, Penelope Santucci. I'm an old man." He cleared his throat, then continued, "A busy old man. If you've come to spin more of your bizarre yarns after all these years, you'd better say so now." He coughed, a deep gurgle rising in his throat.

When I didn't answer immediately he said, "Penelope?"

"Yes, Father. I, I just happened to be in the neighborhood and thought I'd stop in." *Forgive me, Father, for I have lied.*

"I didn't think I'd ever hear from my little wanna-be Catholic again. Ah yes, you certainly made confession an interesting experience."

"Really? I did?"

Even with desperation *and* uncertainty nipping at my heels, I really wanted to know what he thought about that little girl of yesteryear.

"If your family had been a member of my parish, I would have spoken to your mother about the ideas you got from all those trashy novels she allowed you to read."

Ma encouraged reading and I benefited greatly from that encouragement. Somehow I didn't think of *A Tree Grows In Brooklyn* or *Lady Chatterley's Lover* as trash. But I suppose they were novels better suited to adults than ten-year-old children.

I don't think Ma knew just how "adult" some of them were.

Yeah, I had a picture of Father Daniel Kopecky giving Mary Santucci "what for." My money was on Ma.

Father Daniel continued, "After you'd read some book, you'd come to confession and tell this bored priest about your sins of promiscuity and fornication."

Red heat climbed up my neck and burned in my cheeks. "I didn't think you would remember me."

"How could I forget? No one in my parish had your imagination. Those were some wild lies you told." He chuckled. "Do you remember coming dressed like a nun and play-acting that you'd been martyred? I especially liked the nun's habit you constructed of bed sheets covered with yellow daises." His playful laugh made me smile.

I squeezed my eyes shut and visualized the child I'd been, a lost girl wishing so hard to be a part of something greater than herself. "I didn't think of them as lies. Confession was like playing house, only I played church."

"Of course you didn't think of your tall tales as lies. You were a child." He switched gears. "Now what do you say we get out of here and go to the rectory, have a cup of coffee and talk about why Penelope Santucci . . ."

"Please, Father, could you call me, Pen? Penelope sounds so stuffy—it's never really fit me."

Over the years, I must have asked Ma a hundred times why she and Dad named me Penelope. She'd smile sweetly, pat my hand and say, "Penelope is a beautiful name." There is absolutely no accounting for bad taste and Ma is the Queen Mother of bad taste.

The priest responded, "Of course, dear, I'll try to remember. Now, as I was saying, let's find out why Pen Santucci has returned to the neighborhood." The partition abruptly slapped shut.

I leaned against the hard confessional wall and rubbed my burning eyes. How could I possibly tell the priest what had happened?

A sharp rap on the door startled me. I sat up and adjusted my shirt before saying, "I'm coming."

I lied to the old priest when I was ten, but I'm older and I know what a lie is, how serious a lie can be—especially to the police. In some states lying about murder can get you five to ten. If you're convicted of that murder you can get life, or, I shuddered, death, courtesy of the state. Thank goodness Minnesota doesn't execute murderers.

I dragged myself from the bench, stood up, threw my shoulders back, plastered a weak smile on my face, yanked open the confessional door and faked a cheerful attitude. "Hello, Father Daniel. It's been a long time."

CHAPTER TWO

Father Daniel ushered me into his comfortable but worn-around-the-edges study. Books and magazines covered every available surface and small stacks of paper, pens, and pencils were scattered across his desktop.

The sofa, chairs, and tables all screamed early seventies. It was a room held hostage in a time warp and probably wouldn't be released anytime soon.

We sat in matching wing back chairs flanking the unused fireplace. Father Daniel briefly reminisced about the "good old days" while I studied him.

He seemed to be the same jovial priest from my childhood—age had replaced the tall, strong, athletic man I remembered with an older model, late sixties I suspected, complete with sagging muscles, an expanded waistline and thinning gray hair. His bushy eyebrows curled in minuscule ringlets at the arch. But his eyes were still a vibrant blue and sparkled with mischief.

He poured coffee from an old, chipped pot. "You haven't changed Penelo . . . Pen."

Reaching for the cup he offered, I said, "No, I always wanted to be blond, tall, and willowy, but five-two is a stretch and I guess I'm destined to be a brunette who's on the cuddly side of perfect."

He laughed heartily, slapping his knee. "You always wanted to be a Catholic. Did you ever convert?"

Slowly I brought the cup to my lips, mumbling, "No, I never did."

Father Daniel dropped four sugar cubes, one after the other, into his cup. Not hard to imagine how his waistline had spread over the years. Thoughtfully he said, "You and your sister were the only Italian kids I ever met who weren't Catholic."

"True." I nodded. "We were the only Protestant Italians in an all Polish Catholic neighborhood."

He clucked his sympathy. "I suppose it was tough at times."

I shrugged remembering all the occasions when I'd felt left out of things. My friends would walk arm-in-arm to the parochial school while I went in the opposite direction to the public school, alone. And since I wasn't a Catholic I'd missed out on the opportunity to dress up like a bride for my first communion. Oh, how I had longed to be the center of attention for an afternoon and parade around in a gossamer white dress. "My cross to bear, Father."

"So what have you been doing these past years?"

I'd taken a drink of coffee and the rich brown brew caught in my throat. I carefully placed the cup on the table. "You know, college, job, marriage."

Father Daniel slapped the palm of his hand against his thigh again. "You got married! Wonderful. Any little ones?"

My throat tightened. "No. No *little* ones."

"And your husband, what does he do?"

The subject matter became headier. "Uh, that's why I came to confession, Father."

His bushy brows knitted, "Go on."

Picking up my coffee cup, I avoided the priest's eyes. "We were getting a divorce."

Despair settled like a storm cloud over his face and I could almost hear his thoughts. Here was another break down of the nuclear family. *Where would it end? Amen.*

Father Daniel placed his cup in the saucer, turned to me and asked, "You *were* getting a divorce?"

My gaze focused on a spot just to the right of the priest's head. "Yeah."

"You've reconciled then?" he asked, hope gushing out.

I rubbed my neck and replied, "Not exactly."

"Well, you either are or you aren't. Which is it?"

"We're not reconciling." My eyes met his. "My husband is dead."

He blinked twice, his face oozed sympathy. "I'm sorry for your loss. Was it recent?" He leaned forward and cupped my small hands in his large gnarled ones.

"Yes, if you call sometime within the last twelve hours or so recent. Then his death was very recent."

His hands shook and his body jerked upright, like he'd been shot from a cannon. But he still held my hands firmly in his. "I don't understand."

"You had to be there," I mumbled.

"When *exactly* did he die?"

With a shrug I said, "Near as I can tell, maybe last night."

A frown covered his face. "You want me to bury him, then? *He* was a Catholic, was he?"

Our conversation wasn't just going downhill it was going over a cliff. I looked directly into his eyes again. "No, Father Daniel. I don't want you to be sorry or to bury him, or anything else. He was pond scum, a bottom feeder, a shark. I just don't have an adequate name for what he was. What I want is help."

"Help? Help with what?"

"My husband is dead and the police are going to think I killed him."

Father Daniel dropped my hands like he'd touched *the* burning bush and asked, "Why on earth would the police think you killed him?" His eyes narrowed as he leaned slightly forward.

"Maybe I should ask, *did* you kill your husband?"

I was appalled that a man of God would entertain the thought that I, Penelope Santucci, could be guilty of murder. Technically I was only guilty of theft and burglary. The difference might be small, but there was a difference. A gargantuan difference! The difference meant probation rather than a life of bed, board and three squares on the state's dime.

My sigh exploded like a bomb. Then again, why wouldn't Father Daniel consider me a possible murderer? A lot of normal looking people went around killing. There are an ever-increasing number of sociopaths running loose. I should know. As a probation officer for a large metropolitan county in Minnesota, I've worked with a lot of them. Some are clients. A few are co-workers. Then there are the judges.

I looked him square in the eye. "No, I didn't kill my husband. Oh, I fantasized about it. But dreams don't count. At least they didn't the last time I checked."

"Then your confession was real, not make-believe." He finally got it. *Nothing lost on God's warrior.*

My head bobbed up and down in agreement. "I don't have an alibi. I was home alone all night."

"Murder." He shook his head.

"Yeah, I found a statue covered with blood next to his body. The back of his head was caved in. Obviously the wound wasn't self-inflicted. Paul was a lot of things, but he definitely wasn't a masochist."

"When did you find him?"

I glanced at my watch. "Earlier this morning. When I broke into the house."

"You what?"

I flung my arms outward in supplication. "It's okay! Well it's probably not okay. But it's my house, or it was my house before we separated."

Excitement erupted from every weary muscle in my body. "Hey, it's my house again!" A moan escaped and I held my head in my hands. "Another reason the cops will think I killed Paul." I peered through my fingers.

"Wait one minute, Penelope Santucci. Oh, I suppose it's not Santucci anymore. Your name I mean."

Still holding my head in my hands, staring at the floor, I mumbled, "I didn't change it when we got married."

"You're one of those modern women? A feminist?" He made the word feminist sound like a disease.

My shoulder muscles tightened. I looked up. "My husband is . . ." I shook my head. It was difficult thinking of Paul in the past tense. "My husband *was* a criminal defense attorney. We . . . occasionally came into contact professionally. I really didn't want the same name."

I sat up, rubbed the back of my neck and noticed that Father Daniel's eyes had a glazed look.

He leaned back in his chair, shifting his bulky form. "Why did you break into your own house? Didn't you have a key?"

"Oh, I had a key. I made an extra one before we separated. But Paul had the locks changed. Our divorce was messy. Paul used every dirty trick to prevent me from getting my fair share."

"Pen, stop! Don't elaborate. It confuses me." He threw his hands upward. "Stick to the facts!"

"Okay, okay. Just a little editorial sidebar." I paused to collect my thoughts. "He had some of my personal belongings and wouldn't give them to me, so I broke into the house to get them."

His brows furrowed in confusion. "How did you get in?"

"Through a window. He'd left one unlatched," *Father, forgive me for I have lied, again.*

Once you've altered the truth, it gets easier and easier. But I didn't think this was the right time to tell a priest about my

19

newly developed talent. Somehow I doubted he'd understand my need to know how to execute the perfect burglary. Except in this case it wasn't perfect. I'd found my husband's dead body. *There's always something to foul up a good plan.*

"What about going through the Court, Pen?"

"The Court? I work for the Court. It's a crap shoot at best."

Father Daniel's brows arched in surprise. "I feel like I'm attending the Mad Hatter's party."

My fingers tapped a beat on the chair arm. "I know, Father, and I'm sorry. I'll stick to the facts. I do this very well at work."

He leaned back into his chair and gripped its arms like he might be thrown from it, like an inexperienced bull rider. "I certainly hope so."

I ignored his response. "So, after I broke into the house, I collected my belongings and put them in my car. When I returned to give the house a once over, I passed the den and saw my first edition of *A is for Alibi* on the desk. *My* book, Father, and a very valuable one. No way was I going to leave without it."

He ran his fingers through his hair and shook his head in disbelief. "You stayed at a murder scene for a book?"

Father Daniel obviously didn't understand the magnitude of Sue Grafton's first novel. "I didn't know it was a murder scene. Yet. Books, Father. All my beautiful first editions on *his* shelves. So I took them. That's when I saw him."

"Paul?"

"Dead. I'd set a stack of books on the corner of Paul's desk and something caught my eye. I glanced down and saw a foot peeking around the corner."

"What did you do?"

"Screamed."

His eyes squeezed shut, a look of pain shot across his deeply wrinkled face. "Then what?" He sounded a tad bit exasperated.

"Oh, you want a sequence of events."

"That would be nice." His patience was long gone.

"Paul was on the floor in a pool of blood. I knelt down . . ." My throat tightened. Envisioning Paul's battered body was hard.

"Take your time." His melodious voice soothed me a little.

I nodded and forced myself to continue. "I felt for a pulse. None. Nada. That's when I saw his favorite statue. You know the one, the guy sitting, with his chin resting on his hand . . ."

"You mean *The Thinker?*"

"Yeah, that's the one. It's funny. Paul never stopped to think much about anything deep or worthwhile, yet he really liked that stupid statue."

Father Daniel gave me what I began thinking of as the "stop rambling look," urging me to go on with my story.

"Anyway, the statue was next to his body. I picked it up before it registered in my mind as the murder weapon." A small moan escaped from my lips. "I panicked, Father. I mean, I watch television. I work in law enforcement. I know how stupid it is to pick up a murder weapon. There's no excuse for what I did. I just freaked out."

My left eye twitched again. "I couldn't leave my fingerprints on the statue, so I grabbed a towel from the bathroom and wiped it down."

Father Daniel flinched. "Yes, I know I tampered with evidence. But I didn't want my fingerprints on that statue. There wasn't anything I could do for Paul. He was already dead, so I grabbed the books and left the house as fast as I could."

Father Daniel leaned forward, interest etched his face as he asked, "And then?"

"Why I called the police, of course. I disguised my voice." His shocked look catapulted me into defense mode. "If I'd given my name it would be like asking to be arrested. I might just as well have driven to the police station and begged for the silver bracelets."

His face fell. "Why did you call them at all? Especially if you were concerned about being arrested."

My voice cracked. "Paul was a stinker, but nobody deserves to lie in their own blood like that!" I shivered. "I didn't know what else to do, so I started driving around. After awhile I found myself in the old neighborhood. I parked in front of the church."

"And what made you decide to come in?"

My voice broke. "When I saw you walk up the church steps, I decided to go to confession. I figured I could talk about what happened but still be anonymous."

His bushy eyebrows arched. "And I ruined your charade."

"Yeah." Terror punched me in the stomach. "You can't divulge what you learn in confession, can you?"

He stopped me with a raised hand. "No, I can't."

Relief flooded through me. "Good. Now what are we going to do?"

Father Daniel stared at me in disbelief. "What do you mean, what are *we* going to do?"

I threw my hands upward. "About finding out who killed Paul. Hey, I don't want to go to prison, Father. I don't look good in stripes. They make me look hippy."

He ignored my feeble stab at humor.

"Pen, this is a police matter. It's not a situation where a priest can have any impact."

I jumped up from the chair. "But Father Daniel I need help! The police won't do anything. The cops will take the easy way out, pin the murder on the estranged wife. Haven't you watched any movies lately? Maybe *Lifetime For Women* on television?" I scowled at him.

He fanned the air with his hand, motioning me to sit down. "What can an old priest do to help?"

"I don't know." I sat down, hard, and leaned forward.

"Father, I don't have anybody that I trust."

"Surely there's someone who can help you, Pen?"

"There isn't, Father Daniel. Most of our friends, Paul's and mine, were originally his. When we separated, he took custody of them. And my friends . . . well, I mean, who wants a bitter and smart lawyer harassing you just because you're a friend of his former wife?"

His nose wrinkled in disgust. "He sounds nasty."

"That's generous." I sniffed loudly.

"You have no friends, at all?"

"A few. But they won't be able to keep quiet."

"Surely . . ."

"Father, trust me on this. My friends are great, but they love to blab and they tend to have a flair for the dramatic."

Now *his* left eye twitched. "I know, I know. They're a lot like me. But, well, this would be too juicy not to share." I slumped over, tried to fight my frustration. "I'm innocent, Father. I don't want to go to jail."

He paused, "You've convinced me, Pen."

My heart soared. "Have any suggestions?"

"You need a lawyer, and I have the perfect man for you."

Yeah, just what I needed, another man in my life. And a lawyer to boot.

CHAPTER THREE

Fear and anxiety rode shotgun on the drive to my condo in the artsy Uptown area of Minneapolis. As I cruised past my building I searched the area for cops. There weren't any squad cars, marked or unmarked, loitering around. Perhaps I'd been given a reprieve. *There is a God!* My date with handcuffs would wait for another day. I hoped.

I drove my prized possession, a 1973, mint condition, ivory-colored Karmenghia, the only thing of value salvaged from my marriage, around to the garages at the back of the building.

I fumbled for the remote, located it under my seat, hit the button, scanned the area again for the boys in blue and drove inside.

I pulled out the box of things I'd taken from Paul's house, closed the garage door, and headed toward my condo. Balancing the box on my hip, I unlocked the door and stepped into a brightly-lit lobby. Across the lobby a tattered OUT OF ORDER sign covered the elevator door. So, what else is new? Maybe the building manager should hang a permanent sign and call it a day. It would prevent false hope from rising in the residents' hearts.

I trudged up two flights of stairs, contemplating the number of calories I'd burn. Exercise is not on my preferred activity list so when forced to participate, my primary interest is the calorie quotient.

At my door I saw a small white card sticking out of the

doorjamb. I wedged the box between my body and the wall and pulled out the card before my traditional struggle with the lock. I made a mental note to put WD 40 on my shopping list.

Inside, I shoved the box into an empty corner, dropped my purse on the kitchen counter, and examined the card.

"No! No! No!" My right foot beat a fast rhythm, like a one-legged flamenco dancer.

The card read Sergeant Clifford Masters, Minneapolis Police Department, Homicide Division. Turning it over, I attempted to decipher the scrawl covering the backside. This guy should take a handwriting class. I guessed he wanted me to contact him ASAP.

"Not on a bet!"

I tossed the card, watched it sail across the counter like a Frisbee and asked, "And who let him in anyway?" He'd probably rung every bell until someone buzzed him in. "So much for a safe and secure building."

I dug in my pocket for the telephone number Father Daniel had given me during our "keep-Pen-out-of-prison" planning session, picked up the phone, and began punching buttons.

The phone rang several times before a deep voice answered, "Law office."

"I'd like to talk to Mr. Marco Silva please."

"This is Marco Silva."

"You answer your own phone?" The words popped out before I could stop them. Sometimes there is no filtering system between my brain and my mouth.

"My secretary's out sick. You think a lawyer who answers his own phone isn't a good one?"

"I didn't mean that." *Well, maybe I did.*

"What do you want?" He sounded annoyed. But then people are often annoyed when I speak without thinking. It's a nasty habit. I'll address it. Later. Oh yeah, I'm a procrastinator too.

"Father Daniel Kopecky gave me your number. He said you could help me."

His voice softened. "Ah, Father Daniel. How is the good Father these days?"

"Fine. He's fine," I mumbled. I wanted to get on with things.

"What did Father Daniel want me to help you with, Ms. . . . ?"

"Santucci. Pen Santucci," I said. "Mr. Silva, the police are looking for me."

"Why?"

"They want to talk to me about my husband's murder."

There was a long silence before he replied, "I see. Perhaps you'd better come to my office so we can discuss this, Ms. Santucci. I'm assuming you're not in custody?"

"No, and I'd really like to maintain that status. Ah, when can I see you? Right away?" I sounded impatient, but who wouldn't be under the circumstances? I'd had a tough day, and it was only just after one o'clock.

"I have appointments until five. Can you be here then?"

"Of course." Hey, the cops probably wanted me for murder. Keeping an appointment with a criminal defense attorney quickly shot to the top of *my* priority list.

He gave me the address and warned, "And do NOT, under any circumstances, speak with the police before we've talked. It's not in your best interest."

"I understand." *I'm not stupid.*

"Five o'clock then."

I cleared my throat. "Mr. Silva, is there a charge for this consultation?"

He paused. "No charge for the initial consultation, Ms. Santucci.

"Thanks." A good deal is the preferred deal. And knowing the rules up front contributed greatly to my comfort level.

26

After hanging up, I paced and for the first time since finding Paul's body, I thought, really thought about his death. I wanted desperately to feel *something*. Some sadness, or regret maybe. But I didn't. At least now he couldn't make my life miserable anymore. Or could he? The fact that the police wanted to talk to me suggested I could be in deep trouble. Even in death Paul could make me miserable.

Fortunately I narrowed the suspect list and was pretty sure I knew who had killed Paul. Unfortunately, I also knew it would be difficult to prove. It might be impossible. I shivered. But I'd give it my all because the alternative was a jail cell. An eight-by-eight box for the rest of my life. And the food! Creamed corn, cream of wheat, creamed peas, creamed everything. Just thinking about it put five pounds on my already ample thighs.

Hopefully, Marco Silva would take my case. I knew from the office scuttlebutt that he came with a high price tag. Yes, he was a high-priced, high-profile lawyer who could afford to pick and choose the people he represented. But then Paul had been a pretty high-profile citizen. And that translated into good advertising for any lawyer, including Marco Silva.

If he took my case, I didn't plan on telling him I'd be contributing to my own defense. Experience and some latent pathology, probably stemming from my childhood, told me I might be the only one that could clear my name. Well, Marco Silva didn't have to know all my moves. A girl's gotta have some secrets.

I kept myself occupied until it was time to leave for Marco Silva's office. Just before I walked out the door, I ran a brush through my hair and pulled it into a ponytail.

The full-length mirror emphasized my disheveled appearance, so I changed shirts, pulled on a clean pair of jeans, praying they would fit. It's my Italian genes. Every year it gets harder not to look full-figured. Eventually I'll just plaster the pasta directly on my thighs. It'll be faster, just not as much fun.

I sucked in my stomach, held my breath, and tugged up the zipper before I slipped into my shoes, raced out the door and down the two flights of stairs. *A few more calories, gone with the wind.*

When I reached the bottom, I rounded the corner, heard someone humming and abruptly stopped. "Oh, no!"

A short, stocky man, probably in his mid thirties, wearing aviator sunglasses and a rumpled sport coat, about ten years out of date, leaned up against the inside door, trying unsuccessfully to look cool.

A toothpick rolled slowly from one side of his mouth to the other. Someone had let the cops in. Allowing strangers free access to the building was definitely an issue for the next association meeting. I'd bring it up if I weren't in jail.

The cop stepped away from the door, took the toothpick from his mouth and flicked it across the lobby. What a slob! This wasn't the Ritz, but it was my home.

He scrutinized me as he hitched up his sagging pants and ran his fingers through thinning red hair. Yeah, he reeked of cop. *Tough break.*

He took a step toward me. "Ms. Santucci? Penelope Santucci?"

To lie or not to lie. Easy choice.

His voice became harsh. "You there, you didn't hear me, huh? You Penelope Santucci?"

As he walked toward me, I took a step backward and frantically searched my purse for the mace I hoped was there.

The guy looked like a cop, but you can never be sure about appearances.

I ordered, "Don't come near me! I'll mace you!"

He stopped short and held out his hands. "Whoa! No need

to get so touchy." He hesitated, then took a step closer. "Come on, you're Penelope Santucci. I recognize you."

That got my attention. I stared at him while I withdrew my empty hand from the bottomless pit of my purse. "How?"

He snorted a laugh. "Picture. Personnel files at County."

Boy, I'd bet a month's salary that tongues were wagging at the probation office. There's nothing like a new tragedy to get the gossip mill going.

I nodded glumly as I slid the strap over my shoulder. I was made. You can try to avoid the cops, but it's much more difficult when they have your photo. "Who are you?"

He pulled out his identification. "Sergeant Clifford Masters."

"Clifford Masters? Really?" He was *not* what I had imagined. He nodded. "Yeah."

My eyes left his ID and shot back to his small, distrustful eyes. "What do you want?"

"To talk about your husband's murder."

I clutched at my chest. "Murder? My husband?"

He snickered wickedly. "You trying to tell me you're surprised?"

"Sergeant, what *are* you talking about?"

"Come on Ms. Santucci, cut the act. We have your voice on the 911 tape." His snicker became a sneer. "You attempted to disguise your voice. If it becomes necessary we'll get a voice expert. Make a positive ID. It'll take some time but with the sophisticated equipment we have . . ." He rubbed his hands together.

The jerk enjoyed his game of torture.

Voice prints. I hadn't considered that. I wasn't very good at this crime game. But if I wanted to stay out of jail, I'd have to get better at it and fast. There is no margin for error when it comes to murder and the Minneapolis Police. They are *that* good. I could already hear my jail cell door clanking shut.

"I get the idea." My left eye twitched. I might need to have that looked at.

I'd have to confess to finding Paul's body and making that telephone call soon enough. For now, I needed a story to buy me time. "Hey, I just got home. I haven't exactly had time to call, know what I mean?"

He nodded. He possessed a limited repartee of nonverbal communication.

"That was from this morning," he said. "You didn't call back. I'm here to personally escort you."

"Worried about me skipping?" I groaned. How stupid. I'd learned a few things over the years, but not enough to know when to shut up. A murder suspect with an attitude can be a dangerous thing. For the suspect.

He shrugged. "You're not exactly distraught over your husband's death are you?" He waited. "Come on, Ms. Santucci, the sooner we go down to the station, the sooner we're done."

I assessed my predicament. Marco Silva had warned me not to talk to the cops. With his receptionist gone and a client in the office, he probably wouldn't answer his phone. I'd have to leave a message that he probably wouldn't get in time. And I'd end up in the slammer because Marco Silva was understaffed. *What to do, Lord, what to do?*

"Where are we going? Which office?" Like I didn't know.

"Downtown. Homicide."

"Do I have to?" I whined.

He shrugged again. I took it as a yes.

I figured physically fighting him was out of the question. He outweighed me by a lot. All he had to do was grab me, fall down, and it'd be over. It didn't look like I had a choice.

"I have to lock up. You can wait here or come upstairs with me."

Impatience covered his face. "We really should be going, Ms. San—"

I planted my feet firmly and stopped him mid-sentence. "Am I under arrest?"

"No."

"Well, then, I am not leaving my house open for just anyone to walk in." I tossed my head in what I considered a haughty manner. "It seems someone in the building is indiscriminately allowing anyone and everyone free access."

I started up the steps and sneaked a peek over my shoulder. He was following me. And he was frowning.

"Make it snappy," he ordered.

"You on the clock or what?" My pace deliberately slowed. *Defiance, another character flaw. I have a million.*

His lack of response probably had more to do with his shortness of breath from climbing two flights of stairs than merely ignoring a smart mouthed murder suspect. I could hear him gasping for breath. How could he possibly catch the bad guys if he had trouble walking up two flights of stairs? Escape began to look better with each step he took.

I opened my door, which I hadn't bothered to lock. I'd have to reconsider that habit with all the unauthorized traffic in the building.

I said, "Stay here. I'll just be a minute." My bag hit the counter with a dull thud.

When he started to follow me I skidded to a stop, whirled around, and ordered, "Stay there!" He stayed.

"Ms. San . . ."

"Where would I go? The back door is there," I pointed at a door, fully visible from where he stood. "Satisfied?"

"Hurry up!"

Yes, sir! I rushed to my bedroom, collapsed on the bed, and covered my eyes with my hands. This wasn't part of the plan.

31

And I hate it when things don't go according to plan. It's inconvenient.

I considered my situation for about three seconds before I jumped up and grabbed a spare set of keys from my bureau drawer.

My purse was in the kitchen but Masters was probably just naive enough to believe a woman wouldn't leave home without her bag. Hey, it's not like it was my American Express card. I raised the window slowly, praying the creaking of old wood against wood wouldn't give me away, removed the screen, tipped out the emergency fire ladder and scuttled down the steps.

As I backed the Ghia out of the garage I heard yelling. Looking up I saw Sergeant Masters waving his arms wildly from my bedroom window. He didn't look like a happy camper. Tough! He should know better than to trust a murder suspect.

I revved the engine, put the car in gear and yelled, "I'll see you later. I have to talk to my lawyer! I'm sorry, but it's important." *It was my freedom.*

I'd probably land in jail over this stunt. Hey, I'd probably land in jail for Paul's murder. So, later looked better than sooner.

I drove down Hennepin Avenue as if I didn't have a care in the world. *Denial. Ah, how sweet it is.*

CHAPTER FOUR

Marco Silva's office screamed money. He was definitely out of my league.

There wasn't anyone at the front desk, but the office door was open. I called out, "Mr. Silva?"

No one answered, so I inched closer to the door. "Mr. Silva? It's Pen Santucci. You're expecting me."

I peeked inside. Empty. "Interesting."

The office was definitely a man's domain. The massive, wooden desk held papers in small orderly stacks. *Ah, a man after my own compulsive heart.* A carpet of soft beige covered the floor and three chairs fanned out in front of the desk. Cream-colored blinds were drawn to keep out the late afternoon sun. Tasteful prints in warm, muted colors hung on the walls.

I glanced behind me, then sauntered to the desk, leaned over and poked at and separated pages of the neat piles, straining to read them upside down. It's a talent that is useless most of the time.

One stack of papers looked particularly interesting, so I picked them up and casually leafed through them. When I finished I replaced them and picked up another promising pile.

"May I help you?"

The papers tumbled from my hands, and I watched in stunned silence as they covered the desk like a game of fifty-two-card pick-up.

I spun around, clutching at my chest. "You scared the

daylights out of me!"

The tall man's dark eyes burned as he slowly turned his gaze from the scattered papers to scrutinize me. His deep voice held a sharp edge as he said, "You're digging around in *my* office and have the nerve to accuse *me* of scaring the daylights out of *you?* You're lucky I didn't have a gun. I might've shot you."

I snapped, "That would be a little extreme, don't you think?"

He crossed his arms and studied me. "The jury's still out. Did you find what you were looking for?" He nodded toward his desk.

I opted to ignore the question. "You must be Marco Silva."

"I am," he replied tersely. "And now that you have the benefit of knowing who I am, would you care to tell me who you are?"

"I'm Pen Santucci."

"I thought so. Is this," he glanced toward the papers scattered across the desk, "a habit with you, Ms. Santucci?"

Remorse would be a good touch, but after the day I'd had, it was tough to muster it up. "I'm sorry, Mr. Silva. There wasn't anyone around."

"And you thought you'd make yourself at home, check up on my business?"

Give it a rest. I had behaved badly, but a lecture I could get from my mother. I opted for a more docile response. I didn't want him any angrier than he was.

"Mr. Silva, I said I was sorry. It's no excuse, but I'm a curious person. My job brings it out."

Marco Silva brushed past me and tossed a file on top of the desk. "Or it could be a bad habit."

I scowled. "It won't happen again."

"No, it certainly won't."

It seemed like a rhetorical statement so I didn't respond. I doubted that he'd ever leave me alone in his office again anyway.

He directed me to sit down. I did, but the papers scattered

over his desk bothered me. It apparently didn't bother him because he ignored the mess and sat in the chair directly across from me.

I studied Marco Silva. He was tall and muscular, with just enough ripples to give him definition but not enough that he looked like a body builder. His hair was a rich, blue-black and his olive skin was a shade darker than my own. He looked delicious, like the cover of a romance novel.

His deep, mellow voice interrupted my thoughts. "You mentioned your job. Just what is it that you do, Ms. Santucci?"

"I'm a probation officer with Hennepin County." Father Daniel told me that Marco Silva's practice was split between Hennepin and Ramsey Counties. Still, he wandered across the bridge often enough, it was interesting that I hadn't met him before.

"I see," he said icily.

It's tough to admit when I'm wrong, but I needed Marco's help and his annoyance meter hadn't diminished, so I'd grovel a little. "Like I said, I'm sorry, Mr. Silva. There's really no excuse for my behavior. Please accept my apology." I almost gagged.

He cocked his head and studied me. "Enough! Don't go overboard. I accept your apology."

"Thank you." I lowered my eyes, striving for remorse. I must have hit the mark because he relaxed a little.

"Would you like some coffee, Ms. Santucci?"

"No. I've had enough coffee today."

Another lie, dear Lord. There's never enough coffee. But sometimes there are more important things than coffee. My freedom was one of them. Making coffee or even going to get coffee would be time consuming.

I'd left Sergeant Masters hanging out the window of my condo like a battered old flag and it didn't seem likely he'd enjoy the scenery or my prank. Even as we spoke, I could visualize a posse in hot pursuit of my sorry self. *Vengeance is mine sayeth the mad, bad cop.*

"Now, Ms. Santucci, tell me why you think the police want to talk to you about your husband's murder? Maybe I should ask, *has* your husband been murdered?"

I nodded vigorously.

He waited then said, "That was a question, Ms. Santucci. It requires an audible response."

I nodded. "Call me Pen, please."

"Pen." He crossed his left leg over his right. "Maybe you could start from the beginning and tell me what's happened up to this point."

"Okay."

I filled him in on my marriage and subsequent separation from Paul, and continued on through finding his body that morning.

I left out the part where I'd ditched the cops. I didn't feel up to another tongue-lashing.

When I'd finished, he folded his hands, resting them on his crossed legs and said quietly, "The cops always look at the spouse, especially when a divorce is involved."

He certainly knew how to shore up a girl's confidence. "I didn't kill him!"

He was all business. "Let's go back and talk about the trial fixing."

A large, long yawn escaped. "Can't this wait? I'm tired," I complained. "Haven't I told you enough that you can divert the cops and send them to look for the real murderer?"

"I can't waltz into the police station, tell them that you're innocent and expect them to look somewhere else. It doesn't work that way. You know that. Lose the denial!" He emphasized denial. "The police want to see you, and they're not going to wait until you've had your beauty sleep."

I gulped. "I don't expect them to wait."

He smiled knowingly. "Yes, you do. I can see it in your eyes. The police have their own rules. They enjoy inconveniencing people they have reason to believe have committed a crime." He paused. "My job as a lawyer is to make sure my clients aren't inconvenienced *or* convicted." He switched tracks. "Now, tell me about Paul's practice."

It sounded like he might take my case. If he needed more information I could delay my nap.

I stretched my sore muscles and continued, "Paul's practice had always been good, but in the year before we split up, it exploded. The people he represented were big time crooks. Several were well-known dope dealers."

I thought for a moment. "He was gone more, out of town a lot. I never could figure out why, and he gave inconsistent reasons."

"What exactly did he say?"

"That he had to interview people before trial. Investigate things or locate documents. But he had investigators for that kind of work."

"I would think so."

"And I found a lot of cash in our home safe."

"How much?" he asked.

"A hundred thousand dollars."

He gave a low whistle and scribbled on the note pad he'd been writing on for the past hour. "That's a lot of money."

"Yeah. I knew it wasn't petty cash."

Marco uncrossed his legs and leaned forward. "Had he been taking more money than usual from his practice?"

"No."

"Did you ask him about it?"

"I wanted to wait for the right time. But when I decided to talk to him, the money was gone."

"I'm surprised he'd keep that much money around the house, especially if it was gained through criminal means."

"It surprised me too. I chalked it up to arrogance." I leaned closer to Marco Silva. "You probably knew Paul professionally, so you must know it wouldn't occur to him that he might get caught at anything shady. Besides he didn't know I knew the safe's combination." I paused for a moment. "But I really don't know if the money was dirty. Do you think it could be from the stock market? He had always invested heavily."

He scribbled some more. "Doesn't sound like it, not that much anyway. His brokerage records might be helpful. Can you get those?"

"I guess so. I could break into the house again. Or call our broker."

He stared at me and frowned. "I think the broker would be the better choice."

I attempted a contrite look.

"What prompted you to look in the safe in the first place?"

I shrugged. "It was pretty innocent. Our accountant needed some records. Paul was out of town, and I didn't want to wait until he got home."

"You had the combination?"

"I overheard him memorizing it after the safe was installed. He mumbled out loud all the time. I memorized it too. You never know when things like that will come in handy."

His eyes narrowed. "No, you never do. You're pretty resource-ful."

I shifted my position, trying to keep the blood circulating through my lower extremities. "I try to be. It's second nature, working in probation. You're a criminal defense lawyer, you work with dishonest people so you know how it is."

He smiled.

"I'd never found Paul particularly ethical but when his

behavior became even more suspicious, I noticed."

He tapped his pen on the notepad. "And then you heard the phone call?"

"Yes. That was sheer luck. I'd come home early one day and heard him yelling. I eavesdropped."

Marco wrote while he questioned me. "That's a habit too?"

I wanted to stick out my tongue at him but didn't. "He was on the phone, barking out orders. Paul threatened him. A judge! By name. Go figure. We've got some crooked judges throwing cases for money."

"That surprises you?" Marco asked.

"Yes, it surprises me!" I raised my hands. "That stuff only happens in the movies."

Marco stood up and stretched. "Maybe. Remember, you only heard one side of the conversation."

I protested. "I know what I heard!" My anger meter rose steadily. "Things had been going down hill in our relationship for a long time. I didn't approve of the scum-sucking vermin he represented. Threatening a judge was the final straw."

Marco's eyebrows arched, and I knew he was trying to make sense of my value system. It was wrong to buy an acquittal, but it was okay to prowl through someone's private papers. *Does that make me a situational ethicist?*

I spat out, "I have my standards."

The corners of Marco's mouth curved upward slightly as he walked around his desk. He placed the pen and tablet in the center and began straightening the pile of papers I had disturbed earlier. "And you broke into the house to get your stuff and that's when . . ."

"I found Paul's body."

He asked, "Do you have any idea where the money from the safe is now?"

"Not a clue." I sat up straight. "The safe!"

"What about the safe?"

I got up and made for the door. "Let's go to the house and check out the safe. There's got to be something there that will prove I'm innocent." I stopped short. "Or Paul's guilt." I reached for the doorknob.

Marco rounded the desk and reached me in two long strides. He put his hand on my arm, lightly restraining me. "Wait a minute. It's only that easy in the movies, Pen."

"But I need to try," I protested.

He tightened his grip on my arm. "You can't interfere with a crime scene. The police *will* want to talk to you. But it's possible you're not a suspect."

"Oh, yeah! You know that old cliché, if you can convince me of that you could sell me some swamp property, too."

He walked back to his desk, leaned against the edge as he crossed his arms. "Well, there is the matter of my representing you. I haven't said that I would."

That got my attention. "But . . . but Father Daniel said you would."

"Father Daniel told you to call me. *I* decide which cases I take."

I stuck out my chin and announced, "It's the money! I don't have any, so you won't represent me."

Marco looked as though he'd enjoy washing my mouth out with soap. "It's not the money. I have too many cases right now. I'm not sure I can take on something of this magnitude and do justice to you *and* my other clients. I can refer you to someone else," he offered.

I turned my back on him, put my hand on the doorknob, and muttered, "When someone says it's not the money, it's always the money."

He reached me in two steps, whirled me around, and glared

at me. "Ms. Santucci! When I say it's not the money, it's *not* the money!"

Marco was angry. A shot at the truth wouldn't hurt. "Mr. Silva, all I know is Father Daniel said you *always* help a woman in distress and that I should remind you of that if you wouldn't help me."

His body rigid, he said, "*Maybe* we can work something out."

"I don't have much money," I reminded him.

"Some insurance on Paul, perhaps?"

I nodded numbly and gave him a figure. He whistled softly and said, "That would more than cover my fees, if I take the case." He looked thoughtful. "If the insurance company will give it to you. We'd have to get an acquittal first. Those guys don't pay out to the murderer of their well-insured clients."

I shouted, "You've got me charged with murder already? You don't believe me!" I stamped my foot. Reverting to a two-year-old's behavior was a new habit. "I knew it. Father Daniel should reassess his friend's character."

Marco groaned. "It's not important that I believe you're innocent. My job is to provide a solid defense."

I glared at him. "It's important to me."

"Get over it. Anyway, I'm just talking worst case scenario here." He reached out, whirled me around so I faced the door. "Come on."

I dug my heels into the carpet. "Where are we going? I'm not ready to see the cops yet. Especially with someone who thinks I'm a murderer."

I didn't want to tell him I'd already seen the cops. Among other things, I could be charged with Obstruction and Fleeing a Police Officer. Sergeant Masters might be angry enough to dump me in the slammer. Cooling my heels behind bars wasn't what I had in mind. I had far too much to do, not to mention my jail cell avoidance issue. I couldn't help myself from behind bars, and while I felt confident Marco Silva would do all he could, I needed control.

He gave me a gentle shove out the door. I barked, "Hey, wait! You've got to stop manhandling me. Just look at the marks you left on my arm." I stared at a mark-free forearm, willing it to turn a brilliant red.

"I didn't hurt you. But if it helps, I'll tell you I think you're innocent. Happy now?" He didn't wait for an answer. "Now, we're going to your place for some clean clothes. I don't want you staying at home right now. I'm stashing you at Father Daniel's while I set up a meeting with the authorities."

Maybe *this* was a good time to tell Marco about Sergeant Masters. Throw myself on the mercy of the attorney. "Uh, Marco . . ."

"Come on, Pen, let's go. I've got a lot of work to do."

Then it dawned on me. "You really are taking the case!"

Without missing a beat, he ushered me through the doorway, pulling it shut behind us. "Somehow I know I'm going to regret this. I may never see a dime of my fee, and you're probably going to drive me crazy, but yes, I'm taking the case. I *do* owe Father Daniel."

I forgot about my run from the cops because I was too happy. Happy enough that I didn't care if he really believed I was innocent. I'd deal with that problem later. If it became a problem.

CHAPTER FIVE

I was thrilled that Sergeant Masters wasn't lurking around, waiting to nab me when Marco and I arrived at my place. Although it was a good bet he was planning his own gala when he finally got his hands on me. And I knew I wouldn't enjoy the party as much as he would.

Marco parked the car, and we walked up the stairs. His plan to hide me at Father Daniel's, while he negotiated with the police, didn't sound so good to me, but I hadn't been given a vote.

To keep my debating skills honed, I'd test Marco's resolve. It was important to know exactly how formidable an opponent he might be. Before I unlocked the front door I stated, "I really don't want to stay at Father Daniel's place."

He leaned casually against the doorframe. "You don't have a choice."

I struggled with the sticky lock. "There's always a choice."

He gave me a teasing smile. "Consider this a benevolent dictatorship, and I'm the dictator."

I pulled open the door. "Tyrant is the word that comes to mind."

He chuckled and warned, "Be careful or we'll head straight over to Father Daniel's place, without clean clothes. Or, I could throw you to the cops right now and get it over with."

My eyes widened in horror. Clothes and cosmetics were non-negotiable items. No way would I face the cops, or the media, looking less than my best. And with Paul's reputation, there would definitely be media. "Hey, anybody ever tell you you're a bully?"

He laughed heartily. "Not to my face."

It figured.

Well, I had my answer. Marco didn't intimidate easily.

He waited quietly in the living room while I filled a bag with all the necessities I'd need for a couple of days.

As an afterthought I added a romance novel. I'm hooked on romance. Unlike real life, you can always count on the white picket fence standing firm, the knight in shining armor coming to the rescue; and there is always a happy ending. It's a rule. I like the dependability of romance novels.

When I had everything I needed, I looked around my cozy home and left without looking back.

The sound of our footsteps echoed in the still air as we walked to Marco's car. I threw my small bag on the floor of his BMW Z4 and was adjusting my seat belt when he gunned the engine and sped off toward "Nordeast" Minneapolis.

The drive to Father Daniel's was far too quiet for my taste. It made me edgy. The entire day made me edgy—and when I get edgy I want a cigarette. Never mind that I haven't had one in three years. I doubt the craving ever goes away. *Another cross to bear.*

Instead of a cigarette, I pulled some original flavor Carefree bubble gum from my purse, popped a stick in my mouth, and chewed hard, relishing the snap each time my upper and lower teeth met. Cracking gum is a true art form and one that I'd perfected when I quit smoking. A calm began to settle over me.

Then Marco shouted, "Stop already!"

I jumped. "What the—"

"Stop cracking your gum," he ordered. "It's driving me crazy."

"Sorry, already." Giving it one last defiant crack, I spit the gum into its wrapper and shoved it into my purse. "You're aw-fully touchy."

He relaxed his grip on the steering wheel and mumbled tersely, "Do you have any other annoying little habits I should know about?" He tapped his fingers in rhythm to a silent melody.

"None that you'll ever have to deal with," I retorted while glancing pointedly at him drumming feverishly on the steering wheel.

He grinned. "If they arrest you and there's a trial, we could find ourselves spending a lot of time together."

He'd made his point. I shuddered, looked out the window and didn't utter a word for the rest of the trip. I didn't have to. His never-ending finger tapping filled the air with its own monotonous sound. *Torture in a luxury car. Who knew?*

We arrived at the rectory, and before my eyes, I saw my life turning into a bad B movie—*desperate criminal hides out in rectory*. I tried to change Marco's mind about staying there. "I can't do this."

He got out of the car and peered through the window at me. "Come on!"

"No."

"There's always the police."

"Traitor."

Reluctantly I hauled my bag and my weary body out of the car. Marco herded me up the steps. When I reached the top, the door opened wide. Father Daniel stood in silhouette, his arms outstretched with the light from the room burning brightly at his back. Well, I'll be. He looked a little like God welcoming the prodigal daughter home.

My eyes misted ever so slightly. Father Daniel's willingness to open up his home and his heart to me after all these years touched me. The need for a group hug loomed, but I stifled the urge. I didn't want to break down completely. Tears were out of character for me. Or at least they had been yesterday. Today, I was tired, scared, hadn't eaten much all day, hadn't called my family, or shown up at work. I hadn't even bothered calling in to God.

God, family, friends, death, the awful day hit me like a bad dream and my emotions unraveled. Those tears I'd struggled so hard to keep buried tugged at the corners of my eyes. I lost the war and fell into Father Daniel's waiting arms, sniffling.

"I want my mother!"

By the time I'd finished a hot soaking bath, my emotions had settled down and my fatigue had almost disappeared. But I still wanted my mother, which meant I really wasn't in good shape. No, when it came to wanting or needing Ma, I had to be on pretty shaky ground. And yet the desire for the familiar, even my mother's voice, was so strong I picked up the phone and called her.

Ma answered on the first ring, sounding unusually anxious. "Hello. Hello. Who is this? Who's calling?"

"Ma, it's me."

"My Goodness, is that you, Penelope? Are you okay? Is this a ransom call? Have they hurt you? If they hurt you, I'll . . ."

I sank into a nearby chair. "Ma, it's me and I'm fine."

"Oh, Penelope! Are you sure? Should I have Pop call the police? Oh, dear, I just don't know what to do."

I shouted, "Ma! Enough already! I'm okay. I'm not hurt and I haven't been kidnapped."

"But—"

"Ma, just listen, please?" I leaned back and closed my eyes.

Mary Santucci had always been a mother hen. She only had two chicks, me and my older sister Germaine, and neither of us kept her busy enough. A few more children with ongoing problems would have helped us all—Pop, Germaine, and me.

Ma had a black belt in driving me crazy. It was her primary mission to be the cruise director of our lives. Her intent was to be helpful, but that rarely happened. Most of the time she had Germaine and me on the edge of insanity.

I just couldn't spar with her right now. On my best day I could keep up with her—just. And this wasn't my best day. In fact it was possibly my worst, ever, and there had been quite a few bad ones along the way.

I continued, more quietly, "I'm okay, Ma. Really, I am."

Her breath came in shallow bursts, and I could swear I heard a sniffle or two. "Where are you? Are you sure *they're* not forcing you to lie? Are they torturing you in some ungodly way? Oh, my poor baby."

Ma crying? Wow! She must be in a bad way. I'd really scared her. It hadn't occurred to me that she might actually be worried about me. I'd always been independent. And even as a child, Germaine had often been my primary caretaker. This was a new view of my mother.

With my free hand I continually twisted a lock of hair between my thumb and finger. Ma will do that to me.

"Ma, you've been reading too many serial-killer books. I'm not going to play twenty questions. I'm beat."

She gasped. "Beat? Did you say beat? You've been beat?"

I sat upright and screamed. "Ma!"

"But—" Her voice increased in pitch.

"Ma, settle down." If I couldn't get her under control, there would be no talking to her. "You know when you get upset your anxiety quotient skyrockets and the heartburn or heart palpitations or whatever they are set in. And then you get sick. Really sick. So settle down. Better yet, let me talk to Pop."

Her voice became a whine. "He's with Germaine, telling her what happened."

"Boy, I don't envy Pop talking to Germaine. She's gonna be frantic."

"She's your sister; it's only natural she'd be concerned about you, Penelope. Such a good girl, my Germaine."

I sighed. "I know. I know."

She switched gears. Ma was easily distracted. *Thank you, Lord, for small favors.*

She started in. "You know I couldn't have put all those hours in at the laundry if Germaine hadn't been there to help with you. You were not an easy child, Penelope."

My sighs became longer and louder. I could hang up the phone, but it would be easier to go along with her and let her get whatever it was out of her system. Patience is a virtue. It was too bad I possessed so little of that virtue.

"I know, Ma. I would have been resentful if I'd been strapped with a snotty nose, smart-mouthed kid."

She clucked audibly. "Not Germaine. She doesn't have a mean bone in her body."

I didn't voice my opinion that while Germaine was a wonderful person, she was pretty neurotic herself. Who wouldn't be, having Mary Santucci for a mother? "Yeah, Germaine's great, Ma."

"Yes she is. You really should appreciate her more."

My frustration increased. "Yeah, Germaine got all the good genes."

"Penelope!"

Father Daniel walked by so I gave him a quick smile and continued, "Come on, Ma. This really isn't the time for reminiscing."

"It's never a bad time to appreciate your family."

Weary now, I held my head in my hand. "Ma, what's going on here? Most of the time you're angry with Germaine. For what she did."

48

"I am not."

Yeah right. I had only talked about converting to Catholicism. Germaine actually had converted. And became a nun! In the scheme of things that was a high level sin, bordering on outright blasphemy to Mary Santucci. There wasn't enough absolution in the world to atone for that detour on life's highway. According to Ma it was enough to hold Germaine in limbo, if she had believed in limbo, for all eternity.

What it boils down to is, Ma loves Germaine, but she hasn't forgiven her for "going into the life," as she calls it. The way she says it, it always sounds as if Germaine had become a hooker. *Ah, life is full of little twists and turns.*

Ma wanted the family to stay Protestant. She didn't trust that old guy with the red shoes in Rome.

"I'll call Germaine later, Ma. I promise."

"She'll be worried. You'd better call her right away. Right away."

"I will, Ma!"

She didn't miss a beat. "Now, Penelope, tell me everything. And I mean everything."

I lowered my forehead onto the desk and inhaled the odor of lemon-scented furniture polish. "Ma, I can't talk right now. I don't know anything. I just wanted to let you know I'm okay."

"You'd better come home so I can take care of you," she ordered. "I have some spaghetti, a little marinara sauce. It will do you some good."

Now why wasn't that a surprise? If there's a crisis, Ma will have food. It's a wonder I wasn't the poster child for overeaters anonymous. "Ma, I can take care of myself."

"Not so you could notice," she retorted.

The conversation was a long slow train to nowhere. "I have other problems right now. Really big problems. You listening to me, Ma?"

She shrieked, "But the police . . ."

I'd had it. "Ma, stop!" *Forgive me, Lord, for I have not honored my mother.*

Her sharp intake of breath was frightening. I knew I'd pay for my outburst.

Rubbing my neck I said, "Ma, I'm sorry. But this has been a truly crappy day."

She railed at me. "Penelope Santucci, how dare you talk to your mother like that. You're not too big—"

"I am too big!"

She stopped talking, was probably considering whether I was too big. Since she was shorter than me by a good two inches and weighed less, by at least fifteen pounds, it wouldn't take her long to realize physical force wasn't an option. Besides, she'd have to catch me first.

I continued, "About the police. What did they say?"

All Ma knew was that Paul was dead, I was missing, and the cops wanted to talk to me.

Somehow, my mother had decided a band of depraved criminals had killed Paul and kidnapped me and it all had something to do with my job. She never did approve of my career choice, always said that it would be the death of me. That's if *she* didn't murder me first.

It hadn't occurred to me that anyone would think I might have been a victim. Paul and I had been separated for months. There was no reason to think I would have been at his house.

I told Ma what I thought she needed to know, tried to put her mind at ease, which is something like trying to rock an elephant to sleep. Finally I hung up while she jabbered about how I'd made the evening news, but my photograph wasn't very flattering.

I didn't want my mother anymore.

CHAPTER SIX

The clock on Father Daniel's desk read ten o'clock, and we still hadn't heard from Marco Silva. I sank into an armchair just as the study door opened.

In a deep, soothing voice Father Daniel said, "How about some hot chocolate, Pen? Or perhaps, you'd prefer some tea?"

Father Daniel held a tray with steaming cups. I preferred coffee, but it hadn't been offered. "I'd like the hot chocolate, Father Daniel."

He handed me a cup. "Me too."

The doorbell rang as he was about to sit down. I placed the saucer on the table and took a long swallow as Father Daniel left the room.

A minute later he returned with Marco in tow.

"Oh, oh," I said softly. Marco's tie was askew and his expensive suit rumpled. Judging by the angry look on his face, he'd found out I'd run from the police. I sank lower in the chair.

Marco eyed me and asked curtly, "I don't suppose I could have a cup of something hot?"

Father Daniel handed him his hot chocolate. "Here. Take this one. Unless you'd prefer tea."

"Nah, the hot chocolate is fine." Marco sat down, settled in an overstuffed wingback and drank deeply.

Father Daniel pulled his desk chair near us and eased his large frame onto it.

"So what's up," I asked cheerily.

Marco, stress lining his face, leaned forward, put his cup down and asked, "What's the matter with you? Somebody drop you on your head when you were a kid?"

I squirmed but remained silent, sneaking a quick peek at Father Daniel.

Marco continued, "Running from the cops like that. And out a third-story window? You must watch too many movies. Really bad movies."

I lowered my head so I didn't have to look at either of the men.

"What's going on, Marco?" Father Daniel asked.

Marco shook his head. "You don't want to know, Father." He pointed at me, "And you, you're going to the police station tomorrow morning, nine sharp."

I groaned.

"Hey, the only reason you're not there tonight, being grilled within an inch of your life, is because some of those guys have worked with you. For some bizarre reason, they like and respect you." He shrugged his shoulders.

I smiled sweetly. "You didn't expect that, huh?"

His finger jabbed at the air. "Don't start with the smug act. Part of the reason you're not in the slammer is because I convinced them to wait. They're not charging you with anything right now, including Murder *or* Fleeing a Police Officer. But that could change in a heart beat," he warned. "Just because some cops like you doesn't mean they won't do their job."

"Gee, that hadn't crossed my mind," I lied.

In my heart, I believed in the unwritten code of the men and women in blue—they protected each other. I wanted to believe that code included those of us who served in Corrections. Probably a stretch.

Father Daniel spoke up. "I wish someone would tell me

what's wrong."

Marco glared at me. "What's wrong? I'll tell you what's wrong. It's her. She's a walking, talking disaster!"

Marco told Father Daniel about my escapade with Sergeant Masters. He finished with, "I have no idea what I've done to deserve her." He looked at me. "But now, I'm stuck with her, and it's your fault, Father Daniel."

Father Daniel had the courtesy to look remorseful. "I'll go with Pen tomorrow."

"That's not necessary, Father," I replied hotly.

Marco blew the air from his lungs in frustration. "It's not a bad idea, Pen. Somebody has to keep you out of trouble. It's obvious you aren't capable on your own."

"Hey."

Father Daniel interrupted. "Now, now, you two. Behave yourselves. You're acting like children. We've got more important things to do than squabble with each other."

"But Father . . ."

"I'll meet the two of you at the station." Marco ran over my words like a steamroller. "It's not a bad idea to have a priest with you. It'll look good."

"Pious?" I retorted.

"Pen," Marco snapped.

"I can do this on my own," I insisted.

Marco waved his hand in the air. "This is your lawyer speaking. Under duress, since I owe the good Father, but I am your lawyer, am I not?"

"Yes, but—"

"No buts. And because I know more about this than you do, you'll do as I say. Got it? And besides, after the stunt you pulled today . . ."

He didn't finish his sentence. From the look Father Daniel gave me, it was clear we all understood.

Marco certainly was excitable. He'd better watch that as he got older; it could become a serious health issue. Reluctantly I said, "Okay. Father Daniel can tag along. But I hate thinking I'm a burden."

Marco huffed. "You are a burden. Accept it. In the past few hours, I've had to."

I sniffed loudly. "I resent that. I followed orders. You told me not to talk to the cops!"

He groaned. "There are other ways. Like telling them you won't talk without your lawyer being present."

I mused over his suggestion. "I didn't want to do that from a jail cell."

He placed his cup on the table. "Obviously not."

I looked from one man to the other and knew when I was beat. I raised my hands, palms outward. "I give up."

"That's settled, now the game plan is this . . ."

For the next half hour Marco explained the nuances of dealing with homicide detectives when one is the quarry, not the colleague. It all boiled down to tell the truth, don't volunteer anything, and keep my smart remarks to myself. *Deliver me from temptation.*

Marco finished his lecture, collected his belongings, and started for the door. He warned me again, "Just remember, no wise remarks. You might be smarter than these guys, but rubbing their noses in it will not endear you to them or make your life easier. Or mine for that matter. Capice?"

I stood at attention and gave him a mock salute. "Yes sir!"

He shook his head, placed a finger under my chin and tilted my head upward. "The problem is you're just too cute and you know it. You definitely need a keeper." He sighed. "Even when you aren't smarting off, you sound like you are. Between now and nine o'clock tomorrow morning get over the attitude, or your life, my dear, will become a real living hell. That's one thing I can guarantee."

He turned on his heel and walked down the steps toward his car. I shut the front door, checked the locks, and considered what Marco said. What did he mean I was cute? Cute cute? Or smart-mouth cute?

I considered the possibilities, but only for a moment. I was just too tired.

As I trudged upstairs I began a bargaining session with The Big Guy. "Get me out of this mess, God, and I'll be a better person, I promise."

Did He remember those other broken promises? I sincerely hoped not. Did He hold grudges? I sincerely hoped not. But I couldn't be sure. Yeah, I knew all about forgiveness, but I'm human.

I could give trying to be a better person the ol' college try. Especially if it would keep me out of the slammer and the clutches of Big Bertha looking for a new friend. I shuddered.

CHAPTER SEVEN

The homicide division looked vastly different from the perspective of a suspect versus being a Probation Officer. Father Daniel squeezed my hand and took a seat on the scarred wooden bench just inside the doors while I paced.

It was nine o'clock, and Marco hadn't arrived. My anxiety was palpable. What if he didn't show? That was easy. I'd have to hurt him. Not a lot, just enough to get his attention.

"Pen?"

My eyes shot upward. The tall, thin, almost-emaciated man stood by the door, his sad brown eyes drooped like a hound dogs. "Ben, what are you doing here?"

"Just talking to the police about one of my clients. Uh, how are you?" He shifted his stance slightly.

I shrugged.

He continued, "I'm not really sure what to say under these circumstances."

I smiled weakly. "I know, Ben. And yes, to answer your unspoken question, I'm here to talk to the cops about Paul's murder."

Ben switched his briefcase from his right to his left hand and ran his fingers through wispy blond hair. "Yeah, I assumed so. How's that going?"

"Well, I'm still on this side of a jail cell door. You know how things were, Ben. Paul and I were having a contest of wills. But I didn't kill him."

Ben Joston took a step toward me and put his free hand on my shoulder. "I know you didn't. I'm so sorry all this is happening. You're a nice woman, Pen." His blue eyes grew hard. "Paul could be a bastard. More than a few people would have liked to see him dead."

The intensity of his statement surprised me. I'd never heard Ben ever say anything bad about Paul. They'd been law partners and friends for years. Sometimes it seemed as if they were joined at the hip.

If Paul had been taking bribes, as I suspected, did that mean Ben was involved? If he wasn't, had Ben found out about Paul's double-dealings and killed him in the heat of the moment?

I'd figured that Judge Kassner murdered Paul. Maybe I was wrong? You never really knew people. Even friends. Even your own husband.

"Ben . . ."

The double doors of the squad room crashed open, and Marco sailed through looking like an ad for *Gentleman's Quarterly*. Without speaking, he nodded, all business-like, at Ben, me, and Father Daniel as he approached the battered chest-high counter separating *us* from *them*.

An air of confidence swirled around Marco. The battle between good and evil would be fought on new ground this morning. The way I saw it, today, I was the good guy and the cops were evil. A different take from most days.

Our eyes were focused on Marco.

He rapped on the counter, and the receptionist looked up. "Marco Silva here with Ms. Santucci. Please inform Sergeant Masters." His words, though pleasant enough, gave the impression he was giving an order that had better not be defied. The chill in the air became colder.

The middle-aged receptionist snapped to attention. "Yes, Mr. Silva. He's expecting you. Please, have a seat, and I'll tell him you're here."

Ah ha. Welcome to the world of the respected and feared defense attorney.

Marco nodded slightly but continued to stand, his eyes closed, fingers tapping impatiently on the counter's worn top.

I glanced from Father Daniel to Ben. Father Daniel sat, staring blankly into space. Ben didn't seem to know what to do. Marco ignoring a colleague? Wow!

I didn't have a chance to question Ben further because Sergeant Masters approached and he didn't look happy. This was going to be a tough audience.

I cleared my throat, looked up at Ben. "I have to go. Can we talk later?"

He nodded, "Certainly. Just give me a call."

"Thanks."

A feeble-looking smile covered Ben's face as he squeezed my arm.

Masters approached the counter, reached his hand across to Marco. "I'm Sergeant Masters."

Marco virtually ignored him as he walked through the half door that separated the white hats from the black hats and motioned me to follow him.

My hands shook as I smiled weakly at Father Daniel, who was still staring off into space. Then I skittered to the door. Marco and Sergeant Masters ignored me. I was adrift in a sea of momentary invisibility. Small comfort since I knew all too soon I'd be the center of a lot of unwanted attention. I almost wanted my mother again. Almost.

Father Daniel suddenly called out, "Booger? Is that you, Booger?"

Booger?

Sergeant Masters spun around and sputtered, "What?"

Father Daniel got up and walked to the counter. "It is you,

Booger? Yes, I thought so."

Sergeant Master's face reddened. "Father Daniel. It's been a long time."

Father Daniel chuckled. "About twenty-five years. When this unfortunate business with Pen is over, we'll have to get together and talk about the old days? Do you still play baseball?"

Sergeant Masters shifted from one foot to the other, his eyes darting furtively around the squad room. "Not much," he mumbled.

"Well, I know you have business to take care of. Maybe we can visit later, Booger. It's nice to see you." Father Daniel gave a small wave.

Sergeant "Booger" Masters glanced at me, looking more than a little annoyed and obviously trying to figure out my relationship with the priest.

Marco shot me a look that warned me not to make any comment. It was almost impossible. I wanted to know how Father Daniel knew this guy. Most of all, I wanted to know how he got the name Booger. I could only speculate.

We ran the stationhouse gauntlet. A few familiar faces turned away when my eyes connected with theirs. It seemed forever before we entered a door on the far side of the squad room. A long table sat in the center of the room, surrounded by mismatched and battered wooden chairs. A lone file folder rested on top of it. Nothing else was in the room. Except . . . I searched the ceiling, a small light hung at an odd angle. It wasn't lit and was too small to interrogate me by. *Smile, I'm on Candid Camera.*

Masters, all professional now, interrupted my observations. "Have a chair, please, Ms. Santucci and Mr. Silva. Sergeant Nash will be joining us shortly."

Oh, two of them! And I didn't recognize this Nash person's name. They were probably going to gang up on us. On me. I speculated on a good cop, bad cop scenario.

Marco nudged me. I looked to see if he approved of me sitting. He'd told me not to breathe without his say so and I intended to follow orders.

"Sit," he said.

I sat. We waited.

It seemed like an eternity until Sergeant Nash entered the room. He was considerably older than Sergeant Masters, in his mid to late forties and much thinner. He was also taller than Masters by at least five inches and had close-cropped gray hair sprouting from his balding pate, whereas "Booger" had avoided bald. There were other opposites. So many that a smile spread over my face. But I caught myself, deciding I'd better focus on my interview. This was serious business. My serious business.

After the formalities were completed, Masters spoke. "Ms. Santucci, we'd like to ask you some questions."

Hesitating for a moment, I glanced at Marco. When he nodded, I said, "Yes. I understand you'd like to know more about Paul's death. There's not much I can tell you though."

Marco coughed, and I clammed up. So much for following my lawyer's orders. Masters eyes traveled slowly from the file he'd been perusing to Marco. Then his piercing brown eyes rested on me. "You were saying, Ms. Santucci."

I stuck my chin out and replied, "Oh nothing. I guess you should ask your questions, sir." The sir was for good measure, hoping he'd like the show of respect. His expression didn't change. Maybe he hadn't heard me. Maybe he didn't care. Maybe he knew I didn't mean it. Oh, well.

Masters withdrew a small recorder from his jacket pocket, nodded at it and asked, "Do you mind if I record our interview?"

Marco and I answered at the same time. It was difficult to remember my place. *Not a surprise.*

Marco warned me off with his eyes and answered, "I have no

objection to your recording the interview."

"Good."

Masters spoke softly into the recorder. I thought I heard the date and time but couldn't be sure. He placed the recorder in front of me, cleared his throat and asked, "Please state your full name and date of birth, Ms. Santucci."

I also cleared my throat. Maybe whatever he had was catching. "Penelope Ann Santucci."

"You'll have to speak louder, Ms. Santucci."

"Penelope Ann Santucci," I yelled.

Marco placed his hand lightly on my arm, leaned over toward me, and spoke quietly into my ear, "Settle down. This is just an interview."

Embarrassed, I looked down at the tabletop and noticed the scratches covering it. Claw marks from former victims, no doubt.

Masters looked at Marco, and, when he nodded, I cleared my throat again and gave my name and date of birth for the record.

The questions didn't get heavy until almost an hour into the interview. Then Masters and Nash took off the gloves.

They continued their barrage, no good-cop, bad-cop in this twosome. They both were vying for "bad cop of the year" award and were sizzling when Nash asked, "You hated your husband, didn't you, Ms. Santucci?"

"No. Well. . . ."

"You hated him because he was trying to take everything in the divorce. You felt powerless, so you killed him."

I bolted up from my seat. Marco grabbed my arm and pulled me back down. "Sit!" he hissed.

"This is ridiculous!" I roared as I wrenched my arm from Marco's grasp.

I looked at Masters and Nash. They were smiling. They got me. Now they could testify in Court that I easily lost my temper. The jurors would be allowed to speculate whether I angered easily enough to kill. The prison doors were swinging shut right in front of my face.

Taking a deep breath, I quietly said, "I did not kill my husband."

"I think you did," Nash shot back.

"Well you think wrong." I glared at him.

"I don't think so."

"You'd better learn to think, Nash. You're not doing such a good job." Marco increased the pressure on my arm.

Masters sat up straight and glared at me. "Okay then, why would anyone want to kill Paul Preston? He was a hotshot lawyer."

A laugh caught in my throat.

Masters cleared his throat and stated, "You seem to be the only one with a motive."

"I don't think so." I shot back. "Lots of people might have wanted Paul out of the way." Hadn't his law partner said something to that effect in the waiting room?

It wasn't time to give Masters the information I had about the judge. Without proof, I'd just look crazy and anger everyone. Not to mention giving the judge time to cover his tracks.

I leaned my arms on the table. "Look, my husband was a sleaze-ball attorney who represented the scum of the earth. You cops didn't like him either, but that doesn't mean you killed him." Marco squeezed my arm again. I wrenched it from his grasp, again. I'd have to talk to him about the evils of physical abuse pretty soon or my arm was going to be black and blue.

I continued with my tirade. "I did not kill Paul. We were getting a divorce, yes, but that doesn't automatically translate into murder." I breathed deeply. "It could have been a random burglary gone bad. One of his fine upstanding clients from the underbelly of the mob could have fought with him and things got out of control. A victim's family member could have extracted their pound of flesh, etc. etc. etc." On the last etc. I felt like the King of Siam in the *King and I*.

No time to wander through movie land. To make my point, I pounded on the tabletop. Everyone in the room jumped. *Gotcha!*

Marco didn't bother with warning looks. He squeezed my arm in plain view of the cops. For the third time I wrenched myself from his grasp, "Ouch. That hurt!"

He glared as I leaned close to his face and whispered, "Don't do that again or I'll . . ." Whoops, bad form. I stopped mid sentence, sat up straight, and plastered a smile on my face. If I didn't get myself under control I was going to walk myself right into a jail cell. The picture of a slamming prison door now included sound effects, locks clunking into place, twenty years to life.

Masters tapped his pencil eraser on the tabletop. "Or you'll do what, Ms. Santucci?"

"Nothing." I rubbed my sore arm. "Just a minor disagreement with my lawyer. Can we go? I'm tired."

Masters glared, realizing he wasn't going to get any response from me. He searched his notes and then stated, "You broke into Paul Preston's house."

"Pen!" Marco warned.

I ignored him. "Doesn't make me a murderer."

"Your fingerprints, yours and Paul's, were the only ones found in the office," Nash shot back.

"I explained that to you an hour ago. The cleaning woman comes the same day each week." I wearily leaned my head on my hand.

Marco's chair scrapped against the floor as he backed away from the table. "You've gone over this ground several times with my client. We're done. Now, unless you're going to arrest Ms. Santucci, we're leaving."

Marco was calling their bluff. It had better work, or I would have some serious contemplation time, courtesy of the county. No one said anything for a long minute. Marco stood up.

Not really knowing what to do, I followed suit.

Masters shrugged and jabbed at the air with his pencil. "Stick around, Ms. Santucci. We want you where we can keep an eye on you. We don't have enough to arrest you yet, but we will, soon."

He was very convincing. My body shook slightly as Marco guided me to the door. Then I got angry. I was innocent, yet here I was allowing some small minded man to intimidate me just so he could get a slap on the back and bond with the other macho cops.

I turned, smiled my broadest smile and said, "I work at the Government Center. Pop across the street if you want to chat. *Booger.*"

Finally, Marco spoke. "That could mean anything, Pen. Maybe he learned about Paul's shenanigans, and he fell from grace."

"I don't think that was it. What do you think, Father?"

Father Daniel looked squarely at Marco. "He did say it rather empathetically."

"Probably means nothing," Marco replied.

"But it's worth checking into? I mean, I might have it all wrong. But I don't think so."

"If it'll keep you off my back, I'll check into it. See if I can learn anything."

My smile grew.

Marco stopped walking and peered at me. "I take it that will make you happy?"

My smile broadened. "Of course."

"Good, we all want to keep Pen happy."

"No need to get sarcastic about it."

Marco chuckled. "You guys better get going."

Father Daniel said, "Yes, come on, Pen. Time for us to make our getaway."

Father Daniel was getting into this cops and murder suspect business. We left Marco and walked through the tunnel under the street to the Government Center in order to avoid the media we'd been told were waiting for us outside City Hall. I love getting the best of just about anyone, and the media just happened to be pretty high on my hit list since I knew they were taking pot shots at me.

As we walked underground I asked Father Daniel, "Tell me about Booger. How did he get that name?"

Father Daniel grinned and told me. It was pretty much as I had suspected.

Father Daniel drove me home. I kissed him on the cheek and

agreed to have dinner with him Friday night, if I was still the bluebird of happiness and flying free.

After I settled in at home, I called work, a little late—about a day and a half—and told them I wouldn't be in for awhile. Everyone, the receptionist Janice informed me, knew about Paul's murder and she wondered if I had been arrested yet. What nerve! I gave her a curt no and said I'd call in later and talk to my boss. I hung up while she was still yakking. I'd never liked Janice, and now I liked her even less.

With the necessities out of the way, I got in my car and pointed it toward the house I'd shared with Paul for four years. Marco wouldn't like it, but then he didn't much like how I did anything. Besides, he didn't have to know about it.

CHAPTER NINE

The large three-story wood-framed house had yellow crime scene tape draped like last week's party decorations across the front door.

The privileged residents of the upscale Lowery Hill neighborhood where Paul and I had lived were probably appalled with the tawdry events that had invaded their insulated world. Paul's murder would have brought home the sharp reality that they were as vulnerable as everyone else in the world.

I continued to stare at the house and the crime scene tape, wondering if it was actually against the law to break the seal. It had never come up in a discussion at work, but I knew from watching television it probably wasn't a good idea.

The tape itself was really nothing more than a minor inconvenience. It's always easier to ask for forgiveness than permission. I'm not sure where I'd heard the saying, but I'd taken to it like a bee to honey. Besides, I'd broken more laws than Bill Clinton in the past twenty-four hours. How bad would one more be? Probably really bad, but I'd take my chances anyway. A stiff prison sentence loomed in my future, and that encouraged risk-taking.

I scanned the neighborhood and didn't see anyone peering at me from parked cars, or behind curtains, or hedges. Satisfied that my movements were not attracting unwanted attention, I strolled around to the back of the house.

I checked my surroundings again, then walked back to the

front and up the steps to the porch. I dug around in my purse, drew out a small black rectangular case, opened it and chose a lovely, ebony-handled pick. Like a lover, I stroked it tenderly, knelt down and gently poked around in the keyhole. "Ah ha. What a good pick you are," I praised the tool. It was a gift from one of my "clients"—and old man named Otis with a record longer than a race-horse pedigree. Otis was undeniably crooked, but he was a sweetie.

I stood, wiped my hands on my clothes before tucking the pick in my purse. I twisted the front door knob. Hearing the distinct familiar click, I grinned and crept through the doorway and into the darkened foyer.

Apprehension flooded over me as I crossed the threshold, looked around, then started down the hall. The closer I came to the den, the more my hands began to sweat.

Pausing at the door, I wrinkled my nose at the distinct odor that I hadn't noticed yesterday. The air conditioning must have prevented the death stench from permeating the house. Or maybe I had happened along before Paul's body had begun to ripen.

I shuddered at the thought of Paul's body but didn't have the time to think about it before the room began to spin. I had just enough time to grab the doorjamb for support.

In spite of how I felt about Paul, my eyes clouded with tears. When the room stopped spinning, I rushed to open a window so I could breathe the clear June air rather than death.

When my stomach stopped lurching, I carefully surveyed the room. Every surface was covered with the residue of fingerprint powder.

I edged my way around the large mahogany desk, avoiding eye contact with the spot on the beige carpet where Paul's body had been and briefly wondered who would have the unpleasant job of cleaning up the blood. Since Paul had died before our divorce was final, I technically was the homeowner. So I was responsible. It wasn't a job I cherished. The to-do list in my head entered a note; hire a cleaning crew, no matter the cost.

I approached the floor-to-ceiling bookcase and removed a half dozen books from the third shelf. A small wall safe beckoned me.

My hands, damp and itchy, trembled with anticipation. I spun the combination. When the last tumbler fell into place, I paused, took a deep breath, and twisted the handle. "Please open. Please," I implored the god of machines. It would be just like Paul to have changed the combination since I'd last snooped around.

Hesitating, I squeezed my eyes shut, then pulled hard. The heavy door swung open. "Yes!" I bent down and peered inside the small, dark cavity.

It was packed! Reaching inside, I drew out a bundle of papers and several envelopes, fat and thin. I walked to the desk as I sifted through them. When I saw the bloody spot on the floor, I steadied myself. I settled into a chair, positioning it so I couldn't see the dark stain that had saturated the carpet giving it the look of a Rorschach test.

I concentrated on the papers. They included birth and marriage certificates, stock holdings, and mortgage papers. The usual things people kept in a home safe, if they had one. But nothing screamed criminal.

I'd need some of them later, when Paul's estate was settled, so I put them aside. I opened the first envelope. It was Paul's passport. I discarded it and opened a large fat manila envelope. Bingo! Three neat packs of hundred dollar bills. I shuffled through them like a deck of cards. "Holy cow! There must be ten or fifteen thousand dollars in here." Not a lot by some people's standards, but a windfall by mine.

I pondered whether this was evidence or if I could use it to pay Marco. It would make a small dent in what I would owe him by the time this thing was over. I'd think on it and decide later. Yeah, right. There wouldn't be a lot of time spent deciding the fate of this money. No attorney debt loomed in *my* future.

Before I replaced the money in the envelope I considered what a trial would cost. The mere thought brought on an involuntary shudder.

The last envelope was so thin I didn't think it could possibly hold anything important. But a girl could hope.

So far I hadn't seen anything that pointed to trial fixing or any other criminal behavior. The money was a little odd, but not necessarily criminal. Paul might have been hiding assets from me, nothing more. The jerk.

If there wasn't something of interest in the last envelope, I didn't know where else to look. It was certain that Paul wouldn't leave anything incriminating in the desk. It would have been too easy for me to find. And I couldn't imagine him leaving evidence lying around his office for a secretary to stumble across. No, Paul would have safe little hidey-holes because that's the way his imagination worked. Yes, his had been a curious little mind.

I drew open the flap. Nothing but an adoption certificate. I'd struck out. Bummer! I began gathering up the papers to return to the safe. "Wait a minute! Adoption?" Whose adoption? I looked at the paper again. "Paul was adopted?" I couldn't believe it. But there it was, written out in plain English, dated and signed by a judge.

Gripping the paper, I leaned back in the chair, trying to process this new information. If Paul had been adopted, why hadn't he or his family ever mentioned it? It wasn't as if it was something to be ashamed of. Lots of people were adopted. Why keep it a secret from me?

I placed the paper on the desk, absently running my fingers

over the raised Hennepin County seal, feeling uneasy in the eerie quiet.

I wanted to know more about this news. But would Paul's family talk to me about it? They hadn't been especially friendly since we'd separated. Now that I was a suspect in his murder, they probably wouldn't welcome my questions about a part of their lives they'd obviously tried to keep secret.

The grandfather clock in the hall gonged. I jumped at the unexpected sound. "Girl, get a hold of yourself!"

This house of death was getting to me. I quickly gathered up the papers, sans the money and adoption certificate, and started to stuff everything back in the safe. Then I saw it. Tucked back in the corner. A small key. I'd almost missed it.

I drew it out and examined it. I'd expected a safe deposit box key, but it didn't look like one. It looked more like a key from a locker, like at a mall or the airport, where you can store your belongings while you shop.

"Now, why would Paul have a locker key in the safe?" That was easy: to hide something he couldn't keep in the house.

But what would he want to hide? Evidence that would tie him to a crime? If he had been involved in trial fixing, that was reason enough.

"Great! How am I going to find the lock to fit this?"

There had to be dozens of malls with lockers in the metro area. A search of them all could take forever and even then I couldn't be guaranteed of success. I ruled out the airport since items stored more than twenty-four hours were probably confiscated by security.

I plopped my rear on the edge of the desk and tried to think like Paul, which was no easy task because I'd never thought like a scum-sucking bottom feeder.

Why would Paul have a locker and not a safe deposit box? Easy answer. A bank required picture ID. A locker could be opened by anyone. Maybe it was all about the money. Paul could have been transferring cash.

If I was right about the locker, I might be able to find some answers to many of my questions.

I put the safe and bookcase back in order, pulled the office window shut and locked it. Gathering my things, I headed for the door, planning my strategy.

I didn't want to go to strip malls or department stores all around the Twin Cities. I wanted this to be a short excursion, not a long-term treasure hunt.

Paul was basically lazy. He wouldn't have wanted to go very far either. So, I decided to start with the major malls to the south of the city, followed by a stop at the Mall of America, then further east, north and around to the west. If none of those locations panned out, then—and only then—would I hit the bus depots and department stores in both St. Paul and Minneapolis. If I still didn't hit pay dirt, I didn't know what I'd do. Start planning my jailhouse décor, I guess.

CHAPTER TEN

The first mall didn't look promising. It seemed a bit small and out of the way for Paul's taste. But that might be a reason for him to choose it.

I wandered around a bit and stopped a cleaning woman as she exited the women's bathroom. "Excuse me. Are there any storage lockers in the building?"

She pointed down the hall. "Over there. Take the first right, by the bank of phones. Can't miss 'em."

"Thanks." I looked in the direction she pointed and began walking away. As an afterthought, I turned and called out, "Are they the only lockers in the mall?"

The woman paused. "Near as I can remember. You know how it is, you see something every day, but you don't really see it."

I nodded. "Thanks again."

Rounding the corner, I found the lockers, but they only numbered to fifty. The key I had was ninety-nine. "Struck out on the first try."

To expect success on the first attempt didn't mesh with my theory on luck. People either have no luck or bad luck. Only on rare occasions do they have good luck.

I was tempted to skip the next mall on my list because it was smaller than the first. It wouldn't have more than twenty-five lockers, I'd bet. But the luck thing reared its head. If I skipped it, I might have to retrace my steps later and that could cost valuable time, time I didn't think I had. I could almost smell Masters and Nash breathing down my neck. They wanted an arrest. They wouldn't care if it was me or the real murderer. *Support your local cop's promotion.*

Twenty minutes later I struck out again. So I got back in my car and headed for the Clearwater mall. No luck there, either. The same held true at the Mall of America. There was a locker numbered ninety-nine, but my key didn't fit.

I checked my watch. Rush hour would begin soon, and I wanted to avoid that mess. The southern part of Hennepin County's Highway 494 was impossible any time of the day, but during rush hour it was one of the worst freeways in the nation. It regularly brought out road rage in the nicest people. Whoever designed the road system should be forced to travel 494 twenty-four, seven, for penance.

I had time for one more stop at Benton Hill Mall on the city's East Side. If I struck out there, I'd have to stop for dinner and then venture on to the next. Maybe I could do a tiny bit of shopping first. I liked this mall, so did Paul. Hey! So did Paul!

I happened to enter the door nearest the bank of lockers. How convenient. My guess was that it wouldn't happen again in this lifetime. It was the luck thing. I scanned the lockers. There was a ninety-nine! But would the key fit?

Paul was a creature of habit and it seemed realistic that he'd go someplace he liked and frequented even if he had something to hide.

I took a deep breath and pushed the key into the lock and twisted. "Yes!"

I turned the handle and pulled, hard. The door popped open! "Oh, my!" I looked heavenward. "Thank you, Lord" I said with as much humility as I could muster.

I looked inside and saw a tattered brown paper grocery sack at the back of the locker. Peering around to make sure nobody had followed me or was watching too closely, I reached inside and grabbed the bag. Gulping audibly, I slowly pulled out the sack. Turning around, so my back was to the locker, I peered up and down the hall. There wasn't anything unusual going on.

When I opened the bag and saw the contents, I couldn't hold back a breathless shriek, "Oh, sweet Jesus!" I slammed the locker shut and headed for the nearest bathroom at a fast trot. "Oh my God, Oh my God, Oh my God!"

When I reached the stall, I locked myself inside, sank down onto the toilet seat, ignoring the open hole. I peered inside the bag again.

I reached in and sifted through the bundles of cash. "My oh my," I whispered hoarsely.

I didn't know what I was going to do with all that cash, but I decided it was important to get out of the mall right away. I stuffed the bag under my arm and left, trying not to attract attention. I didn't even bother to check out the sale racks. This was that serious!

My hands shook as I started the car. Breathing evenly, my mantra became, "drive slowly and carefully, slowly and carefully." I didn't want the police to stop me for some moving violation and find me with money I couldn't account for. I was too addled to think of a lie realistic enough to explain that much money.

When I got home, I double locked and chained the doors, drew the shades, stared at the sack and asked some philosophical questions. "Where did this money come from?" Why had it been stuffed in a locker? What would I do with it? Would anyone be looking for it? Would they kill to get it back? My condo was eerily quiet. My voice echoed through the rooms. "What have you done, Paul? What in the world were you involved with?"

The one thing I knew for sure was that the money belonged to someone and I sincerely doubted they were going to just forget about it.

Never in my life had I ever *seen* so much money. It was a powerful feeling. The thought of keeping it made me dizzy with joy. This money could help people, promote worthwhile causes, and help stamp out poverty. Who was I kidding? The only charity on my list was me. It was *my* poverty I wanted to stamp out.

I counted it twice because I couldn't believe how much was there. One hundred thousand dollars was strewn around my living room floor.

Yes, somebody would certainly miss this tidy little sum. It had to be tied to Paul's murder in some way. Maybe if I found out who it belonged to, I could clear my name. Or, it could make me dead. Dead, as in stiff toes six feet under. People did some ugly things for a lot less money. *Deliver us from evil!*

Several hours after counting the money, I was still sitting in my darkened living room, frightened out of my wits. I didn't know what to do, so I called Father Daniel. He'd been pretty helpful so far. If you couldn't trust a priest, if you couldn't tell him about your marginal and perhaps illegal behavior, who could you trust?

When he picked up the phone, I mustered my casual voice. "Hey, Father, Pen here. We need to talk."

He chuckled. "We do? When?"

I twisted my hair around a finger. "Now would be good."

He paused. "It's pretty late, Pen."

"I know, and I wouldn't ask, except it's really important." He had no idea how important.

He hesitated. "Then, come on. I'll have some hot chocolate waiting."

"Could you make it coffee?"

"Sure, but won't coffee keep you up?"

It wasn't coffee that would keep me up tonight. "No, caffeine

doesn't bother me, Father." *Father, forgive me for I continue to lie.*
"Then coffee it is."

"I'm on my way," I said.

I hung up the phone, transferred the cash to a duffel bag and jumped in the Ghia. All the way to Father Daniel's I checked the rear view mirror for suspicious vehicles and thought about what I should tell him.

Father Daniel wouldn't like it that I'd gone to Paul's house. And he'd like the bag of money part even less. Tough. I'd done it and I couldn't take it back. I'd tell him the truth and throw myself on his mercy. He'd take pity on me and help. After all, he *was* God's right hand man. Isn't there a rule about helping people in distress? The Church always had rules.

By the time I parked in front of the rectory, I'd wavered about telling the truth. No surprise there. Truth was seldom my friend, so it was logical that I'd be reluctant to use it during a crisis of this magnitude.

As I walked up the steps I tossed a mental coin. Truth won. Tough luck for me. Must be something in the air. I hoped it would pass on to someone else soon.

When we'd settled comfortably in the same chairs as the night before, drinking hot coffee, me clutching the bag in my lap, I decided to get everything out in the open

"Father, forgive me, I went to Paul's house."

It didn't seem to be a news flash. He merely asked, "When?"

I ran my finger around the cup rim. "After I left you."

He put his cup on the table. "Pen, you shouldn't have done that."

I shrugged. "Probably not."

He opened his mouth, but I interrupted him. "Please, Father. Let me continue." I chattered like a runaway train telling him the whole story. I finished with, "In this bag is one hundred thousand dollars, and I want you to keep it for me."

He laughed until he saw my face. "You're serious aren't you?" He began to blink furiously. "You really have a hundred thousand in cash, don't you?"

I clutched the bag to my chest and nodded somberly.

He pulled his rotund frame out of the chair. "Oh, my! You haven't gone completely over the edge and robbed a bank or something, have you?" He approached me with a look of concern on his face and extended his arms. "Come here, Pen. I'll talk to Marco about his fee. You don't have to do anything you'll be sorry for."

I didn't go for the comfort he offered. "Father Daniel. I haven't robbed a bank." I looked up at him. "I told you the truth about finding this money in a storage locker. And I don't have a clue who it belongs to." I clutched the bag tighter. "But I don't think I'm giving it back."

Father Daniel cleared his throat, sounding like a motor misfiring. "Is your life always like this, Pen? Or is this a temporary aberration?"

I groaned. "My life isn't usually this exciting. It's pretty boring most of the time and right now, boring looks good. Frankly, all this excitement is highly overrated." I pinched the bridge of my nose, trying to stave off a headache.

He plopped back into his chair. "Pen, you're going to get in more trouble than you're already in if you keep doing things like this."

I sighed. "It's a possibility. But there's also the possibility that I can clear my name. And I have to try. Prison is not an option. Anyway, I have this money and someone is going to notice it's gone. When they start looking for it, I don't want it in my possession. I might be where they start looking."

Father Daniel mused, "A logical place to start since you were married to Paul."

"Yeah. But hey, if the cops search my place, and it's only a matter of time before they do, I'd be hard pressed to explain this much cash. It's not like I can claim it's my weekly allowance. Not on a probation officer's salary. If I deposit it in the bank, how much attention do you think that will draw?"

He was very, very still. "Father?"

"Pen, could anyone get hurt holding this money?"

"Of course not." I didn't think so, but then Paul *had* been killed. Surely no one would hurt a priest. I didn't even know for sure if there was a connection between Paul's death and the money.

"Are you sure?"

I thought hard about his question. "No one but you and I even know I've got it."

He stroked his chin, combing through a beard that didn't exist. "I don't know. It might constitute a criminal act."

I sat up straight. Time for some hard-core convincing. "Come on, Father. What's criminal about me asking you to hold some money while I try to find out who it belongs to?"

He became quiet again. "Well, if you think . . ."

I handed Father Daniel the duffel bag and he assured me he would stash it in a safe place. As he walked me to the door, I decided to ask for another favor. But first I told him the short version of my suspicions about Judge Kassner.

When I'd finished, he groaned. "Are you sure?"

"Yes, I am. So I was thinking—"

He interrupted me. "Why do I think I smell a problem?"

"Father Daniel, how can you say that?"

He ticked off the reasons on his fingers. "Yesterday you found your husband's body and became a murder suspect. Today you waltz in here with a lot of money you can't explain. No one keeps legitimate money in a mall locker in a tattered paper bag. They keep it in the bank."

He had a point. I stayed silent.

He eyed me warily. "Now what is it? What are you thinking?"

I shifted my weight from one foot to the other. "I checked out Judge Kassner. He has a meeting every Thursday evening. And since Thursday is tomorrow, I thought I'd go over to his house and see what evidence I could dig up." I tried to sound as matter-of-fact as I could.

His eyes grew round and filled with suspicion. "What exactly do you mean, dig up evidence?"

I attempted to sound casual. "I mean, just go in and look around. You know."

"No, I don't know. Just what exactly does go in and look around mean?" His eyebrows pinched together in worry. "You don't mean break into his house, do you?"

"I suppose you could call it that."

Realization registered. "That's what you did at Paul's, wasn't it? There was no unlatched window, was there?"

I looked away.

"Answer me Pen. Did you break into Paul's house?"

I mumbled, "Not really. Technically it's still my house."

He ignored my response. "Penelope Santucci, what has led you to a life of crime?"

My head shot up. "What do you mean life of crime? I'm trying to avoid a life in prison."

"But the ends do not always justify the means, child."

I huffed my disagreement. "They do if you're a situational ethicist."

"Pen, you don't really believe its okay to break into someone's home."

"I do believe." I tried to sound sincere. "It's my freedom we're talking about, Father. I don't have the luxury of your convictions. This isn't a black and white situation. It's not just about right and wrong." I blinked quickly. "Just because you pray, it doesn't mean God will answer."

I didn't bother waiting for Father Daniel's response. I knew what it would be and I didn't want guilt to snake dance through my head.

I left Father Daniel, opened the front door and started down the steps. Pausing, I turned around, walked back inside, and yelled, "I'm doing it. Judge Kassner leaves the house at seven-thirty. It gets dark around nine. I'll be heading over there after that, if you want to help."

I grabbed a piece of paper and a pen from my bag and left the judge's address on the front hall table before running down the front walk.

He wouldn't come. I knew I was asking too much. Hey, he was a priest, and I was planning an evening filled with felonies. If you thought about it, it *was* ridiculous. Not to mention dangerous. And illegal.

Father Daniel called out from the front door, "I can't do it, Pen. I won't contribute to your delinquency. But I will pray for you."

Hopefully he had a direct line to the man upstairs because I needed some help.

I was disappointed but realistic. At least he'd agreed to keep the money. How could I expect a priest or anyone else to help me burglarize a home?

I shifted the car into drive and squealed away from the curb.

Maybe I wouldn't need any help. I could do it without Father Daniel. After all, Otis had been a good teacher. When this mess was straightened out, I'd have to remember to find Otis and thank him for the lock-pick tools. Maybe I'd drop a couple hundred in an envelope. The old guy could use it since his long life of crime hadn't involved any contributions to the social security system. And since I'd tucked away some cash at my condo, I could afford to be generous.

I'd better stash *that* cash too. A storage locker of my own wouldn't be a bad idea. The thought of the police or the owners of the money finding *any* hard evidence to explain cash in my home gave me goose bumps.

CHAPTER ELEVEN

On my way to bed, I noticed my answering machine's call alert flashing. I hit the play button.

"Penelope, this is your mother." Ma didn't sound happy.

She screeched, "Where are you? Have you disappeared again?" Her voice receded then called out, "Stanley, she's not there." There was mumbling in the background. "No. How would I know where she is, Stanley? She doesn't tell me anything. I'm just her mother."

More mumbling followed, but I couldn't understand the words. Finally, Ma spoke into the phone, "Honestly, Penelope, if we don't know where you are, how are we supposed to help you?" I didn't remember asking for help.

"Astrid called." Ma sighed and her voice sounded strained. Small wonder. Astrid was Paul's mother. Always a piece of work, my mother-in-law, but under these circumstances I could guess it had been a conversation straight from the seventh circle of Hell. Ma continued, "She said the police released Paul's body, and the funeral is Friday." Hmmm, the day after tomorrow.

"Astrid is making the funeral arrangements. And she would rather that we didn't attend. Can you believe that?"

Her message abruptly ended. She'd talked too long. I hit play for part two of Ma's speech. "Well, I'm not going to let Ms. Hoity-Toity Astrid bully me. She's just being childish. Of course, we're going to the funeral. Paul was my son-in-law. We'll pick you up." Oh, no they wouldn't. A funeral with my mother and

Astrid within fifty feet of each other—that was a hair-pulling, name-calling drama I planned to avoid at any cost. I'd rather clean toilets.

Silly me, just when I thought Ma was finished with her tirade she added, "Just where are those media people getting the lousy pictures of you, Penelope? Do you want me to give them something more flattering?"

I groaned and punched the erase button. My head throbbed.

The next message was from the local newspaper, wanting an interview. I hit erase. The following three messages were from local television stations wanting interviews. "I don't think so." I erased them all.

The last call was from Sergeant Masters. He wanted me to call. Well, go fish, *Booger*. If he wanted to talk to me, he could go through Marco.

I had money now, even if it wasn't mine, so I could afford to pay for my stubbornness.

I climbed into bed and as tired as I was, tossed and turned, until finally, at four A.M. I got up and made some coffee. I sat at the kitchen counter until I heard the morning paper hit the door. Opening the door, I gasped at the front page staring up at me. "Oh, no!" Square in top center was a picture of me with the caption, "Corrections Department Employee is Suspect in Prominent Attorney's Murder." I picked it up and cringed again. Ma was right about one thing. My photo was awful. Maybe it was a good thing it was so bad. People on the street wouldn't be able to identify me. I hoped.

I heaved the newspaper across the room. It thunked against the far wall.

At sunrise I finally fell back into bed and slept for several hours. When I awoke, the sun was high in the sky and peeking around the edges of my bedroom curtains. I stretched and lay silent, listening to the street noises below.

When the phone rang, I groaned and rolled over. I didn't want to talk to anyone.

The phone continued to ring. "Go away!"

When it didn't stop, I stretched and grabbed the phone. Picking up the receiver I said, "Who ees colling, please?"

"Give it up, kid. The French accent needs more work than you have time or talent."

I giggled and ran a hand through my disheveled hair. "Hey, Germaine. I must have turned the machine off by mistake last night. I'm screening my calls. What's up?"

"Pop told me what happened to Paul. I'm not sure if I'm supposed to say I'm sorry."

It was easy to believe that my sister, the nun, hadn't heard about Paul's death. Germaine was an English Literature professor at St. Margaret's, a Catholic women's college, in St. Paul. She didn't watch the news or read newspapers. Her premise was the stories were not about truth but someone's perception of the truth.

I grunted. "We've talked before. You know how I feel . . . felt about him. But well, dead is a little more permanent solution than I had planned. Even I'm not that strict."

"Pop said the police are looking at you for the murder."

"Yeah." I punched my pillow, shoved it up against the headboard, and nestled into it. "So hard their arteries could clog in the process."

"Sorry, kid. You need any help?"

Bingo. The magic word help. I told her about my suspicions and the clandestine trip I intended to make that night. Since Father Daniel refused to help, perhaps Germaine would hop aboard the bandwagon and help save my skin.

When I finished explaining my predicament, I asked, "So, you want to tag along?"

Air exploded from her lungs. "You want me to ride shotgun with you while you burglarize the home of an extremely popular judge?"

"Yeah, that's about it."

After a long pause, "You off your feed? Pen, you might want to consider seeing a doctor. My God, you're actually considering a burglary? Breaking and entering—what does that get you? Five to ten with good behavior? And 'good behavior,' well, it is *you* we're talking about. So just plan on ten years . . ."

"Not just considering, I'm doing it." It wasn't a good time to tell her it wouldn't be my first burglary.

"I don't believe this! Tell me you're in shock over Paul's death and it's temporarily affected your mind."

I sat up and threw my legs over the side of the bed. "Come on, Germaine. It's not like it's a for real burglary. I'm not gonna *steal* anything. I'm just looking for evidence."

"Oh, no. What you're going to do is break into someone's house and paw through their belongings. Ick!"

I walked out of my room toward the kitchen and began a full-blown whine. I'm good at whining, and it's usually effective with my sister. "Germaine. You want to visit me in jail?"

I could already hear the capitulation in her voice. "There has to be another way. This is stupid. Not to mention dangerous. It could get both of us locked up."

Opening the cupboard, I reached for the coffee. "Stupid is allowing someone time to get rid of evidence."

All I needed was someone to act as my lookout so I didn't get caught. I decided to stir up some good old-fashioned guilt. Guilt works on Catholics. Even converts—especially this convert. After growing up in Ma's house, Germaine has had a lot of practice with guilt in its highest and most refined forms.

I held my breath, then said quickly, "If you don't come with me, I could get caught. I'd go to jail. Like you say, five to ten in the big house." She didn't have to know about first offenses and probation. "And then you'll be responsible for Ma."

She groaned.

I poured water into the coffee maker, coffee grounds into the basket and turned on the machine. "Yep, with me locked up in the slammer, she'll only have you to fuss over. You'll be the one to get all the calls, the demands, the complaints . . ."

She groaned louder.

I sauntered to the kitchen table and sat down. "Are you ready to step up to the plate? It's a gigantic job. And there'll be no vacations, no parole or early release. Ma is a full-time job, Germaine. She is the living definition of high maintenance." I figured I had her now but had saved the best for last. "You'll become old before your time."

She hissed audibly. "You are so low, Pen. We're not going to get caught, are we?"

The brewing coffee smelled delicious. "No way!" I said it with a certainty I didn't feel.

"You're sure?"

"I'm sure!"

"Okay. I'll help, but just to keep you out of jail. And just as a lookout. I am not going inside."

"Hey, we're not going to be in any danger." *Forgive me, Father, for I lied yet again.* I could almost feel my nose growing longer.

The you'll-have-to-be-responsible-for-Ma threat worked. Germaine loved Ma but she'd face the devil himself in order to avoid frequent and long periods of contact with her.

I told her my plans, and she said, "I don't like this one bit. And I won't ever do it again. Ever! Do you understand?"

I pulled a coffee mug from the cupboard. "Got it. Wouldn't think of asking." *I want to stop lying, God. Are you gonna help me?*

"And the only reason I'm doing this at all is to help clear your name." Rationalization works every time.

The rich dark brew slowly filled my cup. "Thanks, Germaine. I owe you."

"Big time. What am I doing? For God sakes, I'm a nun."

I took a long swallow of the sweet nectar called coffee. "Just remember, it's for a good cause."

She grunted her disgust. I didn't think I should push it, so I got down to business.

"Meet me at my place at eight-thirty. That's tonight, Germaine."

"I know it's tonight. I'll be there."

"How about we go in your car?" I suggested. "It's less conspicuous than the Ghia."

"Right."

"Oh, and lose the frock. It could slow you down if we have to run."

She snickered. "I rarely wear my habit. And anyway, I could out run you with my legs tied together."

I knocked back another swig from the mug. "Let's hope we don't have to test that theory."

"Pen!"

"Just a little levity."

"No. Just a little smart mouth."

I accepted her statement with grace. I pretty much had to since I needed her help.

We hung up, and I filled my coffee cup again. The clock said it was noon. On the way to the shower I turned on the answering machine and heard it catch a call as I closed the bathroom door.

After I got dressed, I called Marco and left a message instructing him to call Sergeant Masters and see what he wanted. He'd do it, but he wouldn't like taking orders. Boss and employee. He would do well to remember that. *Ouch!* Even I realized I was becoming a bit cocky. Not a good sign. Utter and complete delusion couldn't be far behind. I'd deal with it later.

I cleaned the bathroom, deposited dirty laundry in the clothes hamper, and was on my way to the trash dumpster when I had my first encounter with the media. Hordes of them.

"Why me?"

I figured there'd be a local gang war, national political scandal, or a new computer virus that would take the heat off me. Wrong. Evidently, I was still the flavor of the hour. And there wasn't even sex involved. One of the news women, blond and plastic perfect, microphone in hand, rounded the corner of my building, running at me like a charging rhino. And I didn't have any make-up on!

I turned to run. The trash bag slowed me down so I tossed it aside. It hit the ground and splattered, covering the grass and sidewalk with coffee grounds, banana peels, spoiled food and—God forbid—feminine hygiene products.

On my way to the door, I sneaked a peek over my shoulder and watched, enthralled, as the blonde's heel got caught in the strap of a ratty old bra I'd thrown out. She tripped and began a free fall into the mess littering the area.

"Wow!" Now this was a Kodak moment.

I bounded through the condo door, slamming it shut just as two other reporters bounded up the steps.

Inside I leaned against the door, my breath coming fast. Then I heard someone yell, "Is it true you murdered your husband, Ms. Santucci?"

Without looking back, I ran up the stairs, into my condo and collapsed on my living room sofa.

CHAPTER TWELVE

Waiting was difficult. To occupy myself, I cleaned the refrigerator, ate, dusted the furniture, ate, made a grocery list, and ate some more because writing the grocery list made me hungry. Sure! That was why. Chomping down on a bag of Oreos didn't have anything to do with nerves. All these calories would only put more unwanted pounds on my already full-figured frame, so I tried to read a romance novel, while also watching the clock.

The steamy scenes captivated my attention. Why hadn't I been able to find a man like Hugo? Get a grip, girl. There *are* no men like Hugo.

At last! It was time to commit a felony. I changed into black jeans, black turtleneck, and skullcap. The skullcap was a bit dramatic, but a nice touch nonetheless. And I thrive on the dramatic.

Dramatic, but hot. And not in the sexy way. Most of today's calories would be lost in the warm June night air. I'd sweat them off. I fanned myself with the romance novel.

My nerves were a mess by the time Germaine rang the bell.

She laughed when she saw me. "Who are you supposed to be?"

"Never mind." Then I noticed her wardrobe. "Hey you're in black too."

"But I didn't go to central casting for my clothes."

"Looks like you did."

Germaine looked stunning in black. But then Germaine looked stunning in everything. Her slim figure, creamy complexion, long dark hair and large, brown, doe eyes stopped traffic, unless she was wearing the old-fashioned habit. I could never figure out why someone who looked like her would want to be a nun. Neither could any of her old boyfriends, some of whom were still licking their wounds years after she entered "the life." But then, as I always say, "there are callings—and then there are callings."

Germaine walked around me. "Honestly, Pen. This is not a movie; it's a burglary."

I grabbed her arm, pulling her toward the door. "Okay, okay. Let's cut the chatter and get out of here. We've got a house to break into."

At the door, I skidded to a stop and held up my hand. "Wait a minute!"

Germaine stared. "What?"

"I forgot something." I walked to the counter, read a telephone number from the paper beside the phone, and punched in the numbers. I let it ring until the answering machine picked up and I heard the judge's voice. "Good, he's not home."

"Or he's just not answering." I could hear Germaine's anxiety meter ratchet up a notch.

"Nonsense. He never misses this meeting."

She crossed her arms and held them close to her chest. "You'd better hope not."

"I have it on good authority. I'll call again before we go in."

"Before *you* go in."

"Yeah. Yeah. Come on."

"What if he has an alarm system?"

"He doesn't. I checked that out on an earlier reconnaissance trip."

Germaine shook her head.

Before we walked out of the building, I checked to make sure the media wasn't waiting to pounce. The area looked clear.

We ran to Germaine's car, and as I started to open the door, I stopped and uttered an epithet that I regretted. *Forgive me, Father, for I have lapsed. Yet again.*

Germaine, hand on the door, stared at me. "What!"

I stomped my foot. "Oh, no! I can't believe it. I am so dumb."

"Tell me, Pen. You're starting to scare me."

"I called the judge's house from my phone. What if he has caller ID?"

Germaine thumped her fist against the car door. "Great thinking! Dumb, dumber, and dumbest. It's a good thing you're not a full-time criminal." She got in the car, fastened her seat belt and muttered, "You'd have to go into another line of work. You're no good at crime."

I let it pass because she had a point. My head spun, trying to figure out what I was going to do. I shot a quick glance at Germaine. "I can explain things. I have a presentence investigation with the judge. I could have called him to discuss something. Or I could check the phone while I'm inside and erase the call." *Yeah, that sounded like a plan.*

I got in the driver's side, and Germaine tossed me the keys. I put the car in gear and started forward.

Germaine asked, "Is that normal? Calling him, I mean."

"Well, no, not exactly. but I can make it work if I have to. I'll give it some thought." I thought, and decided checking the phone for caller ID was the better idea.

She rolled her eyes. "You do that. Now, I expect you to tell me the plan on the way. I don't want any surprises. Explaining to my superiors why I'm in jail would be a piece of cake." She snapped her fingers. "Compared to facing Ma if we're caught."

Boy, she had that right.

I started to explain my plan and finished up after calling the judge's house again, this time from a pay phone at the corner pharmacy. I don't always carry my cell phone because I don't like being available to the world twenty-four-seven. Nah, that wasn't true. It was really about Ma. She'd drive me crazy if she thought I carried it all the time.

But, if the judge had caller ID and I couldn't, for some reason, erase the calls, I also didn't want a cell number displayed for all to see. One call, I could explain, but a second one would be too suspicious.

I parked Germaine's nondescript '98 Honda about three blocks from Judge Kassner's house. Although nondescript, her car, because it wasn't a Beamer, Lexus, or Mercedes might attract some attention in the upscale Lake Harriet neighborhood. But most important, I wanted a clear getaway path.

Before we got out of the car I handed Germaine the car keys and thoroughly scanned the sidewalks, fore and aft, and announced, "All clear."

Germaine shook her head. "You watch too much television."

"Yeah, other people have told me that recently."

I stashed my bag, and we first walked to the house and then around the block, checking it out from the front and back. Finally we crept around the west side of the neighbor's darkened house. Our quarry, the judge's large two story brick house, loomed in front of us.

Anxiety did a little conga dance that snaked through my body. I sucked in my breath and started walking.

I searched the hedge separating the judge's house from its neighbor for an opening large enough for us to crawl through. When I found one, I whispered, "Come on, Germaine, through here."

I got down on my stomach and using my arms shimmied through the opening, soldier style. On the other side, I stood up and brushed myself off, looking warily around me.

Germaine's whisper was raspy. "I can't believe I'm doing this. It's like a bad movie. Are you sure no one's home?"

I kept walking and whispered back, "He's a widower. No children. No girlfriend. Lives alone. I'm sure." *Lord, please, let me be right. Are you listening?*

Germaine followed me, brushing twigs and dirt from her clothes. She took off a shoe, shook it, and stumbled when she tried to put it back on. I grabbed her arm, steadied her, and pulled her around to the back of the house.

I leaned in to her and whispered, "This will all be over in about thirty minutes or so."

"Thirty minutes!" She had me by the throat. Technically she had her hands twisted around the fabric of my turtleneck and was tugging, hard. My discomfort grew. "What do you mean thirty minutes?"

Nose to nose, I clamped my hand over her mouth. "Be quiet! Do you want the entire neighborhood to hear us?"

The yard light beamed down from the top of the judge's garage, illuminating Germaine's expression. Deep furrows lined her forehead with concern. I looked in her eyes. No. That was a bad call. She had passed concern and gone straight to panic.

I removed my hand slowly from her mouth, warning her, "Shh. Don't disturb the neighbors."

Her words were clipped. "Thirty minutes is too long. Fifteen, tops."

Still locked in our private dance, I responded in a firm voice. "I can't do it in fifteen, Germaine. It's gonna take me five to pick the lock, then lock up again when we leave. Then I have to search his den, study or office, whatever he calls it. I can't do it in less than twenty-five."

Her saliva sprayed across my face. "Twenty! Or I'm not going in."

"Jeez, Germaine. I hadn't planned on you actually going *inside.*" I expelled my breath and stepped back quickly; breaking her death grip. I held my hands outward, a sign of giving up. "Okay, twenty minutes it is." Amazing, lying just got easier all the time. "Now come on."

We rounded the corner on the way to the side entrance when I bumped into a large, dark moving object. "Oh, my God!" *Father, deliver me from evil, and I'll be so good.*

"It's me, Pen."

I clutched at my chest with one hand, threw my other arm around Germaine's neck, and covered her mouth. She'd scream long into tomorrow if I took my hand away, and our capture would be all over, except for our respective criminal trespass trials.

"What are you doing here?" I whispered harshly.

Germaine bit my hand. "Ouch!" My hand fell away from her mouth.

Germaine hissed. "Shut up and tell me who this is, or I am going to start screaming and won't stop until we're out of here or in jail. I don't much care at this point."

I clamped my hand back over her mouth. "Well, I do. Shut up! It's okay."

The interloper ignored the argument between Germaine and me. "I decided to help. I didn't want you to try doing this on your own, may the Lord forgive me." Father Daniel's hastily made sign of the cross was barely visible as the yard light's beam stopped just short of where we stood.

I slowly lowered my hand from Germaine's mouth as I warned, "I'm telling you, don't scream."

Her high-pitched voiced filled the air. "Penelope Santucci! Who the dickens is this?"

See, as soon as I took my hand away, she's chattering like a runaway train. And she's so loud.

"Germaine. Quiet. It's my friend, Father Daniel Kopecky. You know, from when we were kids. In the neighborhood."

She held her forehead like she had a headache or something. "Father Daniel? You've got me and a priest helping you burglarize this place?" She took a step backward and shook her finger at me. "Oh, you're good, Pen. You're really good." She leaned forward at the waist and stared into my eyes. "Are you sure you're not possessed? Maybe we need an exorcism." She turned and began walking back toward the hedge. "You're scary. I'm getting out of here."

"Germaine," I whined.

She turned as Father Daniel's hoarse whisper sliced through the air. "Pen. Who is this woman?"

Not the most convenient place to make introductions, but it would have to do. "Father Daniel, this is Germaine, my sister, the Sister."

"She's your sister?"

Germaine, always polite, calmed down, walked back and stood by my side. "Father Daniel, eh?"

"Yeah. He's here to help."

She stepped forward and extended her hand. "Hello, Father. I'm Sister Germaine."

"Oh, you're Pen's sister."

"Yeah, but she's also a Sister," I stated emphatically. I whispered in his ear, "She's one of your fraternity members, sort of."

He looked confused. "What does that mean?"

I was tired of this game of "Who's on First?". "She's a nun, for goodness' sake!"

"A nun? You have a sister who's a nun? I don't understand, Pen."

"You don't have to. Not now, anyway."

Germaine smiled demurely. "I am a nun, Father."

"What in the world is a nun doing at a burglary?" he asked.

Germaine's smile froze; her muscles became rigid. "I might ask you the same thing, Father."

I'd had just about enough. Boy! This would teach me to invite amateurs to my crime scenes in the future. "I told you before, this isn't technically a burglary. Now come on, you two. I thought you were here to help me. Not debate about which one of you is holier." I turned to walk away. "Or, are you both here to *make sure* I go to jail?"

The religious faction in our little group became awfully quiet. They stood next to each other, not moving, probably contemplating their guilt quotient.

I decided to ease up on them. "Come on. Let's get this over with."

I cringed at the sound of their footsteps crunching nosily across the stone-filled flowerbed. These two had a lot to learn if they wanted to be successful burglars.

At the door, I ran through the now familiar routine of surgically inserting my picks into the keyhole, and delicately manipulating them until a satisfying click signaled success. I quietly opened the door a crack and flashed my penlight around. There didn't seem to be anyone home, so I stepped quickly inside. "Done."

Germaine poked her head through the door and asked, "Where did you learn to do that?"

Father Daniel leaned over Germaine's shoulder asked, "What I'd like to know is *why* you learned it?"

"Not now!" I turned to my cohorts in crime. They were beginning to get on my nerves. "You guys wait here. I'll be back." I sounded like Arnold himself.

"Hurry up, you've got fifteen minutes," Germaine ordered.

"Twenty, remember?"

She grumbled.

"I'll be out as fast as I can," I said.

"You'd better. This entire scene is making me nervous. And I have to go to the bathroom."

Great! The situation continued to deteriorate. It seemed I'd brought along a two-year-old. "Just hold it, Germaine. Keep watch. You know the drill if there's a problem."

"Yeah, I'll whistle. Two long and one short."

My first problem was fingerprints. I didn't want to leave any behind, I pulled on the latex gloves that had become as much a part of my job as the paperwork, essential when taking the dreaded, but court-ordered urinalyses on clients. The second problem was the phone. I found it and the dreaded caller ID in the kitchen. Luckily it was just like mine so I punched both numbers I had called from. Erased. One job completed successfully. Now, for the tough stuff.

I pushed open the door to the right of the kitchen and gasped. "Oh!" A long-haired white cat bounded from the dining room.

"What's wrong?" Germaine was framed in the doorway.

"Just a cat."

"Well, be careful!"

I ignored her, walked down the hall, and looked into open doorways using my penlight until I located the judge's office. I started with the desk and then searched the file cabinets. Nothing incriminating anywhere. I'd drawn a blank.

I checked my watch—I'd been inside for about ten minutes.

I quickly made my rounds on the lower level of the house, checking all the rooms to see if there was another place that looked like it would hold any sort of evidence. I didn't have a clue what it would be, but I'd know it when I saw it.

Time flew too fast. I'd already been inside for fifteen minutes. I'd have to be out in another ten. That might be pushing it. Better make it five. If Germaine got too nervous, she might come looking for me.

I bounded up the stairs and contemplated the bedrooms. Maybe he kept important things in his bedroom. I checked three closed doors. Nothing. I opened another that might be the master bedroom. "Yes!"

Then I heard a low growl. I focused my penlight on the beast. A dog, not a big one, quite a small one, in fact. A fluffy white powder puff with a protruding under bite. It would have been adorable if it weren't baring its teeth like a crazed monkey. He or she definitely didn't want me intruding on his or her personal space.

Before I had a chance to pull the door shut, the long-haired rag bounced off the bed and lunged at me. I turned tail just in time and ran down the steps as fast as I could.

The nasty little monster nipped at my ankles in between growls. I ran into the kitchen with Fido hot on my heels. There was a sharp bark and then a hissing noise.

The dog and cat met, like two alien warriors, under the table.

I stopped at the open back door and peeked under the table. The dog and cat were silently stalking each other. Suddenly, the cat thrust his paw at the dog and bopped him on the jaw. The chase was on.

"Oh, no! This can't be happening!"

The dog retaliated, the cat jumped backward, hissing, then they flew at each other, launching a domestic disagreement of grand proportions.

Not knowing what to do, I shouted for my back up team. "Get the dog!"

Germaine popped through the door. "What?"

"Get the dog! Father, get the cat! We have to separate them."

The barking and hissing grew louder, more intense.

"They're fighting!" Germaine yelled.

"You think?" And believe it or not, my tone was somewhat less sarcastic than I felt.

The animals were really scrapping now; it sounded like a barroom brawl.

"Get in here, Germaine. We have to get them separated so I can lock up before the entire world knows we're here and they broadcast our arrests on CNN and Fox News."

Germaine slipped through the door and pulled on my arm. "Come on. Leave them. We've got to get out of here."

Father Daniel stood behind Germaine, shaking his head. "I told you, no good would come of breaking the law." He made the sign of the cross and added, "Let this be a lesson to you, Pen."

I planted my feet wide, and shoved my fists on my hips; John Wayne couldn't have done it better. Then I gave orders. "Save the lecture, Father. We've got to get those animals. Now!" I almost shouted.

"My God!" Germaine screamed.

The dog chased the cat right between my legs and darted out the open back door.

"No!" I dove for the door.

My troops followed.

"Go after the dog, Germaine."

She grabbed at the zippy wad of fluff, missed, and fell forward screaming.

Lights from the house to the east of the judge's went on. The curtains wiggled. "Hit the deck," I ordered.

Germaine was already down. Father Daniel followed her example. The rotund priest flopped to the ground and covered his head. Maybe he thought if he couldn't see them, they couldn't see him. Father Daniel, spread eagle on the ground, was huffing and puffing. I sure hoped the Parish had a good medical plan.

I squeezed my eyes shut and moaned. "The neighbors have probably called the police by now."

That's when the dog started barking again and the cat yowled and scurried up a tree. I crawled back toward the house.

"Follow me, you guys," I whispered as loud as I dared. "Hug the edge of the house, and let's get out of here."

For once, they did as they were told without a theological debate. I looked back at the mess we left behind. The back door flapped open in the night breeze. And in the distance, a familiar sound grew louder with each passing second. "Sirens!"

Germaine whined, "Why me, Lord?"

"Spiritual questions later, Germaine. It's the cops. Get Father Daniel out of here. Get him to his car, and I'll meet you at yours in five minutes."

"But—"

"Don't argue. Go!"

They crawled around the side of the house as fast as they could.

I glanced back one last time, surveying my botched up job, and groaned. Oh, yeah. I'd done it up good this time. The teeny tiny mop dog yapped enough for a pack of frenzied hunting beagles at the yowling cat stuck up the tree.

Nope. Absolutely, no way could I get the two of them back inside and locked up before the police arrived. Not without getting caught. But I might be able to undo some damage. Divert the authorities. Thwart their efforts to piece everything together. Make this look like a good old-fashioned random act of violence.

Hunched over, low to the ground, I ran back to the door, shut it, then stuck my hand up inside my sweatshirt for protection and punched in the glass. Now it would appear to be a simple break-in. But I was going to have to figure out a way to pay for the glass. Costs were mounting.

Using my sweatshirt, I rubbed the doorknob clean of any prints left behind by Germaine and Father Daniel, and left the door standing wide open, swaying in the breeze. I started down the steps just as the squad screeched to a stop in front of the house. It would be close. But I was betting on me.

I ran to the hedge and searched frantically for the opening. Finding it, I slithered through just as I heard Minneapolis's finest round the corner. Close. Too close. I peeked through the hedge.

CHAPTER THIRTEEN

"Over here!" the first cop yelled.

"Punched in the window." The second cop drew his gun and leaned into the open door. "Most likely they've been and gone."

The yapping and yowling had died out entirely. The cat sat calmly in the crotch of the tree mewing meekly, and the rag doll dog rested nonchalantly on the grass below. Waiting.

The first cop drew his service revolver and hugged the edge of the door. Just as he was about to enter, the dog took exception to the strangers about to invade his territory. His growl began deep in his throat and rose in pitch and ended in a loud bark.

I clamped a hand over my mouth to muffle my plea, "Oh, no!"

I scooted backward through the shrubbery on my butt and peered through the leaves. Another fierce growl was followed by the dog's sharp yipping. As it scampered toward the cop, and when he was about three feet from his target, he launched off the ground like a jet-propelled rocket.

"Get this mutt off me, Ralph!"

Curiosity won out over personal safety. I had to see what was happening, so I stood and peered over the top of the hedge. Fluffy might be small but he was one determined pooch. He clamped those little bulldog teeth onto the cop's pant leg and wouldn't let go. The officer hopped on one leg and shook the other, trying to free himself. Suspended in air, the dog hung on, growling fiercely.

"Get him off me, Ralph!" the cop ordered again.

"How do you propose I do that, Joe?"

"Shoot it, if you have to." He and the dog hopped, fused together in their own circle dance.

"I can't shoot him! The dumb mutt's gotta be Judge Kassner's dog, Joe," Ralph replied calmly. "He's just trying to protect the place."

The dog continued to growl, Joe continued to shake his leg, trying to loosen the dog's grip, and Ralph, arms and legs widespread, edged closer to his prey.

"Do something!" Joe yelled.

"Even if I could shoot it, I don't have a good position. I might hit you," Ralph yelled back.

"Then mace him or something. Just get him off me!"

The dog's voice sounded hoarse from all the growling.

"No can do, Joe. I don't want a desk job."

Joe groaned, continuing to shake his leg. The mop-like dog, followed, swinging through the air. "Do something! Stun him, anything, but get him off me!"

"I told you, I'm not hurting the judge's dog, Joe."

This was going nowhere. It looked like a very good time for me to leave. I'd tarried too long at the fair. Crouching low, I scurried across the darkened back yard of the neighbor to the west of the judge's house. Just then I heard the dog's piercing yelp and glanced back toward Kassner's yard. My legs lost solid ground. Splash!

I surfaced sputtering and clutching at the side of a swimming pool. A pool? Who has a pool? Didn't these people know they live in Minnesota? What a waste of a backyard for only three months of the year.

Holding onto the edge, I stayed low in the water and prayed the homeowners or Joe and Ralph hadn't heard me take the plunge and might decide to investigate. Holding my breath, the silence became deafening. Waiting for a few moments and hearing nothing, I took a chance, hoisted myself over the side and dashed around the far side of the house to the street.

I ran like the wind all the way to Germaine's car. Except Germaine's car wasn't where it was supposed to be. I looked around to make sure I was in the right place. I was. It wasn't. Evidently, my getaway car had gotten away.

I stomped my feet and the sloshing just made me angrier. Wouldn't you know it? You just can't trust clergy turned criminals. They're completely unreliable.

"I don't believe it!" Dripping wet, chilled to the bone in the night air, I plopped down on the curb to consider my predicament. I was several miles from my home and there was no way I would be able to find a cab in this neighborhood. With no other choice, I hoisted myself to my feet and began walking, my tennis shoes squished with each step, leaving a trail even a dumb rag mutt like Kassner's dog should be able to follow.

"So what if the cops stop me," I muttered. After the night I'd had, I could use some rest, even if it was in jail. It'd almost be a relief.

I still had a long way to travel. To occupy myself I concocted the various ways I could make a priest and a nun suffer for leaving me behind. None of them were pretty.

Chapter Fourteen

The wood door rattled like chattering teeth each time my fist made contact.

"Open up you cowards," I snarled. "I know you're in there, Germaine. You've got a key and this is where you'd come."

Silence.

I pounded harder, with both fists this time. "You heard me. Open up! You'll have to come out sometime!"

The door flew open, Germaine reached out and yanked me inside. "Pen! My God! Where have you been?" She pushed me away and wrinkled her nose. "Phew! Maybe I should ask, what have you been doing?"

"Swimming, Germaine." I grumbled, gave her my most ferocious scowl, reached for a dishtowel, and began drying tangled clumps of hair.

"I decided it was such a nice night that I'd go swimming. Isn't that what everybody does after committing a burglary?" My left eye twitched. It must have been stress related. "Okay, now you know what *I've* been doing, Germaine." I flicked the towel at her, and she jumped backward. "The real question is, what have you and the good Father been doing while I was out there in the dark, hiking home, soaking wet? Been taking tea with the Queen?"

"Pen, I'm sorry. Let me explain."

Ignoring her, I bent over and began towel drying my hair.

Germaine leaned down, moved the towel, and peered at me.

"Pen, please."

"So, go ahead, already. Explain," I mumbled through damp strands of hair.

Father Daniel said, "I don't understand. Why on earth would you go swimming at this time of night?"

I stood up, flipping limp clumps of hair back over my shoulders. Mouths agape, Germaine and I stared at Father Daniel, then giggled.

"What's so funny?" he asked.

"She didn't go swimming, Father Daniel."

"But she said—"

When Germaine burst out laughing, I scowled at her and said to Father Daniel, "I know what I said, Father."

"What happened then? You're all wet." He looked confused.

I ran my fingers through my hair, trying to untangle it. "I fell into the neighbor's pool making my getaway from Judge Kassner's house."

"Are you all right? You didn't get hurt, did you?" he asked.

"Only my pride."

Germaine sobered. "Are you sure, you're okay?"

"Yes, I'm sure." I pointed my finger at Germaine. "You . . ." Then the same finger arced through the air until it zeroed in on Father Daniel. ". . . And you. Where were you? When I got to where the car was supposed to be, you were gone." My earlier frustration had receded some. Now, it grew to a new level. "You left me out there."

"Pen—"

I stamped my foot. "Don't Pen me, Father."

"We took my car to Germaine's, but when you didn't come . . ." Father Daniel offered.

"A car came down the street with a—what do they call it?—a bubble on top, going like crazy. We didn't think we should stick around," Germaine interrupted.

"You mean a lousy squad car scared you away?" I asked.

"Yeah, and that squad car stood between us and our freedom," she answered.

"Don't be so melodramatic, Germaine. The cops weren't after you. They probably didn't even notice you. It was most likely a back-up car heading to the judge's house."

Germaine threw her hands up in the air. "I realize that now."

"You weren't thinking clearly," I accused.

"I don't normally do burglaries, Pen. The sirens scared me. Besides, you're resourceful. I knew you'd get home, if you weren't caught."

How could I argue with that kind of logic? I sniffed loudly. "Thanks for your vote of confidence."

Germaine tilted her head in Father Daniel's direction and looked hard at me. Her voice became soft and I had to strain to hear her. "Pen, I'm sorry. I had to get Father Daniel out of there." She eased over to me and whispered, "Have mercy, Pen. I thought he was gonna have a heart attack."

My stomach lurched as I realized what my little escapade might have cost the people who care about me, who tried to help me.

I plopped down on a stool. "I'm sorry. I didn't think it would turn out like this."

Father Daniel clucked his sympathy. "None of us expected it to turn out like this. But we knew the risks when we agreed to help."

"You could have been arrested, ended up in jail, or worse." I focused on Father Daniel. "You could have been shot by the police!"

A smile cracked Germaine's face, and then a small giggle erupted deep in her throat. She looked at Father Daniel, and his grin widened, and a guffaw escaped from him. And while I was feeling shame and guilt, a Catholic's solace, and I wasn't even Catholic, these two were doubled over in laughter.

"What are you guys laughing about?"

Germaine snickered. "I can't believe it. Pen, I'm a nun!" She nodded toward Father Daniel, "And he's a priest. We don't *do* burglaries."

"Well you did," I accused.

"Yeah, we did. Your twisted thinking started this process. And we went along for the ride. All of us could have ended up in jail."

Father Daniel gulped between episodes of laughter. "You convinced *us* to commit a crime, Pen, you could rule the world if you put your mind to it."

"That's why we're laughing, Pen. It's all so . . . so . . ."

"Three Stooges," Father Daniel finished for her.

The prickly heat of embarrassment snaked up my neck.

Germaine reached in a drawer, pulled out a dry towel, and offered it to me. "You know, Father. It's bad enough that she needs a keeper," she rolled her eyes and shook her head. "But what about us?"

Father Daniel sobered, then gave warning, "You just can't continue breaking into houses, Pen. It's wrong, not to mention against the law." He looked toward Heaven. "Forgive me, Father."

Germaine said, "While we're on the subject of breaking and entering, care to fill us in on the neat little trick you've acquired?"

"What trick?" I asked innocently.

Father Daniel grumbled, "Don't play dumb, Pen. We watched you with your set of tools. Just how did you acquire that skill?"

"More importantly," Germaine continued, "are you into stuff that's really bad? Do you supplement your salary with crime?"

I huffed. "How can you suggest that?"

"It's not hard. You're pretty proficient at picking locks." She held her hand out, palm upward. "Let's see the little devils that work so well under your tutelage."

I stood my ground. "Come on, guys. This is stupid."

Father Daniel chimed in. "Give, Pen. You asked us to break the law; the least you can do is show us your tools and tell us how you've acquired such an interesting skill."

I rubbed the back of my neck. I was tired and dirty, not to mention damp and probably a little on the ripe side. The swimming pool smelled like its owners hadn't properly maintained it.

My partners in crime wore grim expressions, and it didn't look like they were going to let the subject die.

"It's late, I doubt with everything that's happened any of us will get much sleep tonight." I nodded towards the coffee-maker. "Germaine, make some coffee. I'll get cleaned up and tell you everything."

She looked at me suspiciously. "Honest?"

"Come on, would I lie?"

They both shouted, "Yes!"

I cringed. "Nah. I won't. Not this time."

After a quick shower, I curled up in the corner of the living room sofa. Father Daniel and Germaine had each shed their shoes, were ensconced in armchairs and clutching coffee mugs.

Germaine was the first to speak. "Okay. No more procrastination."

I took a long drink of the hot, dark brew. "It all started with one of my clients . . ."

Germaine closed her eyes and pinched the bridge of her nose. "I knew it." She cocked her head and eyed Father Daniel. "What did I tell you?"

"Be quiet, Germaine."

"Yes, hush. I want to hear this," Father Daniel ordered.

She looked at him knowingly. "It figures. I'm beginning to

think you're an excitement junkie."

He scowled at her. "Nonsense. I'm just interested, that's all." He turned to me. "Go ahead."

"Thank you, Father." I made a face at Germaine. "Now, as I was saying, one of my probationers was going 'off paper.' That means he had successfully completed all the conditions of probation. He picked locks. That's how he did his burglaries."

Both of God's soldiers were paying rapt attention to my every word, proof that voyeurs come in all shapes, sizes, and occupations.

I continued, "Well, I was curious about his, uh, talents. We'd talked about it several times. One day he brought me a board with different kinds of locks. Then he pulled out an ebony set of picks, the set you saw. And he gave them to me."

"No!" Germaine had a stricken look on her face.

I gave her a disgusted look. Father Daniel ignored her. "Go on, Pen."

I shook my head. "You both need to get out more. At least see a movie now and then. It's un-American not to have any more knowledge of crime than the two of you do."

Father Daniel huffed impatiently. "We just don't have the same opportunities you have."

"As I was saying, my client, Otis, gave me the lock picks as a gift because I'd always been fair with him."

Germaine snorted derisively.

"Cut it, Germaine. I am fair. And I didn't plan on keeping the tools. It's against department policy to accept gifts from clients. But I did let him teach me how to use them."

"Bored, were you? Thought you'd spice up your life, give lessons to budding young criminals, maybe?" Germaine's smug sarcasm oozed out like stinky dog doo in the small room.

"No, Germaine. I wasn't bored. Paul had changed the locks on the house—I couldn't get my personal belongings. I figured lock-picking might come in handy. And it did."

She clapped her hands. "You learned your craft pretty well, I'd say."

"It's not a craft, Germaine."

"So why did you keep the tools?" Father Daniel asked.

I held my head high. "I plan on returning them the first chance I get."

Germaine threw her hands in the air. "Sure! Oh, I believe that."

"Germaine!" Father Daniel warned. "If Pen says she intends to return the lock picks, I'm sure she will."

Germaine covered her mouth to stifle a chuckle.

I scowled at her and smiled sweetly at Father Daniel. "Thank you, Father. I appreciate your faith in me."

He didn't miss a beat. "Now, Pen, just when are you going to return them?"

Cornered! I snuck a peek at my sister and saw a grin spreading across her face.

I stared at the floor. "I . . . I'm not exactly sure. You see, I don't exactly travel in the same circles as Otis does."

Germaine crossed her arms across her chest. In a singsong voice she pinned my feeble excuses, "And just exactly when do you intend to return the picks, Pen?"

I jumped up. "Cut it, Germaine . . ."

"Now, now, Pen. Bickering will get us nowhere," Father Daniel admonished me.

I wandered to the kitchen for more coffee. "Okay. So I don't have any intention of returning them. They're a handy little set of tools." I returned to the living room, set my cup on the table and flopped on the sofa.

"See, I knew it." Thinking she'd proven her point she jumped up gleefully. "Ma was right. This job of yours is ruining your life."

I sat, rigid. "How dare you! We've been lucky, Germaine. We've got parents who love us and want the best for us." I stopped and thought about Ma. "Well, you know what I mean. Otis didn't have the opportunities we've had." I sucked in my breath. "He's taught me a valuable skill."

"You really should reconsider this, Pen. No good can come of having and using these tools. I'll pray for you." Father Daniel shook his head sadly.

I ignored him.

"He gave you lock picks, taught you how to use them. How are you going to help him?"

"I've got a little money."

She slapped the palm of her hand against her forehead. "How did Ma produce a liberal like you?"

"I'll just pay for the tools."

"Hey, what money? You don't have any money." Germaine didn't know anything about the money, and I preferred to keep it that way for now.

I gave Father Daniel a meaningful look. "I'm just thinking about Paul's insurance money." I looked upwards. Well, it wasn't exactly a lie. *Lord forgive me for the growing number of half truths.*

Father Daniel must have thought partial truth was better than none at all. He glared at me, but let the statement pass.

Germaine glanced at her watch. "It's one in the morning. I've got to get home."

Father Daniel stood up. "I am not going to be able to get up tomorrow, I mean today."

"Hey, sleep in." He looked shocked at the suggestion. As he walked to the door he said, "I'll take care of a few things and meet you at church for Paul's funeral." He nodded toward Germaine. "She told me while we were waiting for you."

A sharp pain stabbed me in the pit of my stomach. I didn't want to think about the funeral.

He took my hand in his large gnarly one. "No matter what you think, you'll need the support of all of us around you."

"Maybe he can protect you from Ma," Germaine said.

I laughed and gave the priest a hug. "I'd like it if you'd come." I shivered. "I don't expect a warm reception from Paul's family. Especially his mother."

He squeezed my shoulders. "I can't say I approve of everything you do, Pen. And as much as I hate to admit it, I sure am having fun. Tomorrow won't be fun. Funerals never are. But we'll all be there together."

I hugged him again and watched as he left. You just never know about people—they can be real stinkers. Then when you least expect it, the saints come marching in.

I turned to Germaine and suggested, "Why don't you stay here tonight?"

She yawned. "I'd like to, but I think I'll go home. I'm not teaching tomorrow. Sister Josephine is covering for me, but there are some other things I need to do. I'll be here a half hour before the funeral. We don't want to be late, on the other hand, under the circumstances, we don't want to be too early either."

I nodded.

She gave me a quick kiss and ordered, "How about I stay with you tomorrow night? I have a feeling that's when you're going to need the support."

"Would you?"

"Of course."

I hugged her, saw her out the door, and breathed deeply. It had been quite a night. I'd need to wind down a little. I went to the corner of the living room, sat down at my desk, and booted up the computer to play hearts. Not one anonymous person knew or cared that they were playing online with a murder suspect.

When I finally got up to go to bed I saw the infamous blinking red light. I hadn't looked at it when I got home. I hit the play button on my answering machine.

"Penelope?" I winced at the familiar voice. "Penelope? Pick up the phone. This is your mother."

I held my head in my hands.

She continued, "Where are you? Don't you ever stay home?" There was a pause, as if she expected an answer. Not receiving one she continued, "About the funeral. I haven't been able to reach Germaine. No one at that *place* seems to know where she is."

Best that they didn't, I thought.

"Honestly, don't either of you ever stay home? Well, your father wanted me to tell you that we'll pick you up tomorrow."

Deliver me from doing evil, Lord.

"It will be a difficult day, but one we must bear. Honestly, can you imagine Astrid Preston telling us we shouldn't come to the funeral? Why, what would that look like?"

Probably like I was guilty of murder, I thought. Maybe that was what Paul's mother was hoping for.

"You be ready, Penelope."

The phone went dead. No good-bye or so long. Just deliver the message and hang up. *See ya later, Ma.*

Suddenly, I wasn't tired anymore. Back to the computer.

CHAPTER FIFTEEN

It was well after two A.M. when I finally fell asleep. When I woke up, my first thought was of Paul's funeral. I wasn't looking forward to the public scrutiny. I don't subscribe to masochism. I snuggled deeper under the sheets as I thought about my day. What I really wanted to do was pull the covers over my head and wait for the boogie man to visit someone else.

The telephone rang just as I was just about to pull back the covers and take on the day. Screening my calls had been a priority. But with everything on my mind, I didn't think about it, and just nonchalantly picked up the receiver.

"Hello."

A weak, raspy voice said, "Penelope?"

I looked heavenward and sighed deep and long. "Yeah, Ma. What's wrong? You sound sorta funny."

Then I remembered that Ma had insisted on attending the funeral with me. Ma was a formidable opponent. If she wanted something she kept at it until she succeeded. Mostly she wore me down, and I gave in just to shut her up. Any strength I had left had sailed south for a much needed vacation, leaving me to sadly accept my fate. I would be attending my husband's funeral with my mother. *Deliver me from Ma, Lord.*

"I might be dying, Penelope."

The Hallelujah Choir belted out a chorus in my mind. I glimpsed the golden rays of freedom on the horizon. She'd just handed me a brief stay of execution. I knew, no way was Ma dying. We'd been over this ground too many times. But her hypochondria couldn't have had better timing if I'd orchestrated it myself. *Yes, there is a God.*

I played along, barely able to contain my excitement. "What are you talking about, Ma?"

"You okay, Penelope? You sound funny."

Of course I sounded funny. I was deliriously happy that I might be spared my mother's companionship at Paul's funeral. There would be no one, other than myself, who could say something stupid that might reflect badly on me.

Ma plodded on. "It might be my heart."

With every statement she made, I became more relaxed. She didn't have a heart problem. Based on her history, she'd probably eaten something that hadn't agreed with her and had a touch of heartburn. But I'd go along with it. "Have you called the doctor?"

She snorted. "Doctors! They don't know everything. They're nothing more than highly skilled mechanics."

Translated, this meant she had called the doctor and didn't get the response she wanted.

I rubbed the back of my neck, weary, because I knew where the conversation was going. We began the Santucci family communication ritual. "But Ma, if you're sick, you should check it out."

Silence. She is a stubborn woman. I would have to coax her.

"Have you said anything to Pop?"

"What would your father know about a heart attack?"

Only that it wasn't a heart attack.

"Ma, what do you want me to do?" Dangerous territory, but I took the risk. No matter what, Ma knew I had obligations today that were bigger than her heartburn.

She sighed wearily. "Nothing. There's nothing anyone can do. It's in God's hands, now." She paused. "Perhaps you could come over, keep me company before the funeral, or after. Let me know how everything went."

That did it. I was attending my estranged husband's funeral, was a suspect in his murder, and Ma wanted me to catch her up on all the gossip. Determined to skip the rest of the script, I went straight to the finale.

"Ma, am I to understand that you are not coming to the funeral?" I could only hope for a reprieve.

"That's what I'm calling you about. How can I possibly go, feeling like this? Why, I could die during the service. It would be so embarrassing for everyone."

Mostly her. Her heartburn must have been a bit touchier than normal. Nothing else would dissuade her from attending Paul's funeral. Or any funeral for that matter.

Running my fingers through my hair, I said, "If you're not feeling well, Ma, you should stay home." Please!

"I don't want Astrid Preston to think she scared me away."

That wouldn't occur to anyone, much less Astrid. "Ma, I'll be sure to tell Astrid you're ill and give her your sympathy."

"Well, okay. That would be all right. But not so much sympathy that she really believes we'll miss Paul."

Leave it to Ma to have the ability to dole out sympathy in miserly increments.

"Sure, Ma, I understand." This conversation needed to end. I began to orbit precariously around her neurotic thought process. If I wasn't careful she'd suck me in and I'd be riding on her planet.

"You'll know what to say, Penelope. That is if you stop long enough to think about it. You know, before you open your mouth." Leave it to Ma, give me a compliment, then take it away.

I changed the subject. It's always best to limit the level of maudlin thoughts Ma is allowed. "Is Pop coming to the funeral?"

Another sigh. "No. I think he should stay with me so if I go into cardiac arrest he can call the ambulance."

Poor Pop. Then again, he probably didn't want to go to Paul's funeral any more than I did. He had a great ready-made excuse. Good for him.

"Okay, Ma. You take care. I'll talk to you later."

It was too much to ask that I could escape that easily. No, Mary Santucci had an agenda.

"You could come by, or at least, call me later and tell me about the funeral—what Astrid wore and everything."

It's too bad it wouldn't be filmed because nothing short of a play-by-play would satisfy Ma's insatiable curiosity.

To avoid an actual commitment I quickly replied, "I'll call you later. Get well."

Before she could say anything else, I hung up and marched off to the shower, like a sacrificial lamb to the slaughter.

A lot of people attending the funeral wanted a piece of me. I prayed the day would pass quickly and I would escape in one piece. I didn't hold out much hope.

CHAPTER SIXTEEN

Tires squealing, Germaine accelerated the old Honda into the church parking lot with the deftness of a seasoned racecar driver.

A sharp turn tossed me up against the door, and my dress snagged on a jagged piece of cracked vinyl. Germaine needed a new car but wouldn't consider buying one because she took her vow of poverty seriously—in most areas of life. She fudged on the little things, like books, fabric, and chocolate.

Peering through raindrops pelting the side window, I spotted several local television news vans, their crews scattered in a casual but definable pattern on the church lawn. Not much hope the vultures would take a day off. No, high-profile funerals were the stuff that made careers.

Germaine braked hard at the edge of the paved parking lot at the back of the church. "Gotcha here and with time to spare." Her face radiated self-satisfaction.

A frown spread across my face, my brows furrowed. "Yeah, I'm *so* lucky."

She retorted with a motherly cluck.

The windshield wipers beat a brisk rat-a-tat-tat against the window glass in a feeble attempt to clear away the dreary weather. Funerals and rain don't mix well. I pushed my sunglasses further up on my nose and slunk lower in the seat. There wouldn't be any respite from the heavy drizzle or the reporters. Today was just a bad weather day.

I held my head in my hands. "Germaine, I don't know if I

can run the gauntlet. I'm tired of dodging the police, news media, and everyone else."

Germaine's eyes scanned the area, checking out the media troops. "You won't have to. Have faith in your big sister."

Her smile broadened as she eased the car forward and picked up speed. When she reached the edge of the parking lot, she slowed down, then bounced over the natural incline. She squeezed the gas pedal until the car leapt up on the lawn.

"What are you doing? You're gonna ruin the grass in this soggy mess."

"Just hang on."

"Yeah, right. I'll have to replace the grass you've just carved up."

She grinned and shifted gears. "I'm making sure those sharks don't get a chance to feed on you for breakfast. They can't see you from here."

Her whacky logic made sense. Hopefully the groundskeeper would understand when he saw the damage she'd done to the carefully maintained lawn.

She drove another hundred yards before pulling up next to the back door of the church, braking hard. She quickly scoped out the area and ordered, "Get out!"

I glanced behind us at the deep ruts in the grass. "We're gonna get into so much trouble for making this mess." I closed my eyes and shook my head. "Less than twenty-four hours with me and you're acting more like a criminal than a nun."

"Don't be silly." But she made the sign of the cross, just to be sure. "Do you want to get caught in that media mess out there?"

"No, but . . ."

"Then get out," she ordered again. "They're going to figure it out any minute. Go!"

"But, Germaine . . ."

She leaned across me and unlocked the door. "Out, now! Before they . . ." she glanced over her shoulder, ". . . devour you. I'll join you inside in a few minutes."

In my haste to outrun the inevitable mob, I stumbled through a puddle, splashing large droplets of muddy water on my skirt and water logging my new shoes. It was that luck thing again. It wasn't going to be a good day. I stepped gingerly to higher ground.

Germaine didn't wait for me to shut the car door before she made a wide loop, crossed back over the lawn, door flapping, and headed for the parking lot.

"There's a job waiting for you somewhere as a getaway driver," I called out to her.

I'd forgotten my umbrella, but it was too late to worry about it now. As I trudged up the church steps, drizzle snaked down my neck, giving me a wet shiver. I was half way up the stairs when someone rounded the corner of the building. A tall slender man sprinted toward me and beckoned to another who followed with a camera. Busted.

Dashing up the last three steps, I slid through the door with time to spare. The media wouldn't be feasting on me anytime soon.

I shook the dripping water from my hair, skittered down the hall and around corners until I reached a small alcove where I waited impatiently for Germaine. When she arrived, we made our way through the maze of hallways to the front of the mammoth old church.

Father Daniel and Marco stood waiting in the large common room at the front entrance. Marco stopped his foot-tapping and stepped forward when he saw me. A frown marred his beautifully chiseled face. "You're late." He glanced fleetingly at Germaine.

"I am not," I snapped. "Anyway, what are you doing here?"

"I'm your lawyer; it's my job to be here. And you are late."

I checked my watch. "We've got at least five minutes before the service begins."

"That's cutting it a little close, isn't it? As the grieving widow, you're supposed to arrive ahead of time."

I lowered my eyes and, for some reason, my voice trembled, "I'm not coming as the widow. I'm here out of some sort of misguided belief that I have to pay my final respects to Paul."

Marco leaned toward me and peered through the lenses of my glasses. "Why are you wearing those ridiculous glasses?"

Averting my eyes, I replied, "It's . . . it's just the funeral." I lightly touched the frame of the sunglasses with my index finger and pushed them up on my face. "I've been crying." *Dear Lord, when will the lies cease?*

Father Daniel stepped forward. "Are you sure nothing else is wrong?"

A small giggle escaped from Germaine as she approached us. "Don't be silly, it's just a disguise."

The look I gave her could freeze hell.

Father Daniel nodded, "I thought as much. Now I don't mean to offend you, Pen, but I don't think the disguise will work."

Marco turned to Germaine and asked curtly, "And who are you?"

She stiffened and replied, "I'm . . ."

I lightly placed my hand on Germaine's arm. "Marco, this is my sister, Sister Germaine."

"Your sister the Sister?" he asked.

"No." I stated firmly, "We're not going there again. Germaine is my sister. We won't go into her job classification."

Father Daniel chuckled as the last few stragglers entered the church and clapped an arm around Marco's shoulder. "I'll explain it to you later, son. We should go in now."

Marco frowned but remained silent. At least his attention had been diverted from me.

As I peered into the church, a thought crossed my mind. Ever concerned about finances, I placed my arm on Marco's and whispered, "Are you charging me to attend the funeral?"

He became rigid. "No. I'm here because I think I should be. If you'd asked me, then you'd be charged."

"Whew!"

Germaine peered over her own glasses. "Where should we sit?"

"Any seats together in back?" I inquired without enthusiasm.

Marco took my elbow and gently guided me through the double doors. "Come on. Everything's taken care of. We've got seats up front, behind the immediate family." My mind whirred. Apparently Marco had taken it upon himself to set up a scenario, where, as the grieving widow, I would actively participate in my dear departed husband's funeral. I didn't much like the idea. It felt fake, bordering on tacky. And I didn't want any part of it.

I skidded to a stop and wrenched my arm from Marco's grip and whispered harshly, "What do you mean up front? Paul's mother won't tolerate that." My eyes burned. "*I* won't tolerate that!"

Marco, his mouth close to my ear, hissed, "Pen, behave yourself! People are watching."

"I'd have to care."

"Well, you should," he growled. He pasted a very public smile on his face and in an even tone said, "Everything's taken care of. I explained the situation, from a legal point of view, and the family awaits your arrival."

"Like the plague."

He shrugged. "Whatever works."

"You blackmailed them," I accused.

He shifted nervously. "It's not like that."

I glowered at him.

"It's for your own good."

"Well I don't like it. We were separated. Nobody expects me to be grieving."

"Appearances are everything, Pen," he wheedled. "The police are watching!"

"Boy, you don't miss a trick, do you?"

He took my arm again and smiled smugly. "It's what you pay me for, my dear."

I stuck my tongue out at him. My childish habit resurfaced. I'd have to work on the maturity factor.

"Nice." He fixed a plastic smile on his face and tightened his grip on my arm. "Put on a good show for the police at least. Oh heck, and while you're at it, why not have an orange jumpsuit made up special for your trial."

My eyes darted around the church. "Do you really think the cops are here?"

"Without a doubt. They always go to the funeral of a murder victim." He pointed to the back row where Sergeant Masters stood. "They want to see who's there, what's going on. Besides, the murderer often puts in an appearance."

My frown did not turn upside down at that statement. It just became longer. "Great. I'm the prime suspect, and I showed up."

"In your case it would look worse if you didn't."

Marco must know what he was doing. If acting like the bereaved widow would keep me from spending the next thirty years trying to dig out of jail with a soup spoon, I'd just have to play the part. "Okay, I'll do it. I won't like it, but I'll do it."

"Good girl." He drew me closer to him and looked around. "And your family. Where are they by the way?"

Father Daniel echoed his inquiry. "Yes, where are your

parents, Pen?"

"Ma is sick," I mumbled. "And Pop stayed home with her."

Marco grumbled low in his throat, then urged me forward. "It would have looked better if they were here."

I jerked my head upward. "For god's sake, Marco, she's ill!"

He patted my arm. "Okay, okay. There's nothing we can do about it now."

"You talk as if appearances are everything."

"Appearances could help keep you out of jail."

That shut me up.

As I walked with Marco down the long aisle, I kept my eyes focused on the wooden cross hanging above the pulpit. I didn't have the courage to make eye contact with any of the people in the pews. Their silent accusations were hard to bear. I could almost hear them mumbling, "There she goes. That's Paul's murderer."

When we arrived at our pew, Marco stopped abruptly. My gaze rested on Paul's casket. I stumbled, fell forward, and clutched at the corner of a pew. A small murmur rose from the onlookers. My face went hot.

Marco grasped my arm, righted me, and then stepped aside allowing me to slide into the pew. As we settled ourselves, Astrid Preston turned around, hatred flashing from her dark eyes.

I attempted a weak smile. She abruptly turned around, her intense anger making me shudder.

The service was a blur. When it was over, I meekly followed Marco, Germaine, and Father Daniel back down the aisle.

The hair on my neck bristled as people's eyes met mine, indicting me without a trial. If this was the old days in the wild west they'd be tossing a noose over a nearby tree. I clung tighter to Marco's arm and walked as briskly as I could without making it appear that I was running away. Which was exactly what I was doing.

The dark sky continued to dump rain as we emerged from the church. While Marco opened his umbrella, I scanned the churchyard for the vultures in journalists' clothing. Drenched, but alert, they were waiting in small clumps, their cameras covered with plastic. When they saw me, the camera covers were collectively ripped off and the feeding frenzy began.

Marco placed his arm protectively around my shoulders and drew me closer. "Just keep walking and don't respond to anything they say. Don't even look at them," he instructed.

He wouldn't get an argument out of me. I leaned closer into him, stared straight ahead and picked up my pace to match his. He dropped the edge of the umbrella, further shielding me from frenzied reporters who called out questions without bothering to listen for a response. From what I could make out, they wanted to know everything but my bra size. I snuck a peek at them. A few looked like they might want that too, what with all the leering.

As the media pressed closer, Father Daniel and Germaine closed ranks. Father Daniel brought up the rear and Germaine gripped my elbow and pushed away the more brazen reporters who wanted to get the story of the day.

One young bearded man had the audacity to reach out and clutch at my arm. I heard a distinct growl explode from Germaine, then a sharp slap and finally the man's yelp of pain as he withdrew his offending appendage.

"Forgive us our trespasses as we forgive . . ."

"Cut it out, Germaine!" This was no time for guilt. As far as I was concerned she was a hero.

She marched silently forward like a stalwart Christian meeting the lions.

We reached Marco's car. He opened the passenger door and ordered, "Father Daniel, you go with Germaine to the cemetery. I'll take Pen. We've got some business to discuss."

He looked as serious as a heart attack, so I didn't argue. I half-heartedly wiggled two fingers at Germaine, and she saluted me in return. "See you at the cemetery."

It was difficult to hear her words with all the yelling coming from the reporters. Marco shoved me into the passenger's seat and slammed the door.

I locked my side and longingly watched the retreating figures of Father Daniel and Germaine. There was no doubt in my mind that I'd much rather be riding with them.

CHAPTER SEVENTEEN

Marco's earlier sympathy disappeared once we pulled out of the parking lot. He mimicked my simple request, "Call Masters and see what he wants, Marco."

I lowered my head and stared at my soggy shoes, figuring they were ruined. They were my favorite pair, and I'd gotten them on sale. What were the chances of that ever happening again? "Well? I'm waiting." His voice startled me.

I'd momentarily escaped to that safe place in my universe. The one I saved for avoiding reality.

I stuck out my chin. "You're my lawyer, I figured that's what you're supposed to do, isn't it? I mean, aren't you supposed to run interference for me?"

"It is?"

The dull, waterlogged scenery looked as flat and empty as I felt.

Marco honked impatiently as a pedestrian stepped off the curb in front of us. "Asking politely will give you better results. Where did you learn your manners?"

He was flat out right. I'd been rude. I felt drained, like the fight had been knocked out of me. The truth was, it had been. There was no excuse for treating anyone, especially someone who was trying to keep me out of a jail cell, so shabbily. It wasn't a behavior that I'd tolerate from anyone.

I pressed my nose up against the window, watching my breath form on the chilled surface. "You're right. I behaved badly."

"Yes, you did. You're old enough to know better."

Now he sounded like my mother, and it rankled me. "Don't treat me like I'm a child."

"You're acting like one."

I sucked in my breath and said in a sing-song voice, "I'm so sorry, Marco."

He shook his head. "I suppose thinking you'll change your ways is pushing it."

I sighed deeply and didn't respond.

"As good as I'm likely to get, I guess." He began tapping on the steering wheel. He knew I hated that. I glared at him, and he smiled smugly. He'd won and would gloat for awhile. So be it. I like to pick my battles.

"The police want to talk with you again," he said. "I put them off, but they won't wait forever."

I muttered, "Thanks, Marco."

"Hey, it's not a permanent fix. You're going to have to talk with them soon."

I leaned my head against the seat. "Please, try to hold them off a little longer. I haven't got any proof just yet."

He scowled. "Proof? Proof of what? Just what are you up to?"

"Nothing." I'd slipped up and now I'd have to wiggle out of it. "My brain is fried." I gently massaged my temples. "I have a headache."

It was important that Marco didn't find out that I was moonlighting as a burglar to clear my name. He wouldn't like it, and I didn't need another lecture.

He must have bought my explanation because he didn't miss a beat as he announced, "They want to search your place."

"Who?"

"The police."

"No!"

He shifted gear and gunned the engine. "You don't have a

choice. They're getting a search warrant."

I sat up straight. "Marco! How do you know that?"

"It's not important. I found out. That's what's important."

Shocked I said, "You're not gonna let them go through my underwear and stuff, are you? You won't let them trash my place?"

He grinned and held up his hand, palm outward. "The police want to pin your husband's murder on you, and you're worried about them handling your underwear?"

"Marco, no one wants strangers sifting through their underwear."

"No, I guess I wouldn't like it either. After I found out about the warrant, I spoke to the police and offered to allow them to search your place."

I reached out and lightly cuffed his shoulder. "Why would you do a thing like that?"

"Believe me. It's a good thing we made the offer. It makes it look like you have nothing to hide. And this way, I'll be able to keep an eye on things."

I sniffed loudly. "I don't have anything to hide."

"They don't know that."

"Did they take you up on it?"

"I've set it up so I'll be there. You too, if you want . . ."

I folded my arms tightly across my chest. "I don't want."

"Okay. That's your call. But don't worry; they won't do any damage with me present."

I trusted Marco, so I reclined on the car seat, adjusted my glasses, and fell silent.

We had driven to the cemetery in Marco's car rather than the limousine that transported family members. We were at the tail end of the procession, so we had a long walk to the gravesite.

It was raining harder, turning the ground into an ugly mud-slick. If my shoes hadn't been ruined already it was a sure bet they would be by the time we plodded through this mess.

Marco reached in the back seat for the umbrella, got out of the car, ran around to the passenger side, and opened it. Nice touch. I looked up at him, hoping my face didn't show the anxiety churning in my stomach.

He took my hand and squeezed it softly. "I know. It's difficult. The media, the cops, Paul's family and friends will be watching you. But you have to do this. It's the most important scene of your life."

I squeezed my eyes tightly shut and blocked out the world for a moment. When Marco gently tugged on my arm, I attempted a smile I didn't feel.

He helped me out of the car. "That's it. Put on a brave face."

I did.

He squeezed my hand again. "Good. My money's on you, kiddo."

I drew in a deep breath and held it, trying to keep my tears at bay. I didn't much care for Paul and what he'd become, but we had had some good times together and I wanted to remember those. Even if those memories also brought pain.

The chilly morning air changed directions, and the rain, falling in sheets now, soaked my clothes. I shivered, and one lone tear slid down my cheek, resting at the corner of my lip. Marco leaned down and wiped it away with such tenderness that I thought I would fall apart on the spot. But I couldn't, not now anyway. People were waiting to scrutinize me, and I had to pass muster.

Marco leaned down and whispered soothingly, "Come on, Pen."

I pushed my shoulders back, smoothed the wrinkles from my damp skirt and linked arms with him.

Patting my arm in a brotherly fashion, he held the umbrella

over our heads and said, "Good girl. Never let them see you sweat."

My stoic mask didn't match the jitters that ran up and down my spine. We walked slowly to Paul's grave. Suddenly, it all seemed so shockingly final, Paul in the ground, buried forever in this horrible mud. I lowered my head to ward off the rain jetting off Marco's black umbrella.

Chapter Eighteen

Paul's family and the minister stood beside the grave under an awning, protected from the rain. Our little group wasn't in that crowd. Father Daniel and Germaine stood together under a shared umbrella. Through the heavy rain pouring off the edge of Marco's umbrella, I glanced around at the other mourners.

The minister droned without thought to the weather. Common sense would suggest that he give it a lick, a promise, and an Amen, and call it good enough. Not this guy, you'd think he was getting paid by the minute. Maybe he was. If I hadn't been ordered to play the part of distressed widow, I would have left.

Despite the rain, a lot of people had shown up—and not all of them were fans of Paul. Frankly, any one of a number of those people had reason to kill him. Judge Kassner just happened to lead my short list. And he was right down in front in the good seats. I studied him until I heard the collective, "Amen."

I jerked my head upright. *Hallelujah!*

Marco produced a rose and shoved it into my hand. I looked at him blankly.

He took me by the elbow and whispered, "Go on, Pen."

Staring at the rose, I asked, "Where did you get this?"

"Never mind." He gave me a gentle push.

Looking up at him, I questioned, "What am I supposed to do with it?"

He spoke slowly, "Go. Toss it into the grave."

My brows furrowed. "Why would I do that?"

He wiped the rain from his face. "It's what people do, that's why. What, you've never been to a funeral before?"

Actually, I didn't go to many funerals. I made it a practice to avoid them if I could. Pity I hadn't been able to avoid this one.

He gave me another gentle push. Father Daniel and Germaine nodded their encouragement.

Shrugging, I picked my way carefully through the puddles, edging past small groups of people who had already tossed their flowers.

I ducked under the edge of the awning, stepping in front of a tall, thin, sophisticated-but-severe-looking woman. She had a broad forehead accentuated by dark hair pulled back into a knot at the base of her neck. She sobbed quietly into a lacy white handkerchief.

Her behavior seemed a bit much for a stranger, but I didn't dwell on it. Who knows, maybe she'd known Paul in high school; maybe she was his long lost sister.

I struggled to edge closer to the grave, which wasn't easy because the sobbing woman hogged the small space. She even had the nerve to scowl at me as I inched forward. Hey, I was the widow.

At the rim of the grave, I froze. I looked down and realized that was Paul down there in that box. And all the brass-trimmed mahogany in the world wasn't going to make this muddy hole more appealing. The rug of green astro turf wasn't fooling anyone. Underneath the plastic grass was more dirt, dirt that would soon cover him over. Paul would spend the rest of forever in this cold, dark, lonely place. Alone.

Tears started falling as other mourners casually tossed their flowers into the gaping hole.

I stepped forward and leaned over to toss my rose when I felt a bump, like an elbow hitting me in my lower back. It was just enough of a jostle that I lost my footing.

"Watch it!" I shouted.

I hadn't quite recovered my balance when I felt another bump, harder this time. As my feet left the ground, I frantically grabbed at the pole holding the awning upright. It slid under my grasp like a bendable drinking straw. My backside hit the edge of the grave and I slid into the muddy cavity, carrying the awning with me. Shrieks from the surrounding crowd were muffled as they scrambled out from under the heavy tarp to avoid falling with me.

Mud sprayed across my face as I landed spread-eagle with a hard thump on top of Paul's flower-covered casket. A shooting pain stabbed me in my backside. "Uhf!"

Gasping for breath, I thrashed in the small space, trying to free myself from the tangle of awning. My sunglasses slid down over my cheeks and rested, lopsided, on my chin as I pushed at the heavy, wet tarp. I forced myself to take a deep breath and slowly assess the situation. The earthen walls of my prison were surmountable. No need to panic. Maybe. The tarp raised up some, and I looked up at the openmouthed crowd peering down at me. They looked like fish gasping for breath.

I whisked frantically at my skirt, making sure all of the vital parts of my anatomy were sufficiently covered.

Squeezing shut my eyes, I lamented, "Why me?"

"Tch, tch, tch," clucked Paul's former secretary. "Such behavior at a funeral!"

"Wonder what happened?" a man asked.

"Who knows," said another.

"She always did want to be the center of attention," fumed my ex mother-in-law.

Ms. Chic, the woman with the bun so tight she would never need a facelift, tossed in her two cents. "I fail to understand why Paul would have married such a common woman."

"Apparently not so common," said another.

I couldn't see who delivered the most vicious blow of all. "Bad for him that he married a murderer."

The voices receded as the ringing in my ears increased. Tears glistened and clouded my eyes as I shoved my glasses up over my nose and back on my face. Shifting my position slightly, I winced from the pain in my backside. I'd been stabbed repeatedly by the rose thorns I'd fallen on.

How did this happen? Why did it happen?

It didn't really matter; it had. Sometimes my life is like a *Seinfeld* episode.

Several men pulled the awning off to the side. Among the chattering and disbelieving onlookers I spied Marco. He struggled to stifle a grin as he reached out. "Are you all right, Pen?" Typical Marco. Without waiting for my response he ordered, "Here, give me your hand, and I'll help you out."

Water sluiced down my cheeks as I pushed mud-matted hair from my face. Breathlessly, I gasped, "Did you see what happened?"

Marco replied, a smirk covering his face, "Wish I had, but no, I didn't."

Ben Josten's voice rang out over the crowd's murmuring. "Leave it to Pen." Laughter ricocheted through the crowd. I fought tears of embarrassment threatening to break free. Biting my lip I concentrated on getting out of the grave.

Just as I reached up to take Marco's outstretched hand, Astrid Preston peered down at me again and snarled, "How dare you, Penelope!"

"Astrid, I'm so sorry, I . . ."

"It's bad enough you murdered him, but this! To make a mockery of his burial."

Carl Preston took Astrid's arm and whispered something in her ear. Face set in a grimace, she shrugged out of his grip and left. The remaining mourners talked excitedly among them-selves.

Carl reached down and smiled broadly. "Come on, girl, let's get you out of there. You don't really want to join Paul just now. It's not your time."

Thank goodness for Carl. The man knew just what to do and say in any situation. At least one person didn't believe I'd killed Paul. I hoped.

I looked up at him with gratitude and grasped his large square hand. "Thanks."

Marco reached down at the same time. "Here, we'll both help."

Carl grinned. "We're going to pull now, so hang on."

"Wait a minute. I'm not ready." I let go of Carl's hand and brushed battered flowers out of the way. My legs straddled the sides of the coffin like a bull rider at the rodeo, and I inched forward. I secured my balance holding onto the top of Paul's coffin, tucked my left leg, and then my right, under my body. After I steadied myself, I rose to a kneeling position. Satisfied with my effort, I reached up with both hands. Carl and Marco gave me a mighty pull.

But their hands were wet and mine were slick with mud—I slipped from Carl's grip and tumbled backward, yanking Marco with me. I slithered down the muddy side of the grave and landed once again on top of Paul's casket. Marco's body came careening after, landing on top of me with a dull thud.

He gasped, "My God!"

Lying on my back, I tottered precariously on the casket. His face inches from mine clearly showed anger mixed with surprise. He didn't swear, I'll give him that. But I think it was because he was too shocked.

I spit mud out of my mouth. "Get off me, Marco!" Tugging my left hand from beneath his abdomen, I swiped at my face so

I could see and sputtered, "I can't take it, Marco! It's just too much. Don't you dare blame me for this."

His hard glare softened. "Ah, Pen . . ."

Maybe compassion was harder to take than anger. I felt fresh tears threaten.

I started crying, deep heaving sobs. He edged sideways so I didn't have the full weight of his body on top of me. "Shhh, Pen. It's okay."

His genuine sympathy made me cry harder. "Now look what you've done. I never cry in front of people."

He inched his hand toward my face, hesitated, then lightly wiped my tears with a muddy hand, first one cheek, then the other.

I hiccupped.

"Shhh, Pen. I'm so sorry."

Our eyes met and held. Slowly he moved his face toward mine. *My God, he's going to kiss me. We're lying on top of my dead husband's casket, and he's going to kiss me.*

I turned my head just before his lips met mine. "We've got to get out of here, Marco."

He became all business. "Exactly."

"Move, then. I can't breathe with you on top of me."

He shifted. "I don't have any room. I've moved as much as I can."

I pushed at him. "Well, try!"

He inched sideways, grabbing the side of the casket for support.

I didn't dare look at him, my cheeks still burned from the near kiss. "That's better."

"Just stay there, Pen. I'm going to try and sit up."

Carl called out, "Are you two okay?"

My head turned toward his voice. "Nothing broken. But we're going to need some help."

Marco had somehow righted himself and was on his knees. He said, "I'm going to try and stand up. Then you pull, okay?"

Carl got on his knees and leaned over. "Right."

Still prone, I watched Carl tug on Marco's outstretched hand. Time for me to make my move. By the time I got to my knees, Marco stood at the edge of the hole, looking down at me.

He glanced sideways at Carl and winked. "Might be better for everyone if we just leave her there."

Carl took in my tear-stained, mud-spattered face, my bedraggled clothes and cautioned Marco, "Better go easy, son. She's reached her limit."

My impertinent lawyer nodded contritely.

I briefly lost my footing and clung to the muddy walls of the hole and growled, "Marco, your life wouldn't be worth living if you left me here."

He laughed. "Stand up. Carefully. You've been lucky so far and haven't broken anything. You might not be so lucky next time."

I slipped again but managed to hold on and slowly brought myself to a standing position. A small crowd stood, silent, gaping at me. Father Daniel and Germaine were among them, smirking. I'd get them later.

I whipped my head around, attempting to shake my matted, wet hair free from my face. "I'm ready."

From my precarious position on the lid of Paul's casket, I leaned forward and tentatively reached out. They grabbed my forearms and instructed me to wrap my hands around theirs. They tugged, and I popped out of the hole like a jack-in-the-box without the music.

I stumbled forward, and Carl righted me, whispering, "You'd better run on home and change clothes, dear. You're a mess, and you really should look your best when you meet these gawkers at the house." He smiled kindly, his eyes twinkling.

His attitude amazed me. Paul's father was a tall man, over six feet, not really good looking, more like everybody's favorite, nondescript uncle. His calm demeanor seemed to rub off on me. "Carl, that might not be a good idea. Astrid won't like it."

He put his arm around my shoulder as if he didn't care that his clothes became muddied. "Nonsense. She's just grieving for her child. She needs to lash out at someone, and you simply gave her an acceptable opportunity. Look, I want you there." His face crumpled in sadness. He looked at me with tears forming in the corners of his eyes. "I need you, there. You have always been a valued member of this family." He leaned closer, "And the most open and honest of the bunch."

Me! Open and honest? What daughter-in-law had he mistaken me for?

I opened my mouth to speak, but he interrupted, "I need you to make me laugh," he looked at the grave, "like you did just now. Only you could do that, Pen." He squeezed my mud-spattered shoulder.

I pushed a clump of hair from my face and stepped out of his embrace. "Carl, are you sure you want me to come to the house? What will people . . ."

"I don't care what people think, Pen. I know you didn't kill my son, and that's what's important."

I reached out to touch his arm, saw my mud-caked hand, and quickly withdrew it. "I'm sorry, Carl. I know this is hard for you. Of course I'll come." I glanced up at Marco and my support team, then turned back to Carl. "I'd like it if my sister, Father Daniel, and Marco, my lawyer, came. Do you mind?"

My father-in-law's eyes were glazed with grief. "Of course not. Come along, all of you."

I smiled. "Thanks Carl. I'll rush home and change and meet you at the house."

"Good girl."

He gave me a big hug, apparently not caring that the front of his suit was now wet and mud-spattered. This big, softhearted bear of a man would be the family member I'd miss most.

"We'll see you at the house then."

He nodded at the four of us and walked away, shoulders bent, toward Paul's mother.

Germaine broke the silence. "Hey, that was some show. Are you okay?"

I glared at her while I wiped my filthy hands on my skirt, but it was useless. It was just as wet and muddy as my hands.

"Sorry. We won't say anything more about it." She pinched her lips together struggling to control the laughter that shook her body. She cleared her throat and found another topic. "That looked like a tender scene between you and Paul's dad."

I told her about the invitation, and a frown appeared on her face. She didn't want to attend the post-funeral get together. But she would. They all would. They'd come for me. As we turned to leave I noticed the unfamiliar woman who stood behind me before I fell. She stood, alone, by Paul's abandoned grave. She held a single white rose to her lips, lightly kissing the petals before tossing it down on Paul's coffin.

I froze in my tracks. Just who was she? And why was she behaving so oddly? So like a loved one. It hit me. "Oh, my God!" Paul—the bastard! He'd been fooling around with her. My blood pressure soared up like a fourth of July firecracker. It was she who pushed me into Paul's grave.

I started toward her as Marco reached out and grabbed my arm. "Let it go, Pen."

I struggled from his grip. "Not on a bet, I won't."

Marco restrained me and said, "It won't serve any purpose. Now come on, you don't want to be late for your final performance."

I scorched him with my worst scowl. But it was hard to stay

angry with a guy who looked like a kid covered in brown finger paint. Marco, impeccable to the nth degree, was a mess. I wondered if I looked as bad, probably looked worse.

A laugh escaped as I brushed a clump of mud from his cheek. "You're really dirty. Your *GQ* image has been totally destroyed."

He sullenly looked down at his sodden mud-caked suit. "This is bad," he looked at me and grinned. "But I can't possibly look any worse than you do."

I ignored him. "Let's get out of here. We've got an appointment."

He plodded after me yelling, "Don't you dare get in that car before I cover the seats with a blanket!"

CHAPTER NINETEEN

Marco pulled up to my place and made a rolling stop, and I jumped out. As I ran up the front steps, he called out, "I'll be back in thirty minutes. Be here."

I waved and let myself in the front door of my building. The elevator "Out of Order" sign was still there, so I hit the stairs two at a time. After a quick shower, shampoo, and change of clothes only ten minutes had passed. It took another ten to blow my hair to damp, five to slather on some make-up and my wait for Marco took another five. When he got to my place I was out front, on the curb, dabbing on a spot of lipstick. I pinched my cheeks, like they did in the olden days, hoping to bring some much needed color to my face as I walked to his car. The sky had cleared, and the sun was shining by the time we pulled up to the Preston home. Father Daniel and Germaine joined us on the front lawn.

Germaine took my arm. "We've been waiting."

Father Daniel squeezed my shoulder. "It's going to be all right, don't you fret so much."

"Easy for you to say." I knew I sounded a bit snappish, so in a much softer voice I added, "I'm sorry. It's just so difficult. And all those people staring, thinking I killed Paul. Let's just get this over with."

Germaine lightly touched my arm. "Keep it cool. We'll stay a half hour, just so people don't talk, and then we're outta here. Besides, we're late already. This thing will break up soon."

"You're a good sport, Germaine." Actually she was more like St. Jude, the patron saint of lost causes. And she didn't even try—it just came naturally.

She linked arms with me as we started up the walk. In an effort to sound carefree she called out over her shoulder, "Come on, troops. We're off to do battle with the unbelievers."

No one answered, but I could hear footsteps sloshing in the puddles of water that had collected in the low spots on the sidewalk.

The front door was open, and when I approached the screen door I could see small groups of people off to the left in the living room. I sucked in some air and stepped into the large front hall.

Carl Preston emerged from a cluster of people. His eyes met mine, and I froze from the sadness in them. He rushed forward and swallowed me up in his arms. When he released me, I looked up at him and whispered, "I'm scared."

He ran his fingers through graying temples, his eyes clouded with what I knew were tears. "Girl, with everything going on you've a right, but not here. Not in my house."

He took my arm, nodded to my sister, "Germaine, thanks for coming. Sorry to hear that your mother is ill."

She clasped his free hand in hers. "Thanks. Don't worry about Ma. She'll be fine. Carl, I'm so sorry about Paul."

He nodded somberly and looked at the men. "Pen, introduce me to your friends."

I did, and we made small talk for several minutes before Carl motioned to Paul's cousin, Jack Preston. Jack, tall and gangly, with an unmanageable shock of blond hair, ambled over.

"Hi, Pen. Quite a performance back at the gravesite."

Carl gave him a meaningful look, and Jack took a small step backward, knowing he'd gone too far. Someone called out to Carl. He waved and excused himself, "Pen, make yourself at

147

home. There's food in the dining room." As he walked away he frowned in Jack's general direction. Jack and I stood alone. Not a good thing. I'd never cared much for him and after his last comment, I liked him even less. Everyone has their crosses to bear; too bad I have so many of them.

Paul's cousin was around my age, but looked older, probably because he wore a perpetual frown. Not a flattering trait. "Thanks for bringing up a sore subject, Jack. You've always had a crude and definitely unbecoming style."

He didn't even have the courtesy to look embarrassed, just snorted his horse-like laugh. "If you could have seen yourself." He slapped his leg and snorted again.

I looked around for my support group, but they were nowhere in sight. Now, how could I get out of this obnoxious little tête-à-tête without raising Jack's ire. Oh, well, live dangerously had become my motto.

"Jack, why don't you go and entertain some half-wit woman who just might appreciate your humor."

"Not feeling guilty are you?" He snorted again, sipped from his glass and fanned the air, nearly sloshing his drink in the process. "Most of them think you did it. Did you?"

I stared at him in disbelief.

"Well, did you? Come on, you can tell me. It's not like I liked him much either."

A growl, low in my throat, began to rise higher and rather than screech at him like medusa. I turned on my heel and stalked away. I wished I had one expletive that would put him in his place. What a horse's ass. If I never saw him again it would be too soon. But, unfortunately I would, because he was an assistant county attorney and worked in the criminal division. That meant he and I saw each other more often than I wanted.

But, the horse's ass had a point; he and Paul had never really liked each other. Paul never talked about it, but it made me wonder. Why had they always disliked each other? Was it enough of a reason for Jack to murder Paul? I discarded the thought. Jack didn't have the brains to pull it off and get away with it. Besides, it had to have been Judge Kassner who killed Paul. He had the motive, means, and the brains. What I didn't know was how to prove it.

I took refuge in a corner of the large, well-appointed living room and studied the people surrounding me. Most were familiar, but there were a few strangers roaming the room.

A voice from behind, soft and measured, startled me. "How are you doing, Penelope?"

I turned and faced Judge Eloise Hunter. Tall, slender, and graceful, she looked elegant, and her face held concern. She brushed a hand through perfect hair, just beginning to gray, then clasped her drink tightly in both hands.

"Okay, I guess."

Her soothing voice flowed over me, warming my chilled brooding heart.

"Don't mind Jack." She took a short sip of her drink. Then the timbre of her voice changed, hardened. "He's an ass."

I blinked. Always polite and respectful, Judge Hunter showed me a side I hadn't seen before. I didn't know her well since she'd come to the criminal bench about a year ago from Family Court where she had reigned as Queen of the May for many years. That meant she was Chief Judge and power broker. She had the reputation of being a good jurist, meaning few rulings overturned by the appeals courts. She was fair, firm, and consistent. And I like that in a judge. Hmmm, I like that in the general population.

Her mouth formed a tight circle; her brows furrowed as she took a long swig. The Queen of judges appeared to be a little tipsy. "Yeah, he's got the manners of a Billy goat," I answered.

A small gurgle escaped from her throat, along with some stray liquid, scotch was my bet, and she quickly wiped the offending dribble away with the back of her hand.

She leaned closer. "The man has no sense of decency. He'd best watch himself in my courtroom." She brought the half-empty glass to her lips for a third time in less than a minute. The way she was going, in no time at all, she'd be out like a light.

Stunned, I reached out and placed my hand lightly on her shoulder. "Are you all right?"

She shrugged away from my touch. "It's all so sad."

What was she talking about?

She ran a finger around the rim of her glass and spoke with a pronounced slur. "People shouldn't have to die." She paused and focused into outer space somewhere over my right shoulder.

I couldn't imagine what she was talking about, but I was already depressed and seeing her, someone I admired, like this, well, I couldn't take it right now.

There wasn't a good response to her statement so I mumbled something about having to greet my mother-in-law and got out of there as fast as I could.

In my hurry I rammed into Miss Snooty-Buns who had pushed me into the grave. We glared at each other as she righted her glass. Without looking she scooped up some liquid that had dribbled down the side. How did she even know it was there? Then she carefully placed her wet finger in her mouth and sucked. My god, it was almost sexual. No, it was definitely sexual.

"Who are you?" I blurted. *That's right, Pen. Get right to the heart of the matter. When in doubt, interrogate.*

Her laugh, a high-pitched gargle didn't fit this statuesque beauty. "Who would you like me to be?"

"No one." I stepped to the side so I could squeeze between a small group hovering around a table. She also stepped aside and planted her tall, willowy frame directly in front of me. She leaned down, her whisper seductive, "I was sleeping with Paul."

She stood up straight and threw her bony shoulders back, showing all that cared to look that she had no bosoms. Bosoms. That's what Ma called them. I cracked out a half a sneer, at Ma, at Ms. Flat-chest, at the whole pathetic day.

"He needed someone on par with his status. You don't cut it there." She cocked her head to the side and stuck out her chin. She had no idea how tempting that chin was. A left hook planted squarely in the middle of her face, rearranging it, would bring her squarely in touch with the rest of us, I was sure of it.

Amazing even me, I refrained from committing the impulsive act. Instead, I stood tall, at least as tall as I could muster given my vertically challenged status, threw my shoulders back, and showed my large, full, perky bosoms. We looked like two little boys playing "mine's bigger than yours."

I snapped back at her, "Paul wouldn't have slept with somebody who would talk about it later. He must have been desperate if you're the best he could do. That's what I think."

A smirk covered her angular face. She stepped toward me. "Ah, that shows you don't know everything." Her mouth settled into a thin straight line. "Murdering little white trash." She shook her long manicured finger at me. "You'll find yourself locked up with the big girls soon enough and what will you do then?"

This was too much. I turned to walk away before I actually did rearrange her face. The B, as I was beginning to think of her, grabbed me, digging her blood-red nails into the fleshy part of my forearm. "I was going to marry Paul." Her shrill accusation penetrated the hum of carefully modulated voices surrounding us. "You ruined it all!" The room fell into a hideous silence. Everyone stood stock-still, like posed statues, staring at the two of us.

Stunned, I wrenched my arm from her claw-like grip and fled to the bathroom rubbing the bruised flesh to take away the sting of her fingernails. Not my style to leave a battle skirmish unfinished. But a cat fight wasn't my style either—especially at my husband's funeral. I'd been pretty close to taking a swing at her. But I was raised in Nordeast Minneapolis, and I knew how to pick my battles. And when.

I felt like I was in a Mel Brooks movie. This whole demented day was Paul's doing. Death was too good for him. He could have had the common decency to wait before replacing me with something like that . . . that manicured barracuda.

CHAPTER TWENTY

As I left the bathroom, Judge Hunter and Astrid Preston exited the master bedroom. Judge Hunter clutched her handbag tight against her stomach, while Astrid had one arm around the judge's shoulders, steadying her.

Another encounter with Astrid was not high on my list of "must-dos" for the day, so I quickly stepped behind the bathroom door and waited.

As they passed by me, Astrid spoke in a carefully modulated tone. "You'll be all right, Eloise. The cab should be here any minute. Go home and get some rest, dear. It'll do you a world of good."

"I don't know what got into me. I guess I shouldn't have mixed alcohol with my medication."

The next few sentences were so garbled, I couldn't understand what she was saying. "Yes, yes, we'll all miss him," Astrid said soothingly.

I flattened myself against the wall and peeked through the narrow opening between the door and the doorjamb. The judge's brow was pinched. "He should have been more careful. He made some enemies. It's all so sad."

I winced. She was talking about Paul, but she shouldn't be saying those things to Astrid. It wasn't the kind of thing a grieving mother wanted to hear.

"What do you mean?" I got a glimpse of Astrid, she was frowning. "Why do you think Paul had enemies?"

The judge's voice was unintelligible as they headed away from the hall, presumably for the front door.

People should know better than to mix alcohol and medication. I shook my head and eased out from behind the door, glanced into the hall and stepped out.

Marco appeared out of nowhere and took my arm, startling me. Sometimes the man was a phantom. "How are you doing?"

"For goodness' sake, can't you warn a girl? You almost scared me to death!"

"Sorry." He leaned closer and looked into my eyes. "You look like you've seen a ghost."

I briefly considered his words, then commented, "Not a ghost, but a couple of weird things."

While I filled him in on my conversation with Jack, the jerk, Germaine joined us. When I finished my story, Germaine offered, "Jack's an ass. Don't give him a thought."

"Yeah, and then I ran into Judge Hunter. Man, you wouldn't believe how upset she was."

Marco interrupted, "I know Eloise pretty well. She's a lovely and warm woman. I'm sure she's grieving in her own way. Everyone in this room is."

I eyed Judge Kassner. "I don't think he's in mourning." I pointed across the room. "Look at him. He looks like the cat that swallowed the canary."

Marco glanced over his shoulder and shrugged. "He looks bored to me."

Germaine gave me a knowing look. "Oh, Pen, don't try to build a case out of nothing. He was a work acquaintance. Of course he's not mourning him like family and friends would."

I ignored her. "He's most likely relieved."

"Why would you say that?" Marco asked.

Whoops. I wasn't quite ready to spill that part of the story to Marco, just yet. There were more bases to cover first. "I . . . I don't know. They didn't always see eye to eye on things. It caused some occasional tension in the courtroom." Lying was becoming so easy it was almost scary.

Marco put his hand on my arm. "Don't look for trouble, Pen. If you have any ideas of looking for the killer—"

"Of course I have ideas." I crossed my arms firmly over my chest.

His body became rigid, his eyes flashed hot. "Let the police, and me, do our jobs."

I tossed my head in defiance. "By the time the police do their jobs I could be sporting that spiffy orange wardrobe you mentioned, residing at a new address, eating a high-carb diet, and fighting off unwanted attention from Big Bertha."

Marco shrugged. "Hey, playing P.I. is just going to get you into more trouble."

I rubbed the back of my neck to ease the tension that was steadily building. "You're probably right." I looked around the room. "It's really time for us to go. I'm going to find Carl and Astrid and say good-bye. Not that Astrid cares." I nodded toward the front door. "I'll meet you guys in a couple of minutes. Try to corral Father Daniel, will you?" I turned and searched the sea of faces. I didn't see Paul's parents in the living or dining room, so I rounded the corner toward the kitchen.

As I suspected, I found my in-laws alone in the large gleaming kitchen. It always amazed me that no matter the occasion, or how many people were involved, the Preston kitchen looked like a scene right out of *Martha Stewart Living*. Everything had a place, and everything was in its place. Always. Nice and neat.

Now if it had been my kitchen, it would be in disarray. I am scrupulously neat and very well organized in all areas of my life, except when it comes to cooking. I splash. And I create mounds of dirty dishes that I hate to wash. I realized there would probably be no more friendly talks shared over coffee at the kitchen table. No more views of the massive and spectacular flower beds Astrid scrupulously tended. It would be a cold day in hell before Astrid would want or permit me in her house again.

"I'm going to leave now." My hands fluttered uselessly at my side. "Thanks for—"

Carl interrupted me with a warm bear hug. Astrid scowled.

Not knowing what to say, I offered the typical trite remarks people give in these circumstances, "I'm really sorry, Astrid."

Her lips a thin, straight line, quivered. She responded curtly, "Did you have to come, Pen? Couldn't you leave well enough alone?"

Carl left me, walked to his wife, put his arm around her waist, drawing her to him, and spoke in a soothing voice, "I asked her to come. This is not Pen's fault."

Astrid's back stiffened. She looked up at her husband. "Carl, how can you say that? She's the prime suspect."

They were discussing me like the antagonist in an episode of *Law and Order*. Not a good sign. Not a good sign, indeed.

I interrupted, my voice low and measured, "I didn't kill him, Astrid. I had no reason to."

A voice from the doorway screeched, "Of course, you did. You didn't want anyone else to have him."

I spun around and faced *her*. Speechless, I stared.

Carl stepped forward. "Stephanie, this isn't a good time."

Stephanie sauntered into the room, her hipless body swaying like a skinny palm tree. She probably thought she looked sexy. I thought it looked just plain stupid and melodramatic.

Hands on her hips, she sputtered, "But Carl, it's true. She took Paulie away from me."

Paulie? Was his girl delusional? No one would call Paul Preston Paulie and live to tell about it. I couldn't help myself. "Paulie?"

"Bitch!" she hissed.

"Stephanie, this is definitely not the time or place." Carl took her arm and led her to the door.

Stephanie shrugged out of his grip and spun around, eyes flashing. "You killed my Paulie, and now I've lost my one true love."

Make no mistake, I was fed up with this insane B movie we were all stuck in. "You! You have no right! Why don't you take your fake sophistication and false grief and get out of here. We're having a family conversation."

Astrid hurried to Stephanie, who was by this time crying crocodile tears. "Now, now, my dear. Don't mind, Pen. She can be rather coarse at times."

Well, I guess we all knew where Astrid's loyalty lay. My mouth gaped. Me? Coarse? She's the one who'd used the B word. Honestly, I'd been gone from Paul's life for a nanosecond, and he'd replaced me with this bimbo. And the bimbo obviously had my mother-in-law's—strike that—*ex* mother-in-law's approval *and* affection. There was no justice in this world.

Astrid tore her attention from the sobbing Stephanie, pointed to me and snapped, "Out! Now!"

My smirk slid right off my face. "What?"

Astrid gave Stephanie a peck on the cheek and turned toward me. "I want you to leave. Your presence is upsetting everyone."

My head snapped toward Carl so fast I thought I'd given myself whiplash. All I saw was resignation. He started to speak, and I held up my hand. "Don't Carl. I can't deal with it just now."

Turning back to Astrid, I said, "I'm sorry about everything. I really am. I wish you could believe me. I'm going now."

No one said anything, so after a moment, I walked from the room, my chest heaving as I attempted to stifle the sobs welling in my throat.

Marco, Father Daniel, and Germaine were huddled by the

front door, talking. As I approached, Germaine asked, "What happened to you? You look—"

"I don't want to talk about it." I breezed on by her, my response clipped.

Without another word, I led my motley crew out the front door. But I wasn't free just yet. Jack stood on the front porch with a small group of men I didn't recognize. Some of them were smoking. I waved at the air, fending off the offensive smoke halfheartedly as I passed.

Jack tossed his cigarette on the concrete, stubbing it out with the tip of his shoe. "So, you met Stephanie. Isn't she a piece of work? Prancing around here all teary eyed, pretending everything was hunky dory between her and Paul."

He'd gotten my attention. I skidded to a stop and waited. I didn't want to say anything or he'd stop talking. It'd be just like him. Jack reached in his pocket for another cigarette. "Yeah. She's something. Pretending she's sad about Paul's death."

He paused long enough to light the fresh smoke. It seemed to take forever for him to flick his Bic. I couldn't stand it anymore. "What are you talking about, Jack?"

The other men snickered. He spit a stray piece of tobacco on the ground. "Got your attention?"

I glared at him. "Yes, Jack, you have my attention. Now, what are you talking about?" The rest of my group had sauntered down the sidewalk without me.

He drew heavily on the cigarette, held it for a long time, and slowly exhaled in short puffs. Perfect rings. It figures. Jack's an attorney who has no talent for the law but he has perfected smoke rings.

I'd made a tactical error. The only way to handle Jack was to make like you didn't care about what he was offering, so I turned to leave. "I'm going home. I'm tired."

He placed his hand heavily on my shoulder. I stared at the

offending hand and slowly drew my eyes upward, my stare penetrating, ready to pounce. "Don't touch me!" I hissed.

The offending hand snapped back. "Hey, no big deal. I just wanted to tell you that Paul was cheating on Stephanie with several other women and she found out about it. Rumor was, he was dumping her."

He paused, used his finger to remove a minute piece of tobacco from his bottom lip. It looked like it was more for effect than anything. Then he calmly said, "You did the world a good deed, Pen. Paul had it coming." I wanted to grab him by the throat and shake him like a rag doll. But he would've enjoyed it far too much so I passed on what would have been at least fifth degree assault. No sense giving folks what they want.

He chuckled. "I suppose I'll see you at work on Monday. That's if the cops haven't arrested you." His eyes flashed pure evil; his mouth curled at the edges in a sneer.

I smiled serenely, which was difficult because I wanted to bite his head off. "I'm surprised they keep you on, Jack, with the shabby job you do. They don't let you prosecute the important cases anymore, do they? What do they do? Toss you a bone every now and then. The loser cases?"

Hatred flashed across his ugly mug and before he had the opportunity to say anything else, I skipped down the steps and headed for the car.

Suddenly, I was very glad that my big sister would be with me tonight. I didn't want to be alone, especially after the day I'd had.

I had some serious thinking to do. My original belief that Judge Kassner killed Paul wavered a bit. If what Jack said was true, then Stephanie had a strong motive. A woman scorned and all that. And Jack, well, he sounded almost violent. Yes, sir. My simple case was becoming crowded with suspects. I didn't know what to think anymore. It was far too complicated. It made my head hurt.

Germaine must have sensed my despair because, when I got to the car, she put her arms around my shoulders and I leaned into her. "I'm here for you, kid."

"Thanks. I know you are and I appreciate it."

"That's what big sisters are for." She gave me a quick squeeze.

Chapter Twenty-One

"You take the bed. I'll take the sofa," I offered Germaine.

She stared into the mirror, examining a nonexistent blemish. "Nonsense. We'll sleep together, just like we did when we were kids."

"Are you going to tell me scary stories too?"

Germaine gave me a gentle push. "Are you kidding? You don't need any. You're living a scary story."

I nudged her back. "Hey, it's a hard-knock life." I pulled a clean nightshirt from the dresser and handed it to her. "Here. You know where everything is. Help yourself."

She gave me a peck on the cheek. "This has been sort of fun. Not the funeral but the rest of it."

I grabbed my pajamas and turned to face her. "You mean our little burglary?"

Her face lit up like a star. "Yeah. I've never been so scared."

I thumped my hand on the dresser top. "I knew it. Deep down, you're a thrill-seeker."

She grinned and marched past me. "Dibs on the bathroom."

A scraping noise niggled at the outer edges of my consciousness. I couldn't tell what it was and didn't much care what it was as long as it stopped. I snuggled deeper into the soft mattress, tugged the comforter up over my nose and turned over.

The vague intrusion persisted until a sharp noise startled me into consciousness. I punched my pillow into shape and strained to identify the unfamiliar sound. It must be Germaine. She'd probably gotten up to go to the bathroom. A chair scraped on the kitchen floor, and I figured she must have a case of the munchies.

I closed my eyes, rolled over, and brushed up against— Germaine. I bolted upright. My heart thumped so loud and fast everyone within a mile could have danced to the rhythm.

The floor in the living room groaned like a weary old man. But there weren't any old men around. Someone was definitely walking across the floor.

A streak of light arced briefly on the wall outside the bedroom. My teeth chattered, and I clenched my jaw, praying Germaine wouldn't wake up. Someone, an uninvited someone, was creeping around my condo, and I didn't want both of us hysterical. I could probably keep myself under control, but Germaine? God, Himself, couldn't know what she might do.

Inching to the edge of the bed, I slid my legs over the side until my feet hit the floor. I slipped off the bed and crept toward the door. As I crawled past the dresser, I ran my fingers over the top until they wrapped around a heavy glass paperweight.

A loud thud echoed down the hall, and the light went out, plunging the condo to inky-black darkness. Hands shaking, I picked up the paperweight, hugged the wall, and carefully peeked around the door.

"Pen, what is it? What's wrong?" Germaine whispered.

"Hey!" I jumped, stifling a scream. So much for my self control.

"Pen!" Germaine was so close I could feel her breath on my neck.

I whirled around, held my finger to my lips, and hissed, "Shhh. Someone's out there."

"Who?"

"Shhh." My lips brushed up against her ear. "I don't know who."

She leaned into me. "What are you gonna do?"

I took a tentative step into the hall. "Gonna check it out."

She clutched at my shoulder. "No!"

"Yes. Now stay here." I shook loose, turned, and crept silently through the doorway.

She followed close at my heels. "Not on your life."

I crouched, straining to hear something. "Be quiet!"

"I'm calling the police."

I whirled around. "No!"

I thought about the money I'd found. Germaine didn't know about it, and I didn't have time to explain. The person, or persons, unknown in the next room, could be looking for it. Or, it could be an old-fashioned burglary. But why now? Why not during the funeral when people would figure I'd be gone? Then again, who knew the workings of the criminal mind? I only knew I couldn't take any chances, and really didn't want the police involved. But I didn't want to die either.

Germaine leaned closer. "I'm calling the police."

I reached behind me and gave her nightshirt a tug. "Why are you arguing with me?"

She dislodged my fist from her bedclothes. "You've recently become a super hero?"

I tiptoed back into the bedroom and cupped my hand around her ear. "Okay, come with me. But stay close."

She pressed her body into mine, and we walked down the hall in tandem. It was like the dance of Moe and Curly.

As we turned the corner, a light flickered on and meandered across my desk in the far corner of the room.

Reality hit like a nuclear bomb. We really could get killed. Suddenly hiding a lot of someone's stray cash wasn't worth our lives. As I turned to tell Germaine to call the police, a large, bulky figure silhouetted in light rounded the corner from the kitchen and walked toward us, his light catching us full in the face.

"What? Lloyd, you said the broad wouldn't be home!"

Germaine and I stood, welded together, our feet riveted to the floor.

It became eerily quiet. Then survival mode kicked into high gear. "Call the cops!" I screamed.

Everyone sprang into motion. I ran for Lloyd's partner while Germaine turned and ran toward the bedroom. Lloyd scrambled down the hall, hot on Germaine's heels.

Her high-pitched scream echoed through the condo, followed by a door slamming shut. She didn't make it back to the bedroom. It sounded like she'd gotten as far as the bathroom.

Heavy pounding followed. He must be battering the door down with his fists. "Open up!" he shouted.

Yeah, she was in the bathroom. Problem was, there was no way out. She'd have to go through Lloyd, and that didn't seem like a healthy choice.

The second guy grabbed me around the waist. I raised the paperweight and started to bring it down on his head when he grabbed my arm and twisted.

"Ouch!" I yelled.

His fist caught the edge of my jaw and the room spun from the impact. Staggering from the force of the blow, I dropped the paperweight and raised my hand, instinctively shielding my face.

Frantic, I tried to think of a way to escape because my jaw couldn't take another right hook. Hey, getting socked in the kisser isn't as painless as it looks in the movies.

As I scrambled backward, he tripped on the vacuum I'd left out, lost his balance, and fell, clutching at my leg on the way down. I kicked, trying to shake free, but he tightened his hold and crawled toward me on his elbows.

My foot made contact with his face.

He groaned, his grip loosened, and I scrambled forward a few steps. In a distant corner of my mind I heard Germaine yell. What followed sounded distinctly like the smashing of a door—my bathroom door. The insurance company wasn't going to like the not-so-random-act-of-violence.

During the diversion, I kicked free of my attacker for a nanosecond, but he lurched forward and grabbed my ankle. I pushed once, hard, and twisted free again.

I struggled to my feet, took a step forward, then stumbled. Time slowed as I felt myself falling. Just before I hit the floor, he grabbed me by the back of my neck and yanked me upward. In one fluid motion he spun me around and slammed me into the wall. My head bounced off the plaster walls like a boomerang and colorful stars whirled around the inside of my clenched eyelids. Really, stars, I'm not foolin'.

"Where's the money?" he hissed. His hands circled my throat and squeezed. I could smell his sour breath.

I sputtered, "What—?"

My eyes bulged as his grip tightened. Thinking and talking is impossible when someone is squeezing the life out of you. One thing was becoming very clear. The bad guys missed their money, and it hadn't taken them long to figure out I probably had it.

Gagging and wheezing from the increasing pressure on my throat, I tried to answer, "I . . . I don't . . ." I stammered, ". . . have any money."

Down the hall, Germaine screamed, "Get out of here, slime bag."

I winced, hoping Lloyd didn't easily take offense.

My attacker shook me so hard my teeth rattled. "Don't give me the dumb broad act. Where is it?"

Time for a bluff. If it didn't work, it might be my last.

He released the pressure on my windpipe, which translated into, "I wasn't going to die just yet," and a small amount of precious oxygen seeped into my lungs.

"I, I have twenty dollars in my purse," I gasped. "Take it!" He pressed on my throat again, and my gag reflex kicked in.

His grip relaxed slightly, probably didn't want me to throw up on him. I gulped as much air as my lungs could accommodate with the vise-like grip on my windpipe.

"My boss wants his money," he growled.

"Who?"

"Shut up, I'm asking the questions."

So much for the rudimentary interview. Best leave the boss out of it. It seemed to bring up some unresolved issues.

I shook with fear and didn't think I could continue. But I knew I couldn't turn these guys on to Father Daniel because they'd scare him to death if they didn't kill him first. I forced tears. Another of my deep well of talents.

"I don't have any money," I wailed. "My purse is on the counter."

I heard bottles hit the wall. Oh! Germaine was having a hissy fit. Poor, poor Lloyd.

"Take that!" she bellowed.

Lloyd cried out, "What the . . . ?"

Germaine's high-pitched screech echoed through the condo followed by a dull thud. It sounded like a body hitting the floor. I'd bet Lloyd was history. Germaine was a Tae Kwan Do brown belt.

"Danny, help me."

Another thud. "You worthless . . ."

"Ugh!"

"Lloyd, you okay?" Danny called out, keeping his eyes trained on me.

Thwack! Lloyd cried out louder. "Get off me!"

"Take that!—assho . . . !"

There was a pause, then Germaine began, "Forgive us our trespasses as we forgive our trespassers."

Germaine was on a roll. Whenever she reverted to being a regular human being, like swearing under stress, she began quoting the Lord's Prayer. Not the entire prayer, just that one passage, over and over.

There was another dull thud followed by a groan. Germaine: one. Bad guys: zero. I always questioned my sister's attraction to violence. It's such an odd hobby for a nun.

"You're gonna be so sorry."

It sounded like a body hit the floor again. What was she doing to him?

"No! Please!"

"You sh . . . ! Forgive us our trespasses as we forgive . . ."

Danny released me, and I slithered to the floor, my head bouncing off the wall on my way down. He must have figured Germaine was a bigger threat than the half dead widow, because he ran down the hall as my battered body hit the floor.

I wanted to warn Germaine, but all I could muster was a hoarse wheeze.

Germaine screamed as sirens echoed from the street below. Time stood still. Could it be true? Were the cops going to save the day?

I crawled a soldier crab crawl to the hallway, gasping for air. The tables had just turned—maybe. The neighbors must have heard the ruckus and called the police.

From the light that seeped out of the bathroom, I saw that Germaine was on both men like a hurricane. Lloyd was doubled over, and Danny was trying to pull him down the hall, out of her reach.

The sirens got louder. Shakily I pulled myself to a standing position, fell into the wall, more for support than anything, and groped for the light switch. I turned it on and the room flooded with light.

I couldn't tell who was who but suspected it was Danny who got a surprise punch in on Germaine. She went down with a thump. Whoops! That might be the knockout count. I wanted to run to her, but I was in their escape route.

They left her crumpled form, turned simultaneously, and ran down the hall. As they passed, I heaved myself from the wall, using my last bit of strength to lurch after them, pummeling them with my fists. It was a half-hearted effort, given the beating I'd just taken.

Danny turned and grabbed me by the throat again. I wish he wouldn't do that. His granite eyes bored through me. "My boss wants his money."

Fist raised, I glimpsed a tattoo, a butterfly, on the back of his hand between his thumb and first finger before he punched me in the jaw again. My head snapped back and everything went black.

Germaine's voice greeted me when I woke from my forced nap. "Pen, can you hear me? Are you okay?"

I opened my eyes, but instead of my sister, I saw two uniformed cops peering down at me.

I opened my mouth, but what came out wasn't intelligible, even to me. My throat and jaw hurt, a lot. Having my neck squeezed like a chicken during slaughter had probably interfered with my ability to speak. I prayed it wasn't permanent.

I gently tested my jaw. It wasn't broken.

"Pen. Talk to me."

I opened my mouth, swallowed, then gurgled innocuous sounds. I concentrated really hard, then sputtered nonsensical sounds again. I lifted my hand to my jaw and felt a giant-sized lump bulging where my lips and chin should be. "Ouch!"

Germaine squeezed my hand. "I was so scared. I thought he killed you."

"It hurts too much to be dead," I lisped.

I moved my head gingerly, trying to focus on my sister's face, but everything was a blur. I blinked a few times and my eyes cleared.

"I hurt all over."

"You should."

"I guess we didn't win?"

"We're alive." Germaine's voice quivered so subtly you'd have to know her well to have noticed.

From between the slits that must be my swollen eyes, I peered up at her. "That is," I coughed, "one nasty bruise."

"You should see the ones you're sporting, love." Germaine smiled.

I struggled to a sitting position, winced from the pain, and we laughed, a little carefully, due to our injuries.

One of the police officers cleared his throat and kneeled beside me. "Miss. I'm Officer Gant. Do you need an ambulance?"

"No!"

"You sure? You took quite a beating."

"Thanks, but no."

"It really might be for the best."

I glared at him because it hurt too much to continue to say no.

He must have gotten the message because he changed the subject, "Do you feel well enough to tell us what happened?"

"No!"

I was conscious enough to realize this was a cop and the cops were trying to pin Paul's murder on me. And right now, they wanted answers that I didn't want to give.

I groaned, laid down again and tried to get comfortable, which was difficult on the hard floor. The alternative was a spinning room.

Officer Gant glanced at Germaine, then asked me again, "Are you sure you don't want an ambulance, Miss?"

I struggled to talk because it didn't appear he was going to let up unless I seemed okay. "I'm all right. Just a little sore."

"Well," the second officer said, "we really need to ask you some questions."

I glared up at him. "I don't have any answers."

Germaine stroked my hair. "Come on, Pen. Two guys broke into your house and tried to kill us, for God sake. Talk to him, please."

Grimacing with pain, I pursed my lips. "I don't think so, Germaine."

I wasn't about to tell the cops that the thugs thought I had their money—mostly because I did.

"Penelope Santucci, I don't like getting beat up. Talk to him," she ordered.

"Santucci," the cop said. "Are you the Santucci who offed her—?" He stopped. Probably figured that what he was about to say might be considered politically incorrect. He'd be right. It'd be offensive too.

"I don't know what they wanted."

I struggled to my hands and knees then faltered.

Germaine reached for me. "Let me help you."

I hesitated, then stood up and stumbled again. Officer Gant reached out to steady me. I shook my arm from his grip and shakily walked down the hall muttering, "You talk to him, Germaine. I'm going to take a hot soaking bath, followed by an ice pack."

The room began to spin so I grabbed the wall. I inched farther down the hall and got to the bathroom before I sagged against the door frame, weak from the clobbering Danny had given me. I grabbed at the doorjamb and surveyed the damage.

The bathroom door hung by one hinge. The wall mirror was shattered and all my personal hygiene items were scattered over the floor. I cautiously stepped over spilled bottles and broken jars, and stripped down to bare skin. I noticed deep red and purple bruises already beginning to form over different parts of my body. Within twenty-four hours I'd look like a bowl of over-ripe fruit.

Germaine's voice droned on, answering the cop's questions as best as she could. I ran the bath and when the tub was full, sank into the water, leaned back, closed my eyes, and shut out the world. The cops could wait.

CHAPTER TWENTY-TWO

The sun peeked over the horizon just as Germaine and I finished cleaning up the mess the henchmen from hell had caused. It had been slow going due to fatigue and our collective injuries. We had to get up in two hours; if we hit the sack now, we'd just feel sluggish for the rest of the day, and I was already beyond cranky.

During the early morning hours, Germaine forgave me for leaving her to deal with the police. She didn't question me any further about the break-in, but her eyes told me she suspected I knew more than I owned up to.

It had been a long and painful night, more painful than long. My bruises swelled up, and I grew a shiner that became more colorful by the hour. The sunglasses I'd sported at Paul's funeral suddenly became a necessary accessory.

The police searched my place over the weekend, but I'd stashed the spare loot in my own locker. Just following Paul's lead. I'd also done a hundred small tasks that didn't need doing but kept me occupied.

I gave Marco the brokerage information he'd asked for and checked it off my to-do list. Our stockbroker, Dan Thomas, didn't bat an eye when I called and told him I needed the account records.

I'd also spoken to Paul's attorney, and his will had been read. Astrid was livid when she learned that Paul hadn't gotten around to changing it after our separation and I was his only beneficiary. Hey, what can I say, we were still technically married.

He tried to calm Astrid by telling her I wouldn't be able to claim anything if I was convicted of his murder. Nice touch on his part. It may have calmed her down, but it didn't contribute to my peace of mind.

I commiserated with friends: a quart of Haggen Daz ice cream topped off with three, maybe four, Hostess Cupcakes. Chocolate and more chocolate. Just another healthy snack. Or as I preferred to think of it, one of the tastier of the food groups.

I returned to work the Wednesday after Paul's funeral, out of sheer boredom. I wasn't any closer to proving Judge Kassner killed Paul, and now I had other suspects muddying the waters. And while the cops hadn't arrested me yet, thanks to Marco's negotiating skills, I was plenty worried.

My discolored eye had faded enough that I could cover it with make-up, as long as no one looked too closely. I was still sore from the beating but the bruises didn't show so it was only the eye that might attract attention.

I got to the office before seven. The doors were locked so I opened them, started the coffee, and sequestered myself in my broom closet-sized office. The mail had piled up into a daunting heap during my absence. So, I did what every normal bureaucrat would do. I put it aside and planned my next move. It was after eight when I heard the first rustling of bodies in the hallway outside my door.

It was now or never. I opened the door, threw my shoulders back, and marched down the hall. Woman with an attitude—on the move. So much better than behaving like "dead woman walking." It was the only way to handle the wolves sniffing around for any new information they could extract from me over coffee. People in my line of work were no different from the general population. If they smelled blood, it was all over but the burp at the end of the meal.

Murmurs of sympathy hit my back and followed me to my supervisor's office. Karen was already at her desk, a mammoth monstrosity that took up a quarter of her office. Pictures of her three chirpy-looking children adorned every wall and flat surface that wasn't littered with foliage. Nothing had changed, unlike my life.

Her poor plants seemed to hang on precariously to life. They wouldn't make it. They never did. It would be a pitiful and parched death as they slowly drew up their spindly little tentacles, withered and finally gave it up and died. *Bless them, Father, for they have not sinned.*

I shook my head, grateful that her lovingly-cared-for children fared better than those countless dead plants that littered the trash cans of her life. "Can I talk to you a minute?"

She looked up from the papers scattered across her desk, took off her reading glasses and replied, "Pen, I didn't expect you back to work so soon." She motioned me inside. "Come in. And close the door."

I sat in a hard wooden chair in front of her desk. "I've been gone awhile, so I'd like to work a couple of evenings to catch up."

Karen leaned back in her chair. "You've got family leave time coming, sick and vacation time too. Joan's been covering your caseload. And Brian's been helping out."

Her office turned warm and stifling, probably my nerves. My story had better be good. I sniffed a little. "You know how it is." My head dipped slightly, just enough to give the effect I wanted. Sadness, maybe despair. Pick a word, any word. "Paul and I were separated, but it's still hard. I don't like all the time alone at home. Nights are the hardest."

She shook her head, her maternal streak erupting. "I should

have thought of that. Do what you need to do."

"Thanks. I've got my keys, and I'll sign out at the guard's station. It'll only be for a couple of nights."

She stood up and walked around her desk. "Whatever you need, Pen."

I started to reply but was interrupted. "For whatever it's worth, no one here believes that you had anything to do with Paul's death. Is there anything that I can do?"

Relief washed over me. "Thanks, Karen. It's nice to hear that you believe in me. Not everyone does. And no, there's nothing you can do at the moment. But, thanks."

She placed her arm through mine and walked me to the door. "Remember, if you need more time, take it. We can get along without you for awhile."

My beleaguered smile did the trick. She laughed and said sternly, "Now, go get some coffee and get to work."

The coffee room was empty when I got there, and I was relieved. I poured myself a cup and meandered back to my office. Calmer now, and less defensive, I chatted in passing with co-workers who offered kind words and good cheer. They probably meant what they said, in their own way, but all the sympathy sounded hollow somehow.

I went back to my office and made plans for later that evening. As much as I hated to think about it, I needed a lookout. My best friend, Connie, was out of town, and I could only think of one other person who wouldn't hyperventilate and pass out if things got sticky.

I didn't have a choice, so I picked up the phone and punched the familiar numbers. After the third ring a melodious voice answered, "Hello."

I cleared my throat. "I'd like to speak to Sister Germaine, please."

"Who's calling?"

I crossed my fingers for luck, something I hadn't had much of lately. "It's her sister, Penelope Santucci."

There was sharp intake of breath. She'd heard about my recent difficulties, no doubt. You'd think a bunch of nuns would have better things to do than watch the news and read the paper.

She chirped, "I'll get her for you, Ms. Santucci. It'll be just a moment."

"I'll wait."

Well, I waited and waited and waited. After eons I heard, "What's up, Pen?"

"Uh, are you busy this afternoon? Late? About five, five-thirty?"

"I don't like the tone of your voice. Are you in some more trouble?"

"Me? Trouble? What would make you say that?"

"You have to ask? Now, what do you want?"

I put my feet up on my desk, crossed them at the ankles. "Ah, Germaine. Don't be so suspicious."

"Suspicious, now why would I be suspicious? You implicated me in the burglary of a well-respected judge. That's why I'm suspicious."

"That's what I wanted to talk to you about."

"The burglary?"

"Yeah."

"Oh, no! Did the cops get fingerprints? Are we going to be busted? If you've gotten Father Daniel and me in trouble, I'll . . . I don't know what I'll do."

Her breathing was so heavy, she sounded like she was in the room with me. Things weren't going well.

I gathered my thoughts. "Now, Germaine. We're not in trouble. It's just, well, it's just that I need some help and since you've already helped me with—and I don't call it a burglary, I call it looking for evidence—I thought you wouldn't mind helping me out one more time."

"What are you planning now?"

"Germaine, please!"

"Don't you Germaine me, Penelope Santucci."

Boy, her "ticked-off" meter had risen sharply. She called me Penelope. This called for another tactic. I took my feet off my desk and planted them firmly on the floor. I'd try the truth. "Germaine, I want to break into Judge Kassner's chambers and search for evidence."

"What? Have you completely lost your mind? They're gonna haul your behind away and lock you up, sister. And I don't mean jail. You are certifiable."

"Settle down and let me explain."

"No. The answer is no. I'm not getting involved in another one of your harebrained escapades. Once was enough. My God, I thought Father Daniel was going to die of a heart attack."

Exasperated, I interrupted, "He didn't, Germaine. The burglary got loused up, sure, but we got away."

"No thanks to you."

I nervously drummed my fingers on my desktop. "I really need your help here."

"No. What don't you understand about that small, two-lettered word?"

"If I get caught . . ."

"Oh no you don't! That's not going to work this time. I don't care. I'll take care of Ma if I have to. There are worse things in life than Ma, and prison just happens to be one of them."

Boy, she was serious if she was willing to throw out the Ma card. If she was bluffing she was good, really good. They could use her in Washington, negotiating with terrorists.

I had to think quickly. I crossed my fingers and said, "They're going to arrest me. I'm going to jail. Forever, maybe."

There was a long pause. "What do you mean they're going to arrest you?"

My fingers were still crossed. "Yeah, they think they have enough evidence for an arrest. Maybe they found something when they searched my place. I don't know what it could be, but they're hot on my trail." My voice actually shook because truthfully I didn't know just how close the cops were in making an arrest. "I need your help."

Five seconds of silence ticked by, I knew I had her.

"No!"

"Please, jail is so, so difficult. And in this case, it's so permanent."

"May God forgive what I am about to do."

Yes! Maybe it was me they needed in Washington.

"Thanks Germaine." I told her my plan. Then she slammed the receiver. The crash echoed in my ears. Not a good sign.

CHAPTER TWENTY-THREE

At nine-thirty P.M. I raised my head from my desk, checked my pocket for my trusty lock picks, stood up and stretched, a motion far more cavalier than I felt. Fear rattled around in my stomach and dread covered me like a suffocating shroud.

"Come on. It's time." I nudged Germaine, who was curled up in a chair.

She looked up from a stack of papers she was grading and snapped, "I can't believe I'm doing this. It's clear that I'm the one who's got a screw loose." Accusation burned in her eyes. "You know I'm going to have to go to confession in another state, don't you?"

"Honestly, I don't understand why you have to tell some man who's probably never had much of a life, all about yours. I wouldn't."

"Oh, and what about you going to Father Daniel?" I figured she was referring to my childhood confessional visits. She couldn't possibly know about my more recent trip to the confessional.

"Ah, that was just pretend. Mostly, I lied."

"Why should that surprise me? You have no faith."

"Faith I have. It's ethics, integrity, and scruples I'm short of at the moment. Fear of being housed permanently in the state penitentiary does that to a person. Let's go."

Reluctantly Germaine trudged after me, mumbling about an afterlife in hell.

Andrea Sisco

I faced the door, carefully opened it and peered into the darkness. It creeped me out, big time, to be in the uninhabited probation offices at night. I shivered slightly and walked briskly down the hall, on the alert for any employees who might be working late. Fat chance. This is government at work. Or, not at work. It was running into a stray judge I worried about. Sometimes they did work late.

We snaked through the maze of cubicles toward the front door. Just to be safe, I peeked through the glass separating us from the shadowy cavernous hall.

"All clear," I noted solemnly.

I unlocked the door, waited until Germaine passed through, still grumbling, locked it again, darted two steps to the elevator and punched the up button.

It took a lifetime before the mellow ding-dong of the elevator bell greeted us and the doors finally opened.

Germaine huddled in the far corner of the elevator, arms crossed tightly over her chest, while I stood in the center, impatiently tapping my foot as the floors whizzed by on the light panel above. We were silent, but I knew what Germaine was thinking, and I hoped that we'd reach our destination before she began another tirade. My anxiety level was high enough and increasing at an alarming rate.

The elevator lurched to a stop and the doors jerked slightly before opening. I peered out quickly checking to the left and right. The hall was pitch black, and I didn't see anything other than dark shadows shifting like apparitions on the Plexiglas barrier that kept jumpers from taking a high dive to the atrium far below.

Germaine whispered, "This is more than creepy."

The Hennepin County Government Center was actually two tall buildings. In the center was a large atrium and to get from one side to the next you had to cross a bridge. Not every floor had one. Judge Kassner's chambers happened to be on a bridge floor so we didn't have to walk up or down the stairwell to get from the Administration building to the Courtside building.

"Come on." I grabbed Germaine's arm. "We've got to walk across the bridge."

"What?"

"Quiet!" I pressed my finger to my lips.

She shook her arm free. "Who's going to hear us? Ghosts?"

"There might be a janitor cleaning the bathrooms or a guard making the rounds." I crept toward the bridge. "You never know."

She grunted her disapproval. "Let's get out of here. It's not too late. We don't have to live this life of crime. God will forgive you."

I whirled around so fast she slammed into me.

"Hey!" she yelped.

I steadied her so she wouldn't topple over. "I'm not going to jail. How many times do I have to explain this to you? This is my life, my freedom we're talking about! If you want to go, then go." I turned and continued walking. "And I don't need God's forgiveness. Yet."

She ignored me and boldly took long strides across the bridge.

I jogged after her, passed her as we approached the bank of Court tower elevators, and kept going until I reached the locked doors that kept the riffraff, meaning anybody the judges didn't want to see, out of their inner sanctum.

Kneeling on the floor, I reached into my pocket and fumbled with the picks. "I don't know if I can do this with such poor lighting."

Germaine shifted her weight from one foot to the other. "Great! Don't you plan your felonies?"

I continued poking at the lock, pretending I didn't hear her. The lock clicked and I reached up with my right hand, pushed the handle down, and gave the door a tug. It released and I walked backwards on my knees, smiling when it gave way. "Ta da! There is a God!"

"I'm not impressed. And don't bring God into this. It's sacrilege."

I ignored her. She was entitled to a little sermonizing. I hopped up, bowed, sweeping my arm outward and ushered Germaine through the door. I couldn't see her face, but it didn't take a great deal of imagination to know she was pretty angry.

I headed straight for Judge Kassner's chambers, having been there numerous times for criminal sentencing. Intermittent lights from various offices allowed me to dart down the hall without tripping over stray furniture or decorative ferns. And as luck would have it, his door was open. Typical judicial arrogance. He must have thought that little lock on the outer office door would protect his privacy. That and a few million statutes prohibiting the interference with the judicial process. I swallowed hard.

It was dark inside, so I pulled my penlight out of my pocket and flicked it on.

Germaine, hands on her hips said, "You had a light, and didn't use it out there? Why now?"

"It's okay. We're on the twenty-first floor. No one's going to see us. If someone had been out there," I nodded my head in the direction of the hall, "we could have been targets."

"Targets?"

I ignored her and tugged on a drawer. It wasn't locked and neither were any of the others. But that was as far as my luck went. There wasn't anything in any of them that meant anything to me or that pertained to Paul's murder.

"Check those file drawers," I instructed Germaine,

She slid open a drawer. "What am I looking for?"

"How should I know?" I huffed. "You'll know it when you see it."

She stood still.

I shined the light directly on her face. "Well, what are you waiting for?"

She tapped her left foot. "I don't have a light, smarty pants."

I groaned. My miscalculation would cost us time since I only had one penlight.

I slammed the last desk drawer and walked over to the file cabinet. "Here, take this."

"Some criminal you are. Why not just turn on the light? There are, after all, other lights on in this wing. The only reason . . ."

As if saying it made it so, the light blinked on. I was temporarily blinded, but a piercing voice made everything perfectly clear. "And what do you think you're doing?" As I spun around I glimpsed the terror in Germaine's eyes. I shielded my eyes from the bright light and did what I do best, began setting up for a lie.

"What?"

"I said, what are you doing here?" Silence, then, "Pen? Pen Santucci? What in the world are you doing?"

I glanced at Germaine who was savagely beating her breasts as she made the sign of the cross, repeatedly. Her wild eyes gave her the distinct look of a martyr headed to a fiery death. I squinted at our captor in the doorway and gulped. "Judge Hunter?"

"I'm waiting." The judge stood rigid, arms folded stiffly across her chest. "Your explanation had better be good."

An audible prayer spilled from Germaine's lips as my mind whirred with possibilities, none of them particularly attractive or fitting our current plight. The scariest thought was of Germaine and me behind bars. *Oh my, what would Ma say?*

"I'm waiting."

My chest heaved. "I don't know what to say."

Recovered from her shock, Germaine took one step forward, grabbed me by my collar with both hands and shrieked, "I'm a nun, for God's sake!"

Her eyes were glistening with what I thought might be tears or then again, it might be unleashed rage. She'd gone from martyrdom to insanity in a millisecond. Her grip on my collar tightened and my eyes bulged with the pressure. For the second time in a few short days, somebody was trying to kill me. And this time it was my own sister. Considering our predicament, who could blame her? Still, the lack of oxygen made me see spots.

I clutched at her arms, trying to loosen her grip.

Sputtering, I managed to squeak, "Germaine!" I coughed and her grip relaxed a bit. "What—?"

She tightened her grasp again and shook me like a rag doll. "I should kill you, God forgive me."

Judge Eloise Hunter brushed against me, her hands covered Germaine's. "Let go, now!" the judge ordered.

Germaine's hold loosened a tiny bit, and I gasped for air.

"I said, let go!" Judge Hunter commanded again.

But Germaine wasn't following orders, so I picked up my leg, aimed as best as I could, and kicked her hard in the shin. *Ah, regression to our childhood fights.*

"Ow!" She let go enough that I could slip away.

I greedily sucked air and struggled to keep my balance. "What did you do that for? You could've killed me!"

Understanding flooded her face, she crumpled into a heap on the floor, her hands covered her face. "My God, my God! What has happened to me?" I followed suit as my legs folded, and I sprawled out next to her, coughing and hacking.

Judge Hunter knelt beside me, a look of concern settled over her face. "Are you okay, Pen?" She looked at Germaine, "Who's this?"

I stammered, "My sister, the Sister."

Germaine leaned back against the desk. "Oh, Pen."

Judge Hunter glanced at Germaine, then me. "Your sister? The Sister? Your sister tried to strangle you?"

I gagged, the sputtered, "You'd have to know our history."

Germaine, recovered from kill mode, whispered, "My God, I almost killed you." She stood up.

I struggled to my knees, then faltered. "Oh!"

The two women each took an arm and helped me to my feet. Leaning into Germaine, I steadied myself and asked the judge, "I suppose you wouldn't believe it if I told you we were going to the bathroom, lost our way, and ended up here?"

The judge's left eyebrow arched slightly, her mouth turned upside down, into a frown. "A ridiculous story like that? No."

Germaine slapped my arm. "This is not funny. Get serious, will you?"

Judge Hunter took a step back and sat primly on the edge of Judge Kassner's desk, her arms folded across her chest. "I'd like an explanation."

Sure she would, but she'd never believe it. Maybe if I told her the truth she'd take pity on us and wouldn't have us arrested. Probably not. The bad news was I'd lose my job. The good news was that Ma would be happy about that. The bad news was that Germaine and I would go to jail. The good news was that I'd be out of the reach of Ma's wrath. Maybe.

With both of her daughters in jail, Ma wouldn't be able to show her face at the butcher's for a long, long time.

My shoulders dropped in defeat as I sank into a chair in front of the desk and said, "It's a long story."

Judge Hunter went around behind the desk and sat in Judge Kassner's chair. She'd trumped me with the power chair. "I've got the time."

"Yeah? Lovely," I mumbled and took a deep breath wondering exactly how much I could trust this woman. She wasn't going to wait forever, but telling the truth of late had become difficult. I took a long look at Germaine who continued to rub her injured knee. The way it shook out was that I didn't have much choice, so I spilled my guts and gave her my sorry saga. After I finished my story I paused and waited for someone to say something.

Finally, Judge Hunter leaned forward and stated, "It's too impossible to believe. And yet, I do. Even you couldn't make all this up."

A ray of hope? I jumped in with both feet. "If it hadn't happened to me, I wouldn't believe it either."

"From a logical point of view, you're really taking a leap of faith to think that Judge Kassner was being blackmailed by Paul and then killed him because of it."

"Hey, I know what I heard on the phone." I threw my hands up.

"You thought you heard something, and that led you to think Judge Kassner was involved in Paul's scheme. What you heard, of course, could have meant something else entirely."

I shook my head. "I don't think so."

"Pen, he's a well-respected member of the bench. He's wealthy in his own right. It isn't logical that he'd take money to throw a trial."

"Maybe Paul had something on him. It wouldn't be the first time a judge had deep dark secrets."

She cocked her head to the side. "No. But I can't believe it of him. It just doesn't fit."

"I give up. If it's not him, what was Paul talking about? Who was he talking to? Somebody killed Paul, and it wasn't me." I looked around for support. No one gave any.

Judge Hunter stood up. "Your imagination has gotten away with you. I know John Kassner very well. I don't for one minute think that anyone on this bench is capable of doing what you've been talking about."

Germaine, finally spoke, "What you're saying is that we should look somewhere else."

Judge Hunter turned toward Germaine. "That's exactly what I'm saying. Paul had enemies. He earned them." She emphasized the point to me, thumping on the desk with her index finger. "You know yourself that Paul skirted the fringe, did business with some of the more unsavory elements in the city. Oh, I'm not saying he wasn't a good attorney, but, at times, he did have a tendency towards unscrupulous behavior."

"Perhaps we should look elsewhere." I sighed and shook my head. "But I just can't rule out Judge Kassner, at least, not yet."

Judge Hunter walked toward me, her mouth a thin line, her eyes hard. "I suggest you sit down and think things through. Make a list of Paul's enemies. Dig further into his dealings. You'll find something. And when you do, tell your attorney, tell the police, but leave Judge Kassner alone." Her expression made it clear that I'd better not argue.

Okay, so that was settled, but now I had to deal with the break-in. "Uh, about tonight?"

"You broke into a judge's chambers, Pen. That's a felony."

This wasn't going well at all. My eyes were riveted on a small dark spot on the floor, a sigh escaped my lips. "I know."

Judge Hunter cocked her head to the side. "What do you think I should do?"

My head snapped up. We'd reached the bottom line. The place where the deal is made, if it's to be made. "Could we just forget it?"

Her head moved slowly from left to right and back again. "I don't think so. What I should do is call the police." She paused, crossed her arms, resting them on her chest. "But I'll make you a deal. I know you, and I know you've been under a great deal of stress. You're obviously not thinking clearly or you wouldn't have done something this stupid. No real harm was done. You leave Judge Kassner alone, and I won't tell anyone."

My jaw muscles loosened. "Really?"

Germaine inhaled deeply as if she had forgotten to breathe for the last five minutes.

Judge Hunter nodded, "You snapped. You're just misguided. I'll let it go, but you have to give me your word that you'll leave the murder investigation to the police. It's what they do."

"If I do what you ask, you won't tell anyone about this?" I stopped. Her eyes and posture told me she wasn't in the mood for my antics.

"You have my word. Now do I have yours?"

"Would you consider watching things around here and if you hear or see something suspicious, tell me."

"You're not in a position to bargain."

"Judge Hunter, I don't want to go to jail for a murder I didn't commit," I pleaded.

Her eyes softened. "I understand. I'll make you a deal. You leave this thing to the police and if I see or hear anything, I'll tell you and you can tell your attorney."

She was humoring me, but I wasn't playing from a power position. I'd better take the deal.

Germaine interjected, "We're not really in a position to negotiate."

Judge Hunter nodded. "Your sister is right."

I slowly brought my arms down to my sides, eased them behind my back, and crossed my fingers, on both hands. "Okay, I promise."

The grim look on Judge Hunter's face brightened. "Good. Now let's get out of here." She pointed to the door. "And you two get on home and stay out of trouble."

I was already moving towards the door. "You, bet." I turned around. "And thanks, I appreciate it."

Judge Hunter shooed us out the door and walked with us to the elevator, pausing as she mused, "I'm not going to ask how you got in here. I don't think I want to know. But obviously, these chambers aren't as safe as we all think they are."

I looked at her sheepishly and started to respond when Germaine grabbed me by the arm. "Thanks Judge." She tugged. "It's time to go, Pen."

CHAPTER TWENTY-FOUR

We were silent as we waited in the eerie darkness for the elevator. When the bell rang, announcing its arrival, I jumped. It had been a long day. We got in, and I punched the button that brought us to the Atrium level.

"That was almost too easy," Germaine said.

"My sentiments exactly," I answered.

Germaine looked hard at me and said, "Do you realize just how close we came to landing in jail? You're obsessed with this . . . this Judge Kassner thing, and you've got to let it go. Otherwise you're going to land in jail, get hurt or—God forbid—killed."

I clamped my arms against my side to keep them from shaking. "The point is, we aren't going to jail!" I'd barked the words a little too loudly. Struggling to lower my voice and calm my nerves, I continued, "At least, you aren't. Judge Hunter will keep her word."

She turned, planted her feet firmly in front of her and said, "You just don't get it, do you? I'm a nun!" she thumped her chest. "A nun breaking laws to save your sorry ass, and so far we've come up with a big fat zero." She crossed herself.

"We just haven't found what we need." I tried to reassure her, but it was tough going. "We will."

"What's with this we will stuff? *We* aren't going to do anything. No more." Her hands chopped at air. "Let the cops do their job."

"Yeah."

Germaine's eyes widened. "You promised the judge. If you don't keep that promise, we could still end up in jail."

If I didn't come up with something good, really fast, my days of Germaine helping me were over.

"I absolutely refuse to go to prison for the rest of my life for a murder I didn't commit. If I'd had the satisfaction of doing the deed, well, it might not be so bad rotting in a cell. But——"

"Nobody wants you to go to jail." She grabbed my arm. "Think, Pen. If the cops haven't arrested you yet, it's because they don't have any evidence."

I shook free of her grasp and spat, "It's only because I've got a good lawyer."

"No. It's because they don't have any evidence. Suspicions, yes. Evidence, no. There's a difference."

"I'm not so sure."

My sister was on a roll. "And another thing, there are too many strange things going on. I don't think you're telling me everything." She shook her head. "No. I know you're not telling me everything."

I feigned shock. "What do you mean?"

"Those guys in your apartment, just what was that all about?"

I didn't know what to say.

"What's going on, Pen?" Her voice rose to a shout just as the elevator doors opened.

"Be quiet."

She stomped her foot. "No. So far I've aided and abetted you on two burglaries, not to mention getting caught at one of them or getting attacked by two hoodlums."

I distanced myself from her, walked over to the security guard's desk, shook my head and smiled. "We were working late. Probation. We're leaving now."

He glanced at his sign-in sheet.

191

"We've been here since this morning so our names aren't on the sheet."

He nodded, and I walked briskly away with Germaine hot on my heels.

"I'm not done talking to you," she called out after me.

I got on the escalator that went down to street level and mumbled, "Well, I'm done talking to *you.*"

She snatched at my sleeve.

I jerked away from her. "Not here."

I clamped my lips together in angry silence, shoving out of the revolving doors and marching briskly toward the parking ramp, with Germaine trotting behind me. The light turned red, but there wasn't any traffic, so I crossed.

Germaine mumbled loud enough for me to hear, "You don't even obey the traffic lights."

That was all I could take. I turned and yelled, "Germaine! I have had a very bad day. A very, very bad day. In fact I have had a lot of very bad days lately." I waved my hand in the air, Italian style, and ticked off each point on my fingers. "My cheating husband was murdered. The cops think I look good for the deed. The media wants to take apart my reputation piece-by-piece. And, every time I try to get evidence on the real murderer, things go wrong. Oh, and then there's the muscle-bound goons bent on knocking the snot out of me." I ran out of fingers so I threw my arms up in the air. "And, lest you forget, I've also got Ma breathing down my neck." I took a deep breath. "So, I don't want to hear about red lights from you. Sister high and mighty, perfect nun. I'm not perfect, Germaine. I'm just bumbling along, trying to stay alive and keep out of jail!"

It all hit me, right there, late at night, in the middle of Sixth Street in downtown Minneapolis. The whole ugly mess, right down to getting caught in Judge Kassner's chambers and what that could have meant. I started crying. Actually, blubbering was more like it.

I hate public displays, even if the mean streets of Minneapolis were dark and deserted, and no one could see me. I don't like to be vulnerable. It simplifies my life. But life was complicated at the moment, complicated and confusing. Germaine rushed over and threw her arms around me. "I'm sorry."

I snuffled and blathered on between ragged breaths. "The cops are gonna pin me with Paul's murder, I just know it. And those goons think I have their money."

She almost knocked me over as she shoved me away. "What? How do you know those guys think you have their money?" The sympathy was all gone. She leaned in and looked me square in the eye, which was difficult because it was dark and we only had the streetlights to see by. The headlights of several cars bore down on us as we stood in the middle of the street. Germaine tugged me firmly to the other side. "I'm not leaving until you tell me."

My chest heaved as I took a deep breath.

She bent so close our noses almost touched. "You have somebody's money? Somebody who can't go to the cops? Somebody that breaks kneecaps?"

"It was an accident."

She groaned and shook her head slowly. "It's always an accident. You're always in the wrong place at the right time—that it?"

I glared at her, a warning not to say another word.

She didn't care. Sister Germaine was used to dealing with unrepentant liars. I could almost hear the ruler slapping in her hand. "Go on," she ordered. "I'm listening. And don't stop until you've told me everything. And I mean everything!"

I knew when I was whipped. Maybe what I really needed was a heartfelt confession. I sank to the curb and patted the sidewalk next to me. Germaine sat down, and I began talking and talking and talking. This was a confession of a lifetime. No priest, just my big sister.

When I finished telling Germaine about the key I'd found in the safe and the money I'd found in the locker, she was still shaking her head. "You gave Father Daniel the money to hold?"

"Yeah."

Hugging her knees to her chest and rocking slightly she said, "Don't you realize how serious this is? Don't you see how much danger you could be putting him in?"

"He's not in danger." I studied a candy wrapper fluttering by my foot, coming to rest in the damp sludge of the gutter. "They don't know he has the money." Yeah, that was it. He was safe for the time being. "What I can't figure out is how they knew I had it."

She slapped her hand against her knee. "Don't you get it? It doesn't matter how they know or what they think they know. They've decided you have it, and that's enough for them. They are not—hear me when I say this, Pen—they are not going to let up on you."

"I don't believe that. Once they're convinced I don't have it, they'll—"

"Believe!" She abruptly stood up, brushing off the seat of her pants. She'd said it as if she was the healer in a revival meeting. I actually waited for her to press the palm of her hand hard against my forehead and miraculously free me of this awful mess.

She didn't, so I continued talking as I got to my feet. "They've left me alone now for a few days. I think we've spooked them. They won't be back."

She started walking. "I'm the nun, and you're the probation officer. You'd think . . . but no, you're the naïve one." She shook her head, like a disappointed parent. "They'll be back. I can't believe Marco has allowed you to do this." She stopped in her tracks, turned, her stare flaming like a Christmas log. "Marco doesn't know, does he?"

My long silence screamed the answer.

She shook her finger at me so hard I thought it would fly off her hand. "I'm going to say this once and only once. You tell Marco everything! And I mean *everything*, or I will. And you get the money from Father Daniel and give it back to those guys, or something." She marched toward her car, her arms slicing through the air as she issued edicts. "Or give it to the police. I don't care what because if you don't, they're going to be back and you're going to get hurt, or killed. They're probably the ones who killed Paul."

It was amazing how clear-headed and calm I became in that instant. I rushed to catch up to her. "Nah. I considered that but decided, even if they wanted to kill him, they wouldn't have. Not until they'd got their money back. These guys aren't that dumb."

"This isn't up for discussion, Pen. You explain all this to Marco and do exactly what he tells you."

I didn't have the strength for another argument. I wanted a hot bath and a soothing cup of coffee. Yes, that was the answer. Those coffee beans, they do God's work.

I continued walking, catching up and passing Germaine on the way to the car. "Okay, okay. I'll tell him."

She walked quickly after me. "Tomorrow—you'll tell him tomorrow," she pressed. "Don't put it off." She reached out and stopped me before she put her arms around my shoulder. "I don't want you to get hurt. You're my baby sister." She punched me gently in the arm. "Besides, I don't want the wrath of Ma."

Not a pretty sight, the wrath of Ma. "Yeah, alright. I'll talk to him tomorrow."

We laughed, me a little nervously, split up, and went to our respective cars.

CHAPTER TWENTY-FIVE

It was almost eleven when I pulled into my parking garage. I couldn't wait to climb into bed, but I had to sort out my problem before morning. If I didn't tell Marco about the money, Germaine would. My sister tended to be fanatical about follow-through. Oh, and honesty. Without the proper spin, this whole money thing might seem a bit, well, a bit underhanded. It would sound much better coming from me. I just needed to think of a way to put it all in a good light.

My purse strap slipped off my shoulder, and I hitched it up as I walked in the crisp night air toward the front steps. All thoughts were interrupted as two hooded figures leapt from the shrubs flanking the double doors. One grabbed me roughly by the arms.

My adrenalin skyrocketed as survival mode shot into high gear. I twisted so hard and fast I felt like a flag whipping in a Minnesota October wind. I couldn't scream because a smelly hand covered my mouth and nose, suffocating me.

Terrified I was about to meet my Maker, I jumped and kicked his shins with both feet. My attacker's grip loosened just enough that I broke free. This probably wasn't the method recommended in a self-defense class. I landed flat on my belly, air whooshing from my chest. My head hit the ground and colorful stars twinkled brightly behind my eyelids.

My attacker fell on me, dodging my fists as I rolled over just in time to pummel his torso, my feet kicking empty air. He slipped his hands under my body, flipped me on my stomach, grasped my left arm and yanked it up behind my back. I screamed.

The other guy, flipped me on my back, leaned close to my face and growled, "This is for the grief you caused me last time." He punched me hard in stomach.

Instinctively, I drew up my legs to protect myself, but I wasn't fast enough. His next blow paralyzed me for a minute or two. One thought gave me hope. They wouldn't kill me because they wanted their money. As long as they didn't have it, I was probably safe. From death that is. Given the level of violence, I wasn't sure which was worse. These assaults were becoming far too regular for my taste.

"Where's the money?" His breath smelled of garlic and booze, and what was that other smell? Cigar? He drew his hand back and made a fist.

How could I convince them that I didn't have it? Denial hadn't worked the last time. I curled in a ball, pushed out with my feet, and rolled sideways to avoid another blow to my midsection. I couldn't take another direct hit. I was on my back and dug my heels into the ground and pushed. I slid backwards and successfully deflected his fist. It clipped my hip and threw him off balance, which gave me time to get to my knees.

"I don't have your money," I gasped, scrambling away on all fours.

As both men converged on me, the sprinkler system spurted on, spraying water directly into the face of the man who'd hit me. "What?"

The shower of water surprised them enough that I was able to stand and sprint up the steps toward the door. My freedom was short lived as one of my attackers caught me by the ankles, pulling me down. My knees hit the steps, and my head slammed into the glass door.

As I lost consciousness, my funeral flashed through my mind. Ma stood in front of a cheap and poorly made pine casket, her head wagging from side-to-side, never mind that I'd asked to be cremated. Ma didn't believe in cremation. Instead, for all eternity, I'd have creepy crawlies, slithering over me, feeding off my remains.

I didn't die, but it might have been better if I had. My entire body screamed with pain, and my head throbbed like the aftermath of a long night of boozing.

With great care I twitched, first my arms and then my legs, noting with satisfaction that they still worked. I kept my eyes closed because I didn't want to find out I was being held hostage by the two thugs who had beaten me silly. A moan escaped from my lips.

"Pen?"

"Marco!" I tried to blink my eyes open but the light hurt too much. "How? What happened to those guys?"

Slowly, I inched open one eye, keeping the other squeezed tightly shut. Yup! It was Marco. I opened the other eye and slowly tried to figure out where I was. Moving, even my eyeballs, any faster would just make the pain worse, and it was already awful.

The room looked familiar. Yes, I was in my condo. I groaned.

Marco leaned over me. "Pen, can you hear me? Are you okay?"

A quirky jazz beat pounded in my head. "I'm dead, aren't I? I feel bad enough to be in hell."

He placed his hand on my shoulders, and I screamed, "Do. Not. Touch. Me."

"Sorry. You *should* be going to the hospital."

Oh, oh, the H word. No, not for me. I'd rather be drop-kicked into hell than darken the halls of a modern-day hospital.

They breed new strains of diseases in those places, super bacteria, uberviruses. A person could die trying to get well.

I struggled to sit up, and my stomach lurched. Oh drat, I was definitely going to throw up. Maybe not. Pain started in my lower back, shot up through my midsection, and ended at the base of my neck. I stifled a groan.

Marco gently cradled my head in his hands, lowering me carefully on the sofa. "Stay put."

"How about forever?"

"Might make my job easier."

Funny man. But I wasn't laughing. I drew in a deep breath and winced. Every muscle cried out for relief.

"Just lie there," Marco ordered.

"No argument from me."

"For once."

Really funny man.

The longer I stayed still the less it seemed to hurt. After a few minutes, I said, "I think I'll live."

His head dipped closer to my face, and he peered into my eyes. "I don't think anything is broken, but you've got quite a bump on your forehead and a fantastic shiner on your left eye. This one would take first place in any competition."

I groaned with disgust.

"I'm worried about the bump though. It might be a good idea to have it looked at. Just to make sure there's not any real damage."

"I'm not going to the hospital. You can't make me."

He sat up. "Somehow, I thought you'd say that."

What was he up to? I studied his face. "Is that why you didn't take me?"

He shrugged. "I have a friend, a doctor, coming here to check out your injuries."

"What?" I tried to sit up, lost the struggle as the pain intensified, and sank back into the sofa cushions.

Marco pointed a finger at the lump throbbing on my noggin. "A head injury is serious. You need to be seen by a doctor."

"No."

He frowned. "I don't care. Now, tell me why those two guys were beating the daylights out of you."

I closed my eyes and silently pleaded the Fifth.

"Ah, then you do know something about it," he insisted, increasing the pressure.

Busted. I tried to cover. "They were muggers, that's all."

"No, that's not all."

For the first time, I took a good look at him, starting at his feet and slowly, traveling up the length of his body to his face. Oh, my. He hadn't just found me. He'd obviously been involved in my rescue. The *GQ* look had taken a walk on the wild side. His hair was a mess, his shirt torn, and his khakis were wet and had grass stains on them.

"You were there?"

"No. I look like this because I had a little accident while dancing Swan Lake. Of course, I was there. Representing you is becoming a dangerous proposition."

"Where are the bad guys?"

He turned to the window, frowning, and murmured, "They got away."

I noticed a purple bruise blossoming on his left cheekbone. "You took a punch?"

The palm of his hand scraped across his five o'clock shadow as he tenderly rubbed his cheek and chin. "Several, but that's not the point."

"I'm glad you're okay," I whispered, feeling guilty.

"They weren't just muggers, Pen. They knew your name, and they were waiting for you. I have a right to know what this is all about."

How to stall. I diverted his attention with a question. "What were you doing here this time of night?"

"I couldn't reach you all day," he bristled. "I was worried. Trouble stalks you like a disgruntled lover. Besides, I needed more information on Paul's brokerage records, and the cops want to talk to you again."

I clenched my fists. "They're gonna arrest me, aren't they? I knew it!"

Marco leaned over me and surprised me by gently pressing my shoulders back against the pillow. "Settle down. They're not arresting you. They just want to ask a few more questions. And I'll be with you."

I relaxed.

He continued, "I was driving by the neighborhood and decided to stop in. I waited for you in the lobby. It wasn't more than a few minutes before you got there."

It finally sunk in. "You were worried about me?" Somehow, that took the edge off my pain. "Wait a minute! How did you get in? It's a secure building."

He grinned.

"You buzzed each place until someone let you in."

His smirk told me I was right. "So how did you get into my unit?"

His eyes darted to my purse, lying by the front door. "I see. My keys."

He studied me for a minute and softly grazed his thumb over a bruise on my arm. "You've got to tell me what this is about, or I can't represent you anymore."

He was serious, and suddenly, I couldn't stomach the thought of facing all this without him. Unfortunately, lying is an illness from which I wouldn't easily recover. "Marco, I don't know."

"I'm not kidding, Pen," he paused, and when I didn't bubble forth with the info he wanted, his jaw muscles bunched. "You really don't play well in the sandbox with others, do you?"

The buzzer rang. "Must be the doctor." I ignored the pain in my jaw and attempted an apologetic smile. Saved by the bell.

Marco jumped up, hit the buzzer, and pointed a finger at me. "We will continue this conversation." A few moments later a sharp knock prompted him to open the door.

I closed my eyes wishing everything and everyone would go away and leave me alone. Briefly, I wanted Ma, then thought better of that idea. I just needed some rest, or maybe drugs. Yes, give me drugs. Something to take away the pain. I glanced in the doctor's direction.

"Thanks for coming." I heard the soft tone in Marco's voice before I saw the reason. I gulped. In the doorway was a very tall, very leggy, very beautiful woman with shoulder-length, silky blond hair. She looked like a shampoo commercial.

"I'm glad I could help," she replied, her tone a bit too syrupy. I bet she didn't learn that in med school. Maybe she'd worked her way through as a stripper.

Marco kissed her on the cheek. "I appreciate it."

I buried my head under the blanket. "Now, let's see the patient."

I snuggled the blanket tighter around my head, closed my eyes again, feigning sleep.

"She's over here. Pen?"

I didn't open my eyes and didn't lower the blanket.

Marco nudged my shoulder. "Pen."

Slowly, very slowly I opened my eyes as Marco forcibly lowered the blanket from my face.

"Pen, this is Jennifer Crockett. She's the doctor I told you about."

I looked up, way, way up at the perfect Nordic specimen standing over me, with her straight, perky nose and several other perky things that were impossible to miss. Doctor Slut, I silently named her. Can you blame me?

Her perfect white teeth smiled broadly as she plopped down on the hassock by the sofa. "Hello. May I call you Pen?"

"Yeah. Whatever." My cranky meter hit overload.

"Well then, let's take a look at you."

I couldn't say no since that would mean my next stop would be the hospital.

As she began examining me, she commented, "You're a little worse for wear. What happened exactly? Marco wasn't clear about that."

I glared at her nauseatingly beautiful blue eyes through my swollen ones and tried to shrug. She smiled. I didn't want to like her, but her soothing manner and sparkling personality made it impossible. By the time she'd finished her exam, I found myself warming up to Dr. Slut. Drat! I had no control over anything these days.

Marco, who had left the room during the exam, returned. She glanced at him, but had the decency to give her prognosis directly to me. "You've had a nasty bit of trauma, Pen. Not enough to require hospitalization, but you need to take it easy for a few days. I'd like you to take the rest of the week off from work and come see me on Friday."

"I can't do that. I'm behind already."

She stood up, towering over me once again. "I'm not asking you." Dr Nazi Slut placed her hands on her hips. "I'm ordering you."

"But, I can't."

Marco butted in, "Pen, if you want me to continue as your lawyer, you're going to have to start cooperating."

I squinted at him, which wasn't easy, through puffy eyes. "You're just full of threats, aren't you?"

"They're not threats. You follow orders, or I'm outta here."

"Oh, all right." I sank deeper into the sofa cushions. I knew when I was beaten, literally as well as figuratively.

"Marco, I'm leaving this for Pen." She dropped her card on the coffee table. "See that she calls me and schedules an appointment for Friday. In the meantime, watch her. That nasty bump on the head gave her a slight concussion."

Marco picked up the card as he walked her to the door. "Thanks. She'll call."

She went all syrupy again and touched his arm, laughing lightly. "I'm sure you'll see to it." She turned to me, and I snapped my eyes shut. They made me feel like puking, both of them.

"Take care of yourself, Pen. I'll see you on Friday."

I mumbled, "Thanks," and opened my left eye slightly. Marco kissed her on the cheek as she left the condo, and I felt like punching something. Which was odd since I'd already had enough punching activities to last a lifetime.

He closed the door and walked back to the sofa.

"And who is she?" I grumbled.

He sat beside me on the hassock. "A friend."

I drew the blanket tighter around me. "Yeah, I could see that. Just how good a friend?"

"None of your business."

"If she's treating me, it is." I rubbed my aching neck, lightly. It hurt like the dickens, which may have been why I snapped at him. "Give it up, Marco."

"A bit touchy, are we?" He ran his fingers through his hair.

"Look, I've got every reason to be touchy. I ache in places I didn't know could hurt. And you're bringing strange women into my condo. For all I know she's not even a real doctor. I mean she doesn't look like a regular doctor, now does she? What is she your massage therap—"

"Oh, lord. Okay! We used to date. We were both overly involved with our careers, so we decided to be friends. And she is a doctor, a very good doctor."

We both fell silent. If there had been a hole to crawl into I would have gladly slithered into it.

Marco cleared his throat, even though it didn't need clearing. "You can't stay here, you know."

That got my attention. I carefully adjusted my position and looked at him. "What do you mean I can't stay here? This is my home." I made a feeble attempt to wave my arm. This was my queendom. The problem was, my arm felt like it had been jerked out of its socket. It probably had been. I gave up and tucked my hand under the blanket.

"Maybe you didn't notice the two guys trying to kill you? And, according to the police, this isn't the first time."

I tried to sit upright but gave that up when every bone in my body screamed "I surrender." "I don't have anywhere else to go." Which wasn't patently true, I mean there was Ma's. But honestly, I'd rather be dead.

"I'm not leaving you alone tonight. Those guys could come back. Perhaps kill you next time."

"Save you some time and worry," I mumbled.

He casually leaned over me, tucked the blanket under my chin and smoothed out the wrinkles. "Tonight we stay here. Tomorrow we move you."

"What's this *we,* thing? And where would *we* be going?"

He ignored me. "Speaking of the thugs. I want an explanation."

"Explanation?" I gave him my best quizzical look, which was difficult, since my eye was nearly swollen shut now.

"Do not start with me. You will not win."

We'd see about that. I might be a little worse for wear, but I still loved a challenge. I gingerly crossed my arms and held them over my chest. "I'm not leaving."

"I could call the police. You were assaulted after all."

His threat trumped mine until I figured something out. "Now that's something we should discuss. Explain to me why *you* didn't call the police."

Marco shifted uncomfortably. I had him there.

"Yeah, you know that's odd. Hhmm." I studied the ceiling as if it was a word jumble, and I just had to rearrange the letters to get my answers. "You didn't call an ambulance. You didn't take me to the hospital. No, you called your ex-girlfriend, even though you weren't sure just how severe my injuries were." I was on to something. "And . . . you didn't call the police. Why is that?"

"Okay, okay." He sighed. "Gut feeling. The cops are looking at you for your husband's murder, and two goons attack you. I didn't figure you were hurt badly enough to go to the hospital." He paused.

"Go on, I'm listening."

He stood up and began pacing. "There's something strange going on here. You're not telling me everything. I know you aren't." He turned and pointed an accusing finger at me again. That might work with juries, but having been raised by Ma, I was immune to finger pointing. When I didn't fold, he gave up and his shoulders sagged. "And okay, I also believe that you didn't kill Paul."

"Hey, that's progress." I sat up, fighting the pain.

Marco walked to the sofa and adjusted my pillow a fraction of an inch, fluffed it a bit and said, "Don't move so much."

"I'm just glad you finally believe me."

He sat back down on the hassock and began to drum his fingers on the coffee table. That annoying habit again. If I'd had a ruler I'd have whacked him on the back of his hands like the nuns used to do to my friends.

"It doesn't matter what I believe. I need you to trust me. You don't and that prevents me from doing my job."

I let the silence hang. There's nothing like silence to keep people talking.

He did, almost as if I wasn't listening. Maybe he thought the concussion would make me deaf. "I made a couple of calls, followed up on some things you said at the funeral." He paused right at the interesting part.

I calmly urged him on. "Yes?"

He changed the subject. "It's time to get you into bed."

"Not yet. Finish what you started to say."

"Maybe. If you tell me what you know."

"Hey, not fair! This is a need to know basis. And I need to know."

His smile was disarming. I didn't want to move. And here I thought I was the one winning the game. A tactical error on my part. I was just too battered, not to mention tired, to play the game right now. Later. "Okay. You win."

He got up and extended his hand. "Here, I'll help you up and into your bedroom."

"I can do it myself." I slid my legs to the edge of the sofa, rolled to my side, and began to ease myself off, and groaned involuntarily.

He chuckled and said, "Let me." He leaned over, and in one fluid motion scooped me into his arms. It was delightfully humiliating. I buried my head into his shoulder, a fallen and broken soldier. At least my defeat was pleasant. He smelled faintly of a sweet aftershave I couldn't name. I breathed deep.

He carried me to my bedroom and carefully deposited me on the bed. "Where do I find your night clothes?"

I pointed to my dresser. "Bottom left-hand drawer."

He opened the drawer, peered inside, and grabbed a Minnesota Vikings' nightshirt. "Nothing sexy I see."

"Just bring it to me and keep your comments to yourself."

He grinned and tossed the nightshirt on the bed. "Need help?"

"No, I don't need help." I started to get up and my head throbbed and a spasm pulsated in my lower back. I needed help. But I'd rather crawl over broken glass than ask Marco. "I'll sleep in my clothes."

"No need for that. I'll get you started. This is no time for heroics, or false modesty." He helped me sit up. "It'll only hurt for a little while."

I turned my head away from him. "Easy for you to say."

"Hey, this isn't my fault."

He took off my shoes, and I didn't complain.

After he had tucked my socks inside my Nikes he asked, "Can you take it from here?"

"Yes," I responded weakly.

"Okay. Call me when you're done."

CHAPTER TWENTY-SIX

I tugged, twisted and pulled at my shirt, but I couldn't get my arms free, much less over my head. And I would have screamed, but my swollen jaw wouldn't cooperate. Every time I moved, another body part ached. It was like miniature spears simultaneously piercing my head, neck, lower back, and abdomen. I desperately needed help, but it was a sure bet I wasn't going to ask Marco. I would never, ever, let my lawyer see me half-dressed—especially a lawyer that looked like the cover of a romance novel.

I swiped away pity tears of frustration. My life had turned into a complete disaster. All the emotions I'd pushed aside for days roiled around in my stomach.

There was a light knock on the bedroom door. "Are you all right?"

"No, I'm not all right." I hiccupped.

Marco's muffled voice penetrated the thick, old wooden door. "What's wrong?"

I swiped at the falling tears. "Nothing."

"It must be something. You sound funny."

"I'm crying, okay? Can't a girl cry?"

"I'm coming in."

"No!"

Several seconds of silence seemed oh, so long. "You're having trouble getting undressed?"

I swallowed my sobs. "Yes, but I don't want your help."

The door opened a crack. "I'm coming in. *Someone* has to help you."

He was right. "Okay, but you have to close your eyes."

The door opened wider, and Marco ambled in, hands covering his face.

"Don't look."

He shuffled toward the bed. "I have to see where I'm going. I'm looking at the floor, not at you."

Head lowered to his chest, he walked into the bed frame and stopped abruptly. "I won't look any more than I have to."

My pride took a sudden nose dive straight into a place called humiliation. "I can't get my shirt off."

Marco chuckled, felt for my shirt, carefully avoiding my chest. His fingers located, then traveled the length of my arm to the bottom of the fabric. He grasped it firmly and carefully inched it over my head, tossing it on the bed. "Now, hand me your nightshirt."

I thrust it into his outstretched hands, and he placed it over my head and drew it down over my shoulders. I inched up the nightshirt and pulled each arm out of my bra straps, turned it around, unhooked it, and casually tossed in on the floor beside the bed.

Marco opened his eyes. "Now let me help you get your arms in."

He pulled the sleeves down low so I could get my arms inside without straining too much. "That wasn't so bad, was it?"

I sniffed.

"It's going to be all right." He carefully slid the nightshirt into place, made sure it covered me completely before he pulled me to a standing position. "Stay." He drew back the comforter, blanket, and top sheet before he gingerly lowered me back onto the bed. Then he reached under my nightshirt.

I would have slapped his hands if I could have moved them. "Hey!"

"I'm not touching, I'm just unfastening your jeans. There. Now I'm going to pull them down. Don't worry, I'm not going to peek."

Embarrassed beyond words, I turned my head into the pillow. True to his word he gently removed my jeans, lowered my nightshirt so it covered me and drew the bedding up over me.

"There." He beamed a satisfied smile. "I can't figure out if you're terribly modest or you just don't want help."

"Both."

He sat down on the edge of the bed and lightly stroked my hair. "You're a funny one."

I couldn't deal with him being nice, not when I'd gotten him into this mess. He'd be better off if he stayed annoyed with me. So would I. I'd feel less guilty. I shut my eyes. He apparently got the message because he stood and brushed his hand against his pant leg. "I'll be on the sofa."

"You don't have to stay here, really. You're my lawyer, not my friend."

He shot back, "I don't think they're mutually exclusive."

Shame rattled around inside me. "I'm sorry. You're trying to be helpful, and I'm not cooperating."

He leaned over, and said, "You are a handful."

I fought to keep my heavy eyelids from closing and mumbled, "And you owe Father Daniel."

As I nodded off, I thought I heard him reply, "I'd do it even if I didn't owe the good Father." But I might have been mistaken.

That night, I dreamed of men in wild, Halloween masks chasing me down the street, brandishing machetes and yelling, "Give us our money."

The aroma of coffee woke me. *Coffee! Give me coffee!* My body ached, and I didn't want to get up, but the smell of fresh-brewed coffee was like a lover beckoning.

I discovered I could actually stand, as long as I didn't mind the room spinning. The dizziness soon passed, and I tested my balance by taking some tiny steps. Satisfied that I wasn't going to dive headlong into a wall or stray piece of furniture, I hobbled to the door where I could hear Marco down the hall, singing in Spanish.

Using the wall for support, I slowly inched toward the kitchen where Marco continued to sing in a rich, deep baritone. When he saw me, he called out, "You're up and moving."

"I heal fast."

I caught my reflection in the hall mirror. Wow! The way I looked I should be dead. Maybe I was. Mirrors do not lie.

I wouldn't be able to quip, "You should see the other guy." Hair askew, jaw swollen, a large ugly scrape across my forehead, and my eye twice as large as normal, obvious proof that I hadn't won last night's brawl. Not even close. Generally, I was black and blue, accessorized with more black and blue. "My God!"

Marco stopped his domestic activities. "Feel as bad as you look?"

I gave him the dirtiest look I could muster. "If I did, I'd be dead."

"Come on, sit down and eat." He pointed a spatula at the table.

"Not sure I can." I tenderly stroked my battered jaw.

He laughed. "Try."

"Okay, but first the bathroom."

A quick wash-up and clean teeth made me feel immensely better. But since I felt dead, that wasn't saying much.

One look at the breakfast he'd prepared and I realized Marco must have gone shopping, because my kitchen had never, ever had this much real food in it. He placed a plate of crisp bacon and two eggs, fried to perfection, in front of me, then offered a glass of grapefruit juice just as the toaster popped out two perfectly toasted English Muffins. Pretty impressive. He'd make someone a good wife.

I still felt queasy, but Marco had gone to so much trouble, the least I could do was try to eat. After all, eating is one of my particular talents. Hey! I'm Italian, eating is like a religion to us.

Gingerly I took a bite of the bacon and tried to chew. "Oh, that hurts."

He sat down across from me and reached for the butter. "Take it slow. Break everything up into small pieces."

I held my jaw. "It's not the size of the food, it's pressing my teeth together that's making me seriously consider dieting."

He dug into his eggs and laughed heartily. "Do the best you can."

It was going to take me an hour to finish at the rate I was going. Unfortunately that gave Marco time to grill me. "Okay, Pen. Tell me what's going on."

I gave my full attention to my food, chewing as carefully as I could.

"No more stalling." Marco wasn't deterred. He was like a bulldog in that respect. "If you don't tell me what's going on, and I mean everything, I'm going to withdraw from your case. I told you that before."

My head snapped upward and a sharp pain shot down my neck like a bolt of lightning. I stared at him as if he had grown two heads.

He stared back. "You've got one minute to decide. Then I'm out of here and you take your chances with those leg breakers and the police. I'm not a betting man, but I'd lay odds you won't win."

If I didn't tell him, Germaine would. Either way it was a lose-lose proposition. The best I could hope for was amnesty if I handed him the story with the right spin. I sighed deeply. "It's going to take time."

He leaned back in his chair, crossed his arms over his chest, and said, "I've got all day."

"Yeah, I was afraid of that. Okay, but I need you to promise me something."

"Tell me what you want, and I'll consider it."

I took a deep breath and forged on. "I want you to promise that no matter what I say, you won't interrupt me until I'm done."

"Easy enough."

I swallowed some egg and wiped my mouth with a paper napkin. "You can say that because you haven't heard the story."

Marco shifted in his chair and ran his fingers through coal-black hair. "That bad?"

I put my fork on the plate. "And then some."

"Shoot."

I winced. "I wish you wouldn't use that particular word."

"Get on with the story."

I learned, at my mother's knee, the irrefutable lesson that if you're flat out caught doing something you're not supposed to do, you'd better spill your guts and plead for forgiveness.

It took over an hour to tell Marco about my recent escapades. He tried not to interrupt, I'll give him that. But ultimately he broke down several times. The first was when I told him about finding all the money. I didn't tell him just how much and didn't plan on doing so unless there was absolutely no way out of it. Always hold something back is my motto. It might become a bargaining chip later on.

His second interruption came when I told him about burglarizing Judge Kassner's house. He yelped and jumped to his feet, flinging his hands around like he'd suddenly become Italian. During his third interruption I was afraid that vein in his forehead might burst. His face turned a bright apple red, and he yelled, "Are you absolutely crazy?!" That's because I'd mentioned, quite casually, about breaking into Judge Kassner's office, reluctantly adding that Judge Hunter caught Germaine and me in the "felonious act."

I didn't bother answering his question about my sanity. Obviously, it was another of Marco's rhetorical questions. Actually *I* wasn't so sure about my sanity anymore.

Alas, I had saved the worst for last.

By now he was so upset, I figured if I held anything back, he'd bolt permanently. Heck, he might bolt anyway. I decided to cleanse my soul completely, confess everything. So, I threw away my bargaining chip and told him exactly how much money was involved and who I had stashed it with.

He couldn't even speak, just huffed and sputtered. I guess that's what it means to be spitting mad. "You did what?" he screamed and jumped up again. As I tried to explain he rocked back and forth on his heels. Finally he took a step toward me, leaned down inches from my face and said more calmly than I thought possible under the circumstances, "You gave possible mob money to Father Daniel for safekeeping? You really are nuts. I ought to wring your scrawny neck."

"You might have to stand in line for that opportunity," I mumbled.

He ignored me and paced the kitchen floor shaking his head and smacking his palm with his fist. "I should walk out of here, right now!"

That's when I got "religion." Marco meant business. He was fed up. I could almost hear him thinking, "I've got to lose this crazy broad as fast as I can." It was time to plead for mercy. Not a very attractive thought because humiliation doesn't look good on me.

Marco leaned in again. "You could be in the slammer right

now. You could be dead. Or worse, Father Daniel could be dead."

Now that smarted. My stock with Marco had fallen considerably. Apparently, my death would be nothing more than a mere blip on his radar screen.

"What is it with you?" He raised his hands to heaven like he yanked down some celestial assistance. "You look so . . . I don't know, so benign. But you're not! You're the most brazen, wacky . . ." He paused, groping for more adjectives. "The scariest woman I've ever met." He stepped back, took a big breath and just when I thought his tirade was over, started in again. "And what scares me the most is that you believe your behavior is *normal*. Justified!" There was another dramatic pause, lawyers are almost as good at this stuff as Ma. "Your mother really did drop you on your head when you were a baby, right?"

I figured *this* rant was rhetorical, too. But he waited expectantly, like it deserved an answer or something. I threw my hands up and cringed with the pain. "So crucify me."

"Oh, wouldn't I just like to."

Enough! I covered my eyes. "Marco, stop. I needed proof. Don't you understand how desperate I was? Am?"

"No, you're just plain crazy. It's odd. Your sister seems perfectly normal. Is it your mother or your father that you take after?"

I peeked at him through my fingers. How dare he bring up Ma. "That's a little harsh."

He jabbed the air in front of my face with his finger. "You haven't seen harsh. I'm gone."

I couldn't let him leave. I'd have to grovel. And I do loathe groveling although I do it well, on occasion. But I'm not fond of prison either. "Marco, please. I came clean. There's been no permanent damage done."

"No permanent damage?" His left eyebrow arched. "Not

216

because you haven't worked damn hard at it." He continued pacing, his steps thumping hard against the tile. He turned, his eyes burning. "You made two innocent people—people of faith, for God's sake, into criminals." A frown creased his forehead, and the veins popped out again, pulsing dangerously. *Ohhh, scary!* If he kept this up he'd have a stroke. And I'd still be minus one lawyer. I sighed, such a young man, too.

Tired, in pain and running out of plans, I whispered, "So leave. I don't blame you. I'm a horror story. It's not the first time someone dumped me, and it probably won't be the last." I waited for him to deny my statements. He didn't. The room became very quiet. Too quiet.

I started to fidget. He still didn't say anything, so I did. "Marco. Bottom line, what's it going to be? Are you going to bail on me, throw me to the wolves all because I tried to keep my sorry butt out of jail?"

Hands on his hips, he glared. "If you were in jail, at least you wouldn't be committing felonies."

I waved my hands in the air, like a white flag of surrender. "I'm sorry. I really am. I don't know what else to do or say. I ache all over and I'm tired." I spat out, "It's not like I really need your help." *Yeah, right, not much.* The jail cell door clanged shut, locked, and Big Bertha, my new cell mate, waved hello.

I started to get up, tripped on the chair leg, and fell flat on my behind.

Marco rushed to me and dropped to his knees. "Are you all right?"

I clenched my teeth. "Oh yeah, I'm fine. Just take a look, Marco. Don't I *look* fine?"

Marco helped me up. "All right. I'm not withdrawing."

I looked at him expectantly. All I had to do was a prat-fall? This was easier than I had anticipated.

His stare penetrated my soul. Or would have if I actually had a soul. The jury was still out.

"I won't withdraw—as long as you behave and do things my way."

My silence must have spoken volumes.

"Pen."

"I heard you," I grumbled.

He led me to my bedroom door and ordered, "Go lie down and rest for an hour while I do the dishes. When you get up, I'll help you pack a bag. You're coming to my house while we figure out what to do about the money and the bad guys."

"First, we probably need to figure out who the bad guys are."

"Get." He pointed to my bed.

I didn't argue.

CHAPTER TWENTY-SEVEN

I was sprawled out on Marco's sofa, aimlessly clicking the remote control, when the doorbell rang. Father Daniel stood behind the screen, clutching a brown paper sack. It was a safe bet that he wasn't delivering groceries.

My imagination zipped through several scenarios that might play out in the next few minutes, and I didn't like any of them. I turned off the television and called out, "Come on in."

Marco rushed into the room. "Thanks for coming."

Father Daniel thrust his sack at Marco and mumbled, "Glad to be rid of it."

Marco nodded, eyed me with disdain, and left the room without saying another word.

Father Daniel hurried to me, his large body heaving with the effort. "How are you feeling?" He stared down at me. "You look like a piece of pulverized meat."

I winced at the mental picture. "Thanks a lot, Father. You really know how to sweet talk a girl. If the church ever changes the rule and lets priests marry, you're going to have to take lessons on smooth talking."

He dropped into a chair shaking his head. "It just took me by surprise. Marco told me about the mugging, but I had no idea—"

"How bad it really was?" I interjected.

He nodded. "Shouldn't you be in the hospital?"

I wrinkled my nose. "No, Marco hooked me up with a leggy

219

Viking who volunteered to nurse me back to health. Personally, I think it's Marco she's interested in."

Marco loomed in the doorway. "Jennifer went out of her way to help you; why would you talk about her like that?"

When had my mother arrived? "Sorry, I'm cranky. Being mugged does that to me." The subject needed changing. "So, Marco, what's with the sack of money?"

He leaned against the doorframe. "I called Father Daniel while you were sleeping and asked him to come over."

"Ordered is more like it."

Marco's brows furrowed. "I'll stash the money until I figure out what to do with it."

"Why not turn it over to the police?" Sarcasm oozed out. "You're always spouting off about playing by the book."

He glared at me. "We'll discuss it later. I've talked to Father Daniel about the felonies you all committed, and he assures me that it won't happen again." He nodded at the priest. "Will it, Father?"

Father Daniel quickly looked away as he shook his head from side to side.

"Good." Marco's frown softened. "Pen, I looked over the rest of the brokerage reports while you nearly put my television into clicking overload." I put my hand over my mouth and stuck my tongue out at him. The childish act exhilarated me. He continued, "I found nothing wrong with them."

I cocked my head. "Nothing?"

He snapped his fingers. "Nothing."

I thought about that a moment. "Then it must be money from fixing trials."

"I'm not convinced of that. It's just too difficult to do."

I sighed. "Marco, you know as well as I do that an awful lot of lawyers judge-shop."

Father Daniel interrupted, "Judge-shopping?"

Marco said, "Lawyers sometimes try to avoid judges that they don't think will be sympathetic to their client's case. They concoct delays that will, hopefully, bring them in front of a more sympathetic judge."

Father Daniel shook his head. "Doesn't sound fair."

"It's not about fair, Father. It's about doing the best job that you can for your client," Marco explained.

"I've been thinking," I said.

Marco cringed. "That could be a problem."

I rolled my eyes. "I won't officially return to work for awhile, but I can make some calls, you know, check on judges who are finding for the defense in cases they shouldn't win."

Marco nodded. "Focus on Paul's cases since he's the one we're looking at. It'll be less time consuming."

"Good idea, but I ought to include Paul's law partner, Ben, in the equation. I want to see if he's involved somehow. I'm still uncomfortable about what he said at the police station."

Marco chuckled. "Widening the loop?"

"What do you mean?"

"From what you told me, you've decided Judge Kassner is the murderer."

"Yeah, but it doesn't hurt to look at other people. I've learned that a lot of people didn't like Paul. No one except his mistress—and she's totally off her noodle. Even Judge Hunter made disparaging remarks about him. So did Jack." I paused, "There's something I just remembered. I'd like to check it out."

Father Daniel asked, "What's that?"

"Paul was adopted. Well, why didn't he tell me? It's nothing to be ashamed of or keep from your wife."

Marco shrugged. "No, the place to start is the Hennepin County criminal cases."

If I'd learned nothing else since Paul's murder, it was to appear to acquiesce to demands and then do what I want. And unless I got caught, technically I wouldn't be breaking any of Marco's rules. "Okay."

Marco seemed pleased I'd agreed so easily. "While you're checking out the criminal cases, I'll ask around about Ben, Jack, and Judge Kassner."

Father Daniel jumped in, eyes flashing with excitement. "And what do I do?"

My eyes met Marco's, and we both smiled. Father Daniel was really getting into this detective thing.

Marco edged into the room and patted him on the back. "Nothing for now, Father. If something comes up, I'll let you know."

Father Daniel didn't look happy.

I moved to get up from the sofa, "Well, let's get going."

Marco's hand waved like a flag. "Whoa. You sit back and rest. You're not going anywhere."

I sank back into the sofa. "But there's so much to do."

"Forget it."

Father Daniel clucked, "Marco is right. You have to take it easy."

"But . . ."

Marco looked thoughtful. "There are two burly mobsters after you, remember?"

"They don't know where I am. Besides my house, the only place they'd look is at work, and I'm not there."

"No."

Drat! I'd laid here like an invalid as long as I could stand. As soon as Father Daniel kissed me on the cheek and left with Marco, I snuck into the kitchen, found some paper and pen, and scrawled out my rudimentary plan—all the things I needed to do to keep my bruised butt out of jail. Right there, at number one was convince Marco to postpone my interview with Detective Booger and his sourpuss partner.

My to-do list grew long quickly. I sighed, I'd be one busy invalid.

CHAPTER TWENTY-EIGHT

Sunday dawned, warm and sunny, or so I learned later. I didn't actually see it happen since I was catching some much needed zzzzs.

Around ten o'clock, several explosions recoiled through the house. My heart thumped like a snare drum as I did a swan dive from the bed, hit the floor, and rolled. Splayed out like I'd been tied to a stake, face smashed into the carpet, terror engulfed me. I sucked in my breath and waited.

"Oh, my god!" They'd found us! Ma was right, my involvement with criminals would be the death of me. I hate it when Ma is right.

I crawled crab-like toward the bed, hoping I could get under it in time. A sharp, jagged pain shot up my leg like a bolt of electricity, scissored through my lower back, and rattled around like a pinball marble. I gasped.

The mob's bullets would be a waste of good ammunition since that dive off the bed was gonna kill me. I clenched my teeth against the pain pulsating in my lower back.

I cautiously glanced at the door. It was far too quiet out there which meant Marco was probably a goner. If he was alive, he'd be fighting back. I scooted under the bed and peeked into the room just as another explosion erupted. It took a few moments to realize the blast came from the television, an early morning shoot 'em up, no doubt.

My head cleared, and I heard cupboard doors opening and

closing. I also realized the first explosion, the one that jolted me awake, was probably pots and pans bouncing off the kitchen floor.

Relief and humiliation played tag in my head. I'd thought it was all over but the funeral dirge. I didn't know much, but I could predict with certainty that this story would never be told, to anyone. It was enough that I knew.

It was time to solve Paul's murder because my nerves were deteriorating at warp speed. I was neither Thelma *nor* Louise.

I slithered out from under the bed and staggered to the dresser. My muscles screamed for a time-out.

I got cleaned up, then happened to glance in the mirror and gasped at the stranger's reflection. My jaw was the size of a lemon, scraped and bloodred. However, it was the shiny, translucent purple and black eye that made me nauseous. I touched the colorful, spongy mess and jumped. Not even a giant pair of sunglasses would cover this damage. But I'd have to do something. Reality is not my strong suit, and delusion is the name of *my* game. Make-up would have to work its magic on my face.

I prepared myself for another of Marco's tirades while I got dressed. I'd set up a meeting with Carl Preston, and he hadn't liked it. His concern was understandable. I wouldn't want any stray muggers following me home either.

I tapped a broken fingernail against the wooden dresser, mulling over a minor little snag—transportation. I didn't have a car. It was a sure bet Marco wouldn't offer to lend me his. Maybe if I told him about my exemplary driving record, but that probably wouldn't impress him much after my recent escapades. I'd ask anyway. What could he do, say no?

I leaned out the bedroom door. "Marco," I shouted. "I have to meet Carl Preston. I need my car, or I can't go."

He yelled back, "We're not going to your place. It's too

dangerous."

"What do you suggest?"

"This meeting is about Paul's adoption?"

"Yes."

He sauntered into the bedroom. "There's enough to do without investigating the adoption."

I shrugged my shoulders. "What else can I do on a Sunday? The Government Center is closed."

He ran his fingers through his hair. "You could rest, which would guarantee a trouble-free day for everyone."

I gave him my best hard-ass stare. "I'm on borrowed time. I need to wrap things up before the cell door locks. It's pretty hard to find a killer when you're busy digging out of Sing-Sing."

He shrugged. "Okay, okay."

Ah, he was compliant today. Why not go for broke. "Could I use your car? I won't be gone more than an hour or two."

Horror covered his face. He didn't even answer at first, just sputtered, until finally it burst out, "No!"

"Hey, it's not like I'll hurt it."

He rippled air through his lips. "With you, there are no guarantees."

"Well, what am I supposed to do? I can't fly."

"How about the bus?"

I rolled my eyes. "Yeah, I've got a picture of that. If I caught a bus now, and made the transfers, I might catch up to him sometime tonight."

A wicked grin spread from ear to ear. "Well, you're not taking my car."

"Get real. Might I remind you that the doctor *you* consulted demanded that I take things easy. *You* demanded I take things easy. A bus is not easy, Marco."

He pursed his lips. "Wait here." He left the room and

returned a minute or so later with a set of keys. Could this be the sweet smell of success? "Here, it's not fancy, but it runs." He tossed me the keys and said, "Come on."

I grabbed my purse, followed him to the garage, skidding to a stop when I saw *it*. I clapped my hand over my mouth hoping Marco hadn't heard my gasp. He wasn't kidding. It wasn't fancy. What it was was an old jalopy, a pick-up truck painted a garish ruby red. Huge rust spots dotted the driver's side door. The rust was accompanied by deep, ragged scratches that criss-crossed the rear panel. Cautiously, I circled around what could only loosely be referred to as a vehicle. The passenger side was worse. Craters disguised as dents ran horizontally from the front to the back. The hood had been primed but sat unpainted, naked, like a forgotten lover. I inched to the back end of the monster. The tailgate was wired shut and several gashes cut a swath across the manufacturer's name. The forlorn relic rested sadly in the stall, as if waiting for its marching orders to the scrap heap.

I grimaced. "Wow!"

Marco gave the driver's door a sharp rap. "She's not much to look at, but she's dependable."

My eyes darted from the hood to the tail lights. "She?"

He leaned against the door, arms crossed. "A figure of speech."

I shook my head. "Where did you get this heap and why on earth have you kept it?"

He turned and looked longingly at the piece of junk. "It was my first set of wheels. We were poor. It took me two summers to earn enough to buy her."

"But why keep it, her?"

"To remind me of where I came from and how fortunate I've been."

This was a new, improved, sensitive, man. I preferred my

lawyer to be a little edgy and all business. My good eye twitched.

I patted the fender sharply. "Aren't you afraid I'll crack her up?"

He laughed. "Look at her."

At least he was realistic. I opened the door and climbed into the cab. The interior was immaculate, unlike the rest of the vehicle. But after seeing Marco's office and home, it didn't surprise me.

He hit the garage door button, and the door groaned upward. I put on my sunglasses, turned the key, shifted in reverse and backed out of the garage.

"Be careful."

"Don't worry; I'll get her back in one piece." I heard his deep laugh as I backed down the drive.

The drive to the coffee shop near Carl Preston's Edina home took a mere twenty minutes. Edina is one of the more affluent suburbs of Minneapolis, and I could feel the residents' stares as I chugged by in Marco's eyesore.

Carl was already there when I pulled up next to his shiny black Lexus.

I stepped out of the truck too fast and winced as pain shot through my lower back. I shuffled around the truck. "Nice car. New isn't it?"

He hit the remote and replied, "Yeah. It's a comfortable ride. Can't say the same about that." He pointed at Marco's rattletrap. "Where did it come from?"

I slapped the truck door and said, "It's Marco's, you know, my lawyer. It's a sentimental thing with him. But she got me here. Now all she has to do is get me back."

"Where's the Ghia?"

I pushed my sunglasses farther up my nose. "Long story."

He nodded his understanding.

As I approached, his eyes widened. The sun glasses only hid so much. "What happened to you?"

"Another long story."

"Care to tell me about it?"

"No, not right now."

He said, "Okay, but I hope you've seen a doctor."

"I have. The diagnosis is that I'll live."

We entered the coffee shop, and Carl pointed to an empty booth by the window. We ordered coffee, his plain black and mine a double skim vanilla latte. After our waitress left, Carl asked, "Now, what's so important that I had to miss my regular Sunday golf game?"

I leaned back in the booth. "Sorry. I didn't know about the golf."

"It's okay."

"I'm sure, under the circumstances, Astrid wouldn't be happy if she knew you were meeting me."

He shrugged. "She thinks I'm on the course."

"Here I drag you out on a Sunday morning and make you miss your golf game and mislead your wife too." I hesitated. "And I'm not sure how you're going to feel about this conversation."

Carl sat up straighter, his neck muscles tightened. "Depends on the subject."

The waitress approached the table and plopped our orders in front of us. I took a big gulp of coffee. "When I was at our house, I mean Paul's house, I found some papers."

He nodded.

"I broke . . . I opened the office safe. There was the usual stuff there, but one thing, in particular, surprised me."

He cocked his head. "What was that?"

I took a deep breath. "I found Paul's adoption papers."

Carl drummed his fingers on the tabletop. "I see."

A long and uncomfortable silence followed. I gave in first. "Carl, I didn't know Paul was adopted."

He put his cup down and sighed. "We didn't talk about it."

I cupped my mug in both hands. "Why?"

He leaned back in his chair, his mouth in a grimace. "Astrid didn't want anyone to know we weren't able to have children. And she was afraid people wouldn't accept Paul if they knew he was adopted."

I nodded, pretending to understand, but I really didn't.

"Back then, things were different." Carl shook his head and fiddled with the napkin under his coffee mug. "People were less accepting. Astrid demanded it be kept secret. When our lawyer located a woman who wanted to place her child up for adoption, Astrid went out east to stay with relatives until the baby was born. She returned with Paul, and no one ever knew that he'd been adopted."

I wiped some stray latte foam from my lip. "That's some secret to keep all these years."

Carl took a swig of coffee and placed his mug on the table. "A burden, actually. Paul didn't know until recently. Maybe a couple of years ago."

"What!"

He shook his head. "I thought we should tell him, but I didn't fight Astrid. It was easier. You know her." As Carl's story unfolded, his sadness grew.

I nodded my understanding.

"Some years ago Paul helped Astrid sort through some old boxes, and he found his original birth certificate. Who knows why Astrid kept it all these years. I suppose she thought nobody would ever find it."

I leaned across the table. "What happened?"

He pinched the bridge of his nose, his eyes glistened with tears. "Paul confronted Astrid. When I got home Paul was yelling and she was crying uncontrollably."

I cringed. "Not a pretty sight."

"No. It fractured their relationship. Now, Paul's dead, and Astrid is overwhelmed with guilt. She lives with the fact that she lied to her son and he died without forgiving her. That's why she's striking out at you so hard."

"I wonder why Paul never told me."

"You knew him. He was always pretty private."

"But I was his wife."

"Doesn't matter. If he didn't want to talk about something, he didn't." Carl looked over my shoulder, staring aimlessly out the window. "Paul changed after he found out about his adoption."

This news peaked my interest. "How so?"

Carl slumped over the table. "It's not something you could really put your finger on. He seemed angry and impatient." He looked at me. "I don't quite know how to describe it. He asked a lot of questions. He wanted to know about his biological mother. Astrid wouldn't tell him anything, and that made him angrier, almost obsessed."

I leaned my elbows on the table and said, "I'll bet he went ballistic."

"Yeah, he did. He couldn't accept that we didn't know who his biological parents were. Our lawyer took care of that. Their names were redacted from the birth certificate." He stared thoughtfully into his mug. "We didn't *want* to know who they were. Astrid thought it would somehow make him less hers. And of course we didn't want his birth mother showing up on our doorstep either."

The waitress returned, topped off Carl's cup and asked if I wanted another latte. "Yes, please."

She hesitated, staring at me, "Aren't you—" Abruptly she scrubbed at an imaginary spot on the table and said, "There.

I'll get that coffee for you." She beat a path to the kitchen.

I could feel the heat burn in my cheeks. I slurped the tepid dregs left in my mug. "She recognized me."

Carl finally spoke, "Don't mind her."

"Wanna bet the help starts making unnecessary trips from the kitchen to see the local Lizzie Borden?"

"Don't pay any attention to them."

I slumped over the table. "I can't help it. It hurts." I watched as the cook sauntered out of the kitchen and made a show of looking for something behind the counter, his eyes darting from me to a shelf. "See."

He reached for my hand. "Stop. You can't control what other people think. I know you didn't kill Paul and so does Astrid. She's just so angry right now she has to blame someone."

"And I'm handy."

He nodded. "Paul changed. It's too bad you didn't know why; maybe you wouldn't have left him." He lifted his cup with both hands and took a long draw. "It was almost as if he tried to hurt people. You, his mother, me and then Stephanie."

So it wasn't a rumor. "They had problems?"

"I shouldn't say anything."

"No, you should. It's important. Any clue that might help me avoid prison would make me happy."

His mouth curled upward into a hint of a smile. "And we want you to avoid prison."

I squeezed his hand. "You're one of the few people who is on my side."

"I don't know much, but before he died he told me he was breaking up with Stephanie."

I sat up. "Why?"

He shrugged his shoulders. "That's all he said."

"Did Stephanie know?"

"Yeah. Paul said she wasn't taking it well."

My brain began to spin with possibilities. "But she was playing the grieving girlfriend."

"Appearances are everything to her. Maybe she didn't know we knew."

I leaned forward. "Do you have any idea why he dumped her?"

"Jack told me he had seen Paul around town with another woman. But then, you can't always tell about Jack. He's been known to stretch the truth."

"Just for the fun of it."

"He and Paul didn't get along. They've always been pretty competitive, even as children."

I chewed on my lower lip. "Carl, Stephanie seems to be, ah, difficult."

"She is."

"Could she have gotten angry enough to kill Paul? Especially, if she knew he was cheating on her?"

Carl shook his head. "You can't think Stephanie would kill Paul."

"All I know is the field of suspects is growing."

"Pen, you don't murder someone just because they break up with you."

"No, sane people don't. But this girl is queen of the fruit loops."

He studied his hands. "But murder?"

"Carl, think about it. Maybe she caught him with someone. Or, maybe she learned about the other woman, went to the house, confronted him, and they had a fight. Things got out of hand and, in a fit of anger, she hit him."

He shook his head. "I suppose it's possible. She has a temper."

"Hey, I work with people who kill because their toast was burned or the boss fired them."

He shook his head in disbelief.

I watched as another employee stood at the kitchen door, staring at me. I turned away. "Carl, what's Stephanie's last name?"

"It's Collins, and she lives in Edina. She owns the day spa. I can't think of the name. It's on the main drag."

"The Place."

"Yeah, but I can't remember the place's name."

"The Place," I said.

"Yeah, I know but I can't . . ."

I snapped my fingers twice. "Carl, the spa's name is The Place."

He laughed weakly. "Oh, I get it."

I patted his hand. "Don't worry about it." I put some money on the table and stood up. "I have to go. Thanks, I appreciate the help."

He wanted to pay, but I told him that it was the least I could do since I'd made him miss church—the church of golf.

We walked to the door, and he hugged me. I moaned silently. "Don't be a stranger."

I raised my eyebrows. "It's probably not . . ."

"Astrid will come around."

"We'll give it some time."

"Be careful. Don't forget there's a murderer out there. If that person thinks you're getting too close, well, you watch your backside."

I smiled. "Don't worry, I can take care of myself."

His eyebrows furrowed deeply. "From what I can see," he pointed at my battered face, "you haven't been doing too well at it, lately."

"I'll have to work on that." I turned to leave then thought of something. "Carl, did you know anything about Paul's finances? I mean, was he having money problems? Or had he come into any large amounts of money that you were aware of?"

"No. But he wouldn't have talked to me about that."

"Well, thanks anyway. I was just curious."

We pushed open the glass doors when someone rushed up behind us. "You. Penelope Santucci?" I turned to face the mop-haired busboy. He glanced furtively around the coffee shop, before shoving a newspaper and pencil at me, eyes darting around the coffee shop, then at me. "Could, could I have your autograph?"

I glanced at the paper where my likeness, sans the black eye and bruises smiled back at me. The media had gotten hold of a better photo of me. I wondered if Ma was acting as my representative without my permission. We'd have to talk.

I didn't bother to read the caption. I could guess what it said.

The tall, lanky teenager said, "So, you gonna give it to me?"

My cranky meter burst through the roof. I clenched my fists and stepped menacingly towards him growling, "You bet I'll give it you!"

Carl quickly stepped between us, lightly restraining me, while glaring at the busboy. "Leave her alone."

"But, I . . ."

"Now!"

The kid took several tentative steps backward. "I just . . ."

I gave the kid my best "make my day, punk" squint.

Carl tightened his grip on my arms and ordered, "Leave now!"

The kid jumped and turned on his heel and scrambled back into the shop. I screeched, "Be careful, you just might be my next victim!"

CHAPTER TWENTY-NINE

Carl calmed me down which was no easy task. I wasn't a murderer, but after that kid's stunt, I was seriously considering a job change.

After I stopped shaking, I waved good-bye to Carl and climbed into the battered old truck, pulled out of the parking lot and headed east. Traffic was light, so I revved the engine, shifted, and stomped on the gas pedal. Marco's jalopy lurched forward, gathered speed, and held steady. The old relic didn't race like the wind, but she still had some oomph.

I rolled down the windows so I could feel the wind on my face and drove without a destination, headed nowhere, anywhere. Hunting freedom. Avoiding humanity. Life was taking a detour to a small prison cell faster than I cared to think about.

In a wild fit of desperation I decided Jack would be a good person to hunt. My gut told me he had a few secrets tucked under that sleazy expression and greasy hair.

I exited the freeway near Jack's, hung a right on Lyndale Avenue until I got to twenty fifth. His apartment building loomed on twenty-sixth like a fat French chef foisting his fare on all. "Open up and say ah, baby."

Jack didn't answer his buzzer, so I rang every unit until somebody let me in. People are victims waiting to happen. Don't open your door to strangers—it's the first commandment of urban survival, and most obey it—except they'll open their *building* to a stranger without a second thought.

I checked out the nondescript lobby, located the resident directory, and zeroed in on Jack's number. It had been a long time since I'd been at his place. Since he didn't answer the buzzer, I didn't expect he'd be home. But it didn't cost anything to check, so I called for the elevator and exited at his floor. I knocked several times, but there was no answer.

As I turned to leave, Jack, laundry piled high in a pink plastic clothesbasket, got off the elevator.

Yes!

He didn't look pleased to see me and walked by without a word. Apparently, I'd become persona non grata. Not a good sign. He opened the door and walked inside.

I hesitated, gathering courage. "C'mon, Jack, I need to talk to you. Can I come in?"

He dropped the laundry basket on the dining room table and asked, "Slumming, Pen?"

I tentatively tiptoed through the door. "Cranky, Jack? Or just the usual poor pitiful whine?"

He grabbed a towel from the basket, shook it out with a loud snap, and began folding it. "I don't want to talk to you. Don't want to see you. Don't want to think about you. Just go."

I sidled into his lair. "A really bad day, I guess. No playmates?"

He smoothed the folded towel and placed it on the table beside the basket. "It's always a bad day when you're around."

The grouch hadn't exactly kicked me out. A little sucking up might make the medicine sweeter. He wouldn't talk if I continued to spar. "I know we haven't always gotten along, but I really need your help."

He sneered. "Give me one good reason why I should help you keep your sorry ass out of prison?"

"Because it's the right thing to do."

He shrugged, a cloud of malice and indifference hovering over him.

Time to appeal to his baser need of self-preservation. "Jack, I'm here to help both of us."

He brushed a clump of dirty blonde hair from his face. "Why would I need help? You're the one about to get twenty to life."

I crossed my fingers behind my back. "Well, my lawyer thought the statements you made at Paul's funeral were interesting." Not a whopper exactly, just a tiny bit of truth stretching.

His interest piqued, he asked, "How so?"

I marched to the center of the room. "You seemed so angry with Paul, said he deserved to die. People might think you had a reason to want Paul dead." It was my turn to feign indifference. I shrugged the same way he had. "They might even think that *you* killed him."

He snorted his disgust. "And what makes you think that anyone will pay any attention to what I said? Everyone in this city, including the cops, thinks you murdered him."

"Well, there's my lawyer for one. It's his job to keep me out of jail. And he's really very good at his job." I sucked in my breath. "Part of his job is to give any leads he has to the police. Put the right spin on it and, well, at the very least, it could cost you a great deal of money."

"Money?" Oh, I had his attention now, even if he did try to sound skeptical.

"Sure. To prove him wrong. Oh, and then there's your reputation to consider." I almost choked on the reputation part. Jack's reputation was mediocre at best. "Now, I personally don't think you had anything to do with Paul's death." I hoped I wasn't laying it on too thick. "Even so, it would be the police's job to examine all leads. And who knows how it might affect your job. Even if you're innocent, the suspicion could taint you for life. Ever think about that, Jack?"

He shifted his weight and looked down at the carpet.

Gotcha.

It was his body language. I may be dense in some areas, but reading people's body language is not one of them. In my line of work it was a skill that kept me on top of my game.

"Well? Do you want to talk with me? Or would you prefer the police? No skin off my nose, either way." I shrugged again, just for the effect.

He hesitated, looked at me, eyes weary. "You are a piece of work."

"What do you expect me to do? I don't want to go to jail. If that means I have to give the police a reasonable alternative, I will." My eyes hardened. "I want information. The more I know the better. I don't like the prison wardrobe, Jack. Orange jumpsuits are not flattering to a woman of my skin tone and stature. Not to mention the food or accommodations. So talk or I'll go to the police."

Jack's face reddened. He dropped into a chair and held his face in his hands. "I hate talking to you. The police are almost better."

"Your decision, Jack." I turned to leave, praying he'd back down. Otherwise, I didn't know what I'd do. I reached the door and had grasped the handle before I heard, "Wait!" *Yes! She scores!*

I looked heavenward. "Thank you Lord," I whispered, my smile growing wide. I made my face a blank canvas and slowly turned. "Well?"

"I didn't kill, Paul." I nodded, in what I thought was the proper amount of encouragement. "Not that I didn't want to. He was a royal pain in the ass. He'd changed this last year. Sure, he'd been a jerk before, but it was different. He got even more short-tempered and mean-spirited. He ran over anyone and everyone to get what he wanted. Leaned on people, hard, to bring cases before the judges that he thought would be more sympathetic. And that's not easy."

I didn't wait for an invitation; I just sank into the nearest chair. "So, how'd he do it?"

"Most of what I know is pretty sketchy. But he had someone in court scheduling, I'm not saying who, in his pocket. And he didn't get her by asking for favors, if you know what I mean."

"No, I don't." I leaned forward, interest oozing like an embarrassing drool. "Explain it."

His scowl spoke volumes.

Both of my hands flew outward, grasping at air. "Jack, this is my life we're talking about here."

"Okay, okay. Someone made a mistake, a big mistake, and somehow Paul found out about it. It could have ruined her career. She could have been charged with a crime."

Jack paused, his eyes narrowing, muscles tightening. This was difficult for him.

"Please, I need this information."

His frown deepened. "You're just like Paul, willing to hurt anyone that gets in your way."

"Jack, life in prison is pretty serious." I scrambled for a way to convince him to tell me. "We can try and keep this person's name off the police's radar screen."

"Paul found out about her, her indiscretion. He promised to keep quiet if she cooperated with him. It was awful for her. But in the end she cooperated. What choice did she have?" He snorted. "Paul sure didn't leave her one."

My voice softened. "What did she do for him, Jack?"

"Everything. She assigned his cases to the judges he wanted, gave him the heads-up on everything going on in the judicial corridors."

"How do you know this?"

"She's a friend." He looked at me pointedly. "I do have friends."

"I know you do. And I know I've been hard on you."

He slumped over in the chair. "I worked late one night and needed a court assignment. When I walked in, the office was empty. At least, I thought it was. But then I heard loud voices. I recognized Paul's. He was royally ticked off." Jack paused. "No, he was enraged. Suddenly the door opened, and Paul was inches from my face. He warned me to stay out of his way, that curiosity would get me into trouble. Then he stormed out of the office."

I tried to picture Paul, the man I married, doing these things—trampling on people as if they were insignificant pawns in his twisted little game. I shook my head. The deeper I got into Paul's murder, the more amazed I became.

Jack continued, "I was shocked. But more shocked when I saw my friend in tears."

My eyes widened. "Did you find out what happened?"

"She didn't want to tell me, but she was scared, pretty soon she just started talking. Like I said, Paul had threatened her professionally. The kicker was he'd threatened her physically too.

I sat back stunned. "That doesn't sound like Paul."

The vein in Jack's forehead pulsated. "You didn't know the bastard, Pen. If you had, you'd never have married him."

He had a point there. Empty air hung between us.

Jack's demeanor slid back into normal mode, and I considered my options. Should I or shouldn't I? Finally I charged forward. "Thank you. It's obvious that this has affected you. But I really need to talk to this woman."

"No!"

I leaned forward. "Just hear me out."

"I said no, and I mean it!"

"Jack, it isn't going to take a genius to figure out who she is. There aren't more than five people over on the court side that have access and control over the things you're talking about."

"Stay out of this. She can't tell you anything else. In case you think she murdered Paul, she didn't. She doesn't have it in her."

I got up from my chair. "That's fine for you to say. But shouldn't that be for the police to decide? It sounds like she had a motive."

He jumped up. "Pen, I'm warning you. Stay away from this, from her."

It was obvious I wasn't getting anywhere with Jack. I could get the information without him, but it would be easier if I had his cooperation. And it was a good bet that *his* cooperation equaled *her* cooperation.

But something else troubled me. My list of possible murder suspects was growing, rather than diminishing. A massive headache started behind my left eye and danced across to the right. I squeezed both shut, and rubbed my temples.

Was Jack protecting a girlfriend, or himself? I'd give it one more try—straight up, no games.

"I can find this woman with or without your help. If you give me her name, I'd be inclined to go easy on her. Perhaps keep her name from the police. At least for now." I stared hard at him. "You know it's futile. Give her up, and we can keep her out of trouble. Stonewall me, and I'll snitch her out to the police so fast she won't be able to hear the cell door clang shut."

"You're a pit bull, aren't you?" Resignation flooded his face.

That smarted. "I'm not talking about embarrassment or a simple indiscretion, we're talking prison. For life. And I'm here to tell you, I am not going to prison just because your girlfriend doesn't want to be embarrassed. I, Penelope Santucci, am not big enough, smart enough, or bad enough to survive prison! Got that, Jack?"

His eyes flashed with what could decidedly be called hate.

"Pit bull? Yeah, maybe," I continued. "I have dreams, and those dreams do not involve forming a new family unit behind bars."

"Okay. But you have to give me some time. I need to talk with her before I tell you anything."

I didn't think about his offer for very long. I knew I didn't have much time before the police picked me up.

I nodded. "Twenty-four hours, that's all. If I don't have her name *and* if I'm not talking to her within twenty-four hours, I'm going to find her myself. And I'm not going to be quiet about it or give any thought to her reputation."

He frowned and ran his fingers through his hair. "I'll call you tomorrow."

Victory was not sweet. I felt like a jerk. "Thanks."

As I walked to the door I thought I heard a breathy, "Bitch."

I still felt like a jerk, so I almost let it pass. Almost. As I pulled open the door I said, "Be careful, Jack. A girl doesn't like to be called names."

I pulled the door shut and walked down the hall toward the elevator contemplating what I'd heard, trying to make sense of the things I'd learned about my ex-husband. Clearly, I knew nothing about him.

An unsettled feeling dropped over me like a net and I didn't like it. No, I didn't like it at all.

CHAPTER THIRTY

Marco wasn't home when I returned, but he'd thoughtfully left the side door open. How dumb is that? He's a criminal defense attorney. He should know unlocked doors are an open invitation to the criminally inclined. Alas, a safety lecture from me wouldn't be appreciated.

There was a note from Germaine plastered on the refrigerator instructing me to call Ma. I'd been out of touch for far too long. If I didn't make contact soon, she'd sniff me out like a hound dog hunting a possum. But I figured I'd better talk to Germaine first because I never, ever, want to talk to Ma without being armed to the teeth with information.

One of the nuns answered the phone. "May I help you?"

"Yes. I'd like to talk to Sister Germaine, please."

"May I ask who's calling?"

Her disapproving tone said it all. The nuns were circling the wagons. They would protect Germaine at all costs. It was probably a good thing that they didn't carry guns. I could feel the target on my back.

"This is her sister, Pen."

Her sharp intake of air confirmed my suspicions. Obviously she'd watched the evening news and was ready to whip me with her rosary if I dared bother her beloved Germaine. "I'm not certain she's available." She may as well have added, "to you."

My cranky meter shot skyward. "Well, check!" I may be a murder suspect, but I wasn't a murderer, and this nun wasn't going to interfere with family business. "Hey, she called me."

She sniffed, and for a nun it was a mighty haughty sniff. Actually it was a stubborn, judgmental sniff.

My cranky meter hovered in the danger zone, spiked, then shot up like a misguided missile. I didn't have time for her theatrics, and I hated being treated like a leper. Shouldn't Sister Stuffy-Bottom be out helping the poor and infirm? "Cut the crap, Sister. She's there. She's always there, unless she's with me or our mother."

After an incensed gasp, she paused. "I'll see." With a sharp thwack, the receiver hit a hard surface. I waited a full five minutes before I heard Germaine's brittle voice. "Penelope!"

Uh, oh, the nun tattled on me. "Yeah, I'm returning your call."

Germaine sounded breathless. "Sister Mary Elizabeth just told me a very short but naughty tale about your phone etiquette. Pen, it's not a good idea to use vulgar street language on a nun."

Crap? Vulgar Street Language? These religious types have no sense of humor and no clue. "Hey, I strongly suggested she call you to the phone, that's all. She got a tad uppity. Vulgar? I don't think Sister Stuffy-Bottom gets out enough. Her imagination is running amuck."

"Cut it out, Pen. Sister Mary Elizabeth does not have a problem with her imagination. In fact, she," I distinctly heard a twitter, "has no imagination whatsoever." She giggled conspiratorially. "You should have seen her. She was blustering."

Whew! I escaped a lecture. I looked heavenward and whispered, "Thank you."

Germaine asked, "What?"

"Nothing." Dodged the bullet. Score one for Pen. "You called?"

"Yeah, Ma is frantic."

Didn't I just know it. "Now what?"

"You know perfectly well what. She's hopping mad. Since this whole mess with Paul, you haven't been over to the house. And she can't reach you."

"Hey, I called her back."

She sputtered a cynical humph.

"I did too. Once."

She sighed. "Once is not enough for Ma. She's been trying to reach you since yesterday. Talk about imagination. She's certain you're either lying dead in some ditch or you're in some guy's bed. And it sounded as if dead in a ditch would clearly be her first choice."

"I know I haven't been around a lot. It's not as if I've been doing nothing. I'm trying to stay out of jail! And that's not been easy. I'm on borrowed time here, Germaine."

"Yeah, I know. But all Ma understands is that you're neglecting her."

"She could be the poster woman for 'It's all about me,' " I chuckled. "What do you want me to do?"

"Call the folks. Have dinner with them. I don't care what you do, but do *something*. Just get Ma off my back. She's driving me crazy."

"I thought that when you became a nun, all your problems blew up a chimney."

"Not if you're a member of this family. Honestly, she's on the edge. She came over to the college yesterday and interrupted my lecture to find out what's going on."

Ouch. "Sorry, Germaine. I had no idea."

"It wasn't pretty. And I don't want it to happen again, so call her."

I sagged against the wall and sighed. "Okay, okay. I will."

"Today."

"Today. Right after we hang up. I promise. And I'll even offer to have dinner with them. I could use some pasta and Ma's marinara."

"Good girl. Now I've got to run."

"Hold it! I need to talk to you."

"Can it wait? I've got prayers in 10 minutes."

My brain kicked into gear. It might be better if I talked to Paul's partner and Miss X at the Government Center before I bounced my thoughts off Germaine. After all, I'd been stretching her good will quota lately. "Sure. You go, pray. It's nothing. We can talk later."

"You sure?"

"I'm sure. Remember to say prayers for me. I need them."

"Always." There was a long pause. "I love you."

Embarrassment flooded through me. We Santuccis are a bit on the reserved side for a bunch of Italians. We yell a lot but aren't particularly exuberant about much else. And we certainly don't run around hugging, kissing, and confessing endearments to each other.

I mumbled, "I love you, too," and hung up.

Now, for Ma. I dialed her number and waited. The answering machine spit out the request for a message. Saved! I left a message and hung up quickly, fearing she would pick up the receiver and life as I knew it would be suspended for as long as she chose. I'd miss the marinara sauce though.

CHAPTER THIRTY-ONE

Marco's car rumbled up the drive while I lay soaking in a tub of soothing hot water. A killer headache had begun at the base of my neck, traveled upward, and settled behind my right eye. I sank deeper into the water.

The bath is where I do most of my heavy thinking, solved most of my problems. The solvable ones, that is. There has to be some pathology there somewhere. No one else I know does all their important thinking in the bathroom. But, like Ma says, "you can't argue with what works."

Deep in thought I heard Marco enter the house and call out, "Honey, I'm home."

I draped a hot wash cloth over my eyes. "Funny, real funny," I mumbled through the thick cloth.

"Where are you?"

I pushed the wash cloth aside. "Taking a bath," I answered.

He must have followed the sound of my voice because he rapped lightly on the door and asked, "Will you be done soon?"

I sank lower into the water. "I just got in. You must have another bathroom in this place."

"Of course I do. I just wanted to talk with you, find out about your day."

The water sloshed up against the sides of the tub as I sat up. Now that sounded too much like a cozy couple for me. "Why do you want to know?"

"Knowing it's not safe to leave you unattended for more than five minutes, I figured I'd better check. As your lawyer, I want to know what you've been up to."

He had a point. "Okay, okay. Just let me soak a little bit longer."

His voice faded as he walked away. "I bought some steaks and salad fixings. I'll put the meat on the grill, toss a salad, and we'll talk over dinner."

Hmmm. Smart, good looking, and he cooks more than just breakfast. Very interesting. I leaned back into the warm water and shut my eyes.

A few minutes later, I stepped from the tub, quickly dressed, brushed out my hair, pulled it back in a pony tail and followed the smell of beef wafting down the hallway.

I walked out the back door to the patio. "It smells good."

Marco turned around, spatula in hand, and grinned until his face lit up. I drew in my breath. It didn't matter where or when, this man just plain looked good. Drooling-all-over good. All the time. He wore a salmon colored golf shirt, khaki shorts, and loafers without socks. It was the no socks thing that got me. I've always thought that going sockless was sexy.

My mind veered down paths I didn't want to travel. I shivered.

He pointed the spatula at me. "There's been a change in plans."

I blinked and looked up. "What's that?"

"Father Daniel is coming over. He's concerned and wants to know what's going on. I figured he might as well join us for dinner and save you telling your story twice."

"Thrice." I held up three fingers.

"Thrice?"

"There's Germaine you know. She's my sister, and she likes to be in the know."

He turned back to the grill. "Yeah well the good padre didn't forget her. They're both coming."

"Let the games begin." I peered at the sizzling meat grilling. "Hey, I thought Germaine said she was busy. Well, no matter."

I offered to set the picnic table and hadn't finished before the dynamic duo rounded the side of the house. Everyone said their hellos, and soon we were behaving like good carnivores. We feasted on some very rare beef and washed it down with everyone's individual beverage of choice. *Ah, the power of tasty beef.*

I filled the trio in on what I'd learned from my conversations with Carl and Jack. And for once no one thought I was chasing rainbows. Or windmills. Or whatever. They all, including Marco, admitted that maybe I'd gleaned some valuable information.

But, while Marco had a newfound confidence in my investigative abilities, he wanted to put the kibosh on the investigation. "If Jack tells you the name of the woman who works in the clerk's office, I want to know about it first so I can talk to her." He tapped his finger on the table beside my plate. "First."

My knife hit the picnic table, clanking loudly before it bounced on the deck. "I don't think so."

Father Daniel's eyes met Germaine's as if to say: "Hit the ground, incoming missiles."

Marco rested his elbows on the table, leaned forward and asked, "What do you mean, I don't think so?"

I slapped the tabletop sharply. "Just what I said. I. Don't. Think. So."

Father Daniel actually flinched. Germaine scooted a few inches farther away from me. *Danger, danger. Incoming missile has landed.*

Marco sat up straighter, ran his fingers through his hair. "Come on. This is something for me to do, not you. It's too important."

I pointed a finger at Marco. "I'm telling you she won't talk to a lawyer. She's frightened. I don't represent authority, the court, or jail . . . I'm merely a probation officer. She'll talk to me, but not to you."

Father Daniel and Germaine's eyes darted, like a bouncing ball, rapidly from me to Marco.

Marco put his steak knife on the table. "I don't agree."

I picked up my fork and stabbed a piece of meat. "Well, then we'll agree to disagree."

Marco's spine stiffened as he cleared his throat. I noticed that Germaine sat up a bit straighter and Father Daniel's mouth formed a large O. I expected him to call out, "Hit the deck!"

Marco didn't miss a beat. "Penelope Santucci. I'm your lawyer and you'll do as I say."

Now that sounded too much like my mother for my taste. As angry as I was, a small smile crept over my face, and I had to breathe deeply to stifle the laugh rising inside me, threatening to hit the airwaves. I looked at Father Daniel and Germaine. Eyes wide, they too struggled not to laugh.

I leaned my arms on the picnic table, rested my upper body on them and declared, "Marco, you are not my mother."

"You don't need a mother," he growled. "You need a keeper. But in the absence of both, you have me. You are my client and my job is to keep my clients out of jail."

I took a bite of steak, chewed, swallowed, and said, "Marco, give it up. You won't win this one."

Marco grumbled, "I didn't want to have to trump you, but perhaps you need to know a couple of things. The drums are beating at the cop shop, and the dinner bell is about to ring. You, my dear, are the main course."

That got everyone's attention. "What do you mean?"

"Let me finish."

With that news, all I could do was nod my head. A first.

"The second thing is, I've had you followed."

I jerked up right. I hadn't seen this coming. "You what?"

He placed his outstretched hands palm down. At least he had the courtesy to look sheepish. "I said, let me speak. Are you aware you don't take directions very well?"

I opened my mouth to answer but stopped when Marco's eyebrows furrowed. He continued, "It was a rhetorical question, Pen."

I folded my arms across my chest and waited impatiently.

He pushed his empty plate to the middle of the table. "I had you followed because I'm worried about your safety."

I jerked forward again, itching for an opening and received another nonverbal warning as he pointed his finger at me. A small hiss escaped from my lips.

"And I'm glad I did because my associate," he paused to look around the table, "has observed a dark, late-model Ford, complete with two thugs, following you."

Father Daniel, Germaine, and I all spoke at the same time, "What?"

Marco cocked his head and responded sharply, "Can it, Pen. I said you'd get your chance. I've let you go off half-cocked long enough. So for once, be quiet and listen. It may keep you out of jail, and more importantly, it may keep you alive."

I slumped down and briefly checked Father Daniel and Germaine's expressions. *Quiet as mice. No help there.*

Marco said, "So far these guys don't know you're here. My associate's car took a hit, or should I say, hit them, when I brought you here. He did it to keep them from following us. Their car was, shall we say, incapacitated, and they weren't able to follow. I have, however, run the license plates and traced the owner. He's a local drug dealer known as Johnny Two Shoes."

I sniggered.

"Pen, the name is funny, I'll grant you that. Sounds a bit movie-ish. But I can guarantee you that he is not a nice man.

He'd just as soon bury you in cement and be done with it. You're causing him too much trouble." He paused to take a long draw on his drink. "And this bad man has, I mean, had a lawyer. Care to guess who it was?"

I didn't want to consider what Marco implied.

Marco nodded his head. "Yes, Pen. None other than your dearly departed husband."

Father Daniel had been squirming around in his seat for the past five minutes. He couldn't stand it any longer. "Then he killed Paul? This Johnny Two Shoes guy?"

Marco frowned at the elderly priest. "Will everyone please be quiet? There will be time for questions." He crossed himself, near his heart, like a twelve-year-old Boy Scout.

Germaine lowered her head. I could feel her anticipation oozing from every pore in her body.

Marco continued, "I don't know if Johnny killed Paul. But I don't think so. I think Paul promised to deliver a favorable verdict in Johnny's drug case. If Johnny were convicted, he would serve anywhere from fifteen to twenty-five this time around. He needed Paul alive to deliver the not-guilty verdict."

I sat up straighter. "You think the money we found belongs to him, don't you?"

Marco's scowl deepened. "Don't you? And I think he figured that as Paul's widow you might have the money, even if you weren't on the best of terms."

"Wow!" I said. My eyes widened. Widow! I still couldn't get used to the word. One small noun transformed me from the blush of youth to an aged crone.

"Johnny probably thought that you'd found the money or that Paul told you about it before he died. Before you killed him."

"I didn't kill Paul" I snapped.

Germaine interrupted, "The bad guys don't know that."

Father Daniel added, "That's right. All this guy knows is that his money is gone."

I shook my head.

Marco said, "I was speaking hypothetically."

I shrugged. "Just wanted to be sure."

Marco sighed. "Anyway, you've got some problems, and time is the biggest concern right now." He stopped, and the silence hung in the air.

Germaine asked, "Is Pen going to be arrested?"

Father Daniel exclaimed, "Surely, you can't mean that the police have enough evidence to arrest our Pen."

I glanced at everyone sitting around the picnic table on this beautiful June evening. Our Pen. I felt like the family pet.

Marco responded, "It's a distinct possibility. I went over Paul's business files and talked to his partner this afternoon."

My eyebrows raised, "Hey, I was going to do that!"

His stern glance silenced me. "More and more, the things you've been saying have begun to make sense. It's my job to cover all the bases. And Ben Joston was a base that needed covering."

"Well, does that mean I don't have to talk to him?"

"I took care of things."

Father Daniel asked, "Learn anything interesting?"

Marco drained his glass and set it on the tabletop. "As a matter of fact I did. His relationship with Paul was strained to the point of dissolving the partnership. But, I don't think Ben is the murderer."

I nodded. I'd known Ben long enough to have some doubts, yet I just couldn't see him doing it.

Germaine fiddled with her spoon, tilting it so it reflected the faded orange of the setting sun. "Did he say why they were going to dissolve the partnership?"

"Because he didn't like the unsavory characters Paul

represented. Actually, representation was one thing . . . Paul seemed to be involved more deeply with several clients. And there had been some unexplained money Paul had received but had not passed through the firm. Then there's Stephanie. Her behavior in public was becoming an embarrassment. Things like that." Marco got up and walked to the kitchen for more iced tea. When he returned he added, "Ben mentioned something else that I found interesting."

My ears perked up. I love information, especially information that might keep me free from the county lock-up. Or worse, the state prison system. Marco wasn't telling his story fast enough for me.

Or for Germaine. She piped up, "What did he say? We're waiting here, Marco."

Marco responded, "Hang on."

Germaine shrugged, and I thought I saw the tiniest spark of fire shoot from her eyes. "Okay, okay."

"Stephanie did find out about another woman. Evidently, several other women."

Now that got my attention. Seems my wayward husband had been spreading himself around town and got caught. Served him right, the philanderer.

Marco continued, "She went to Paul's office about a week before he was murdered, and Ben overheard a fight between them. In fact, everyone heard it. Ben had to ask them to stop."

"How tacky," I giggled.

Marco obviously didn't think I was serious enough about the story because his glare burned into my skin. Boy, he'd better be careful, or he'd have permanent frown lines before he was thirty-five. "Pen."

Curiosity got the better of me. "Hey, I just want to know what he heard."

Marco smiled like a fellow conspirator. "I'm getting to that."

255

He rubbed his hands together. "Ben said Stephanie threatened Paul. Said that he wasn't going to get away with cheating on her. That he should stop it or she'd stop him, permanently."

I jumped to my feet, threw both hands in the air and yelled, "Yes!" Then I doubled over in pain. In my excitement I'd forgotten my aches and pains.

Everyone stared. I slowly lowered my arms and said, "Hey, it takes the heat off me. Let's tell the police." I slowly moved toward the house and the nearest telephone. "Stephanie obviously killed Paul, and we should tell the police." I inched my way to the door.

Marco interrupted, "This really doesn't mean much."

I stared in disbelief. "What do you mean? This is my ticket to the ballgame, my get out of jail free card." I looked heavenward. "Thank you Lord, I will do my best to refrain from all sin in the future."

Father Daniel chuckled and said, "Pen. Stop it. That's sacrilege."

Germaine got to her feet. "No, she's got a point. It means that someone, other than Pen, had a motive. This has to be good news."

Marco held up his hands. "Stop it! All of you. Yes, it's good news but—it's not good enough. It just points toward other possibilities."

I crept back to the bench and dropped slowly onto it. "No fair. You always rain on my parade." I put my head in my arms.

Germaine sat down next to me on the bench and began rubbing my back. "It'll be okay."

Father Daniel chimed in, "Your sister is right, Pen. You've got a good lawyer and the police aren't going to arrest someone for a murder they didn't commit."

I peeked at Father Daniel through my arms. "I don't mean to offend you, Father Daniel, but you are really naïve." I sat up.

"The police will arrest anyone that they think they can convict. And right now, I'm the prize behind door number one."

Marco jumped in. "It's not that it isn't good news. It is something I'll talk to the police about, and they'll talk to Ben and Stephanie."

"Well, get on it. If we tarry too long at the fair, it'll be over and I'll be the target in the penny arcade."

Marco sighed. "The most that will happen right now is that you won't be arrested immediately. They might put that off for a bit."

"Gee, thanks for the encouragement. You make a girl feel so safe and secure."

"Hey," Germaine said as she got up from the table and started clearing the dishes, "anything that keeps you out of jail until the real murderer is found is a good thing."

I couldn't deny that. But the damage was done. My personal parade was canceled due to rain. But just when I thought it couldn't get worse, Marco said, "Now, there is the thing about the money."

Oh, the money again. I was beginning to wish I hadn't found the dratted money. I wrinkled my nose and asked, "Now what?"

Marco replied, "Well, two things, really. The money and you."

I started to speak, but he held up his hand. I was learning—I sat and listened. "I put the money in a safe deposit box. It's going to stay there until things get straightened out."

I couldn't resist. "Well, straighten them out because that's your fee for representing me."

Everyone's eyes bored holes into me. I shrugged. "Well, hey! I don't have any other real funds at the moment."

Germaine waved me off. "Pen, you're something else."

I didn't get a chance to defend myself because Marco ignored my comments and kept talking. "You're going to stay with Germaine for a few days."

I started. "What?"

My eyes darted toward Germaine, and it became clear she was in on this part of the story. My gaze started with Marco, drifted to Father Daniel, and settled on Germaine. They were *all* in on it. The entire dinner was a setup. Oh, they would pay dearly for their treachery. My motto: If you're going take a shot at the queen you'd better darn well kill her, 'cause she's isn't taking a bullet calmly and she doesn't ever forget. Revenge will be mine.

My whine began slowly and built to a crescendo. "Marco, I can't stay at the convent. There are, well, there are too many nuns there!" In particular, I figured Sister Stuffy-Bottom would make my life miserable. I could just see myself stuck scrubbing the priory steps with a toothbrush while she stood over me rapping a thick ruler against her palm.

Germaine started, "Pen, you have to."

I slowly turned toward Germaine and pointed my finger at her. "Pen, nothing. I do not, I repeat, I do not want to live with nuns. I'm going to go home. To my cozy condo, free from all things religious."

Marco countered, "It's safer if you stay at the convent." His arms swept outward. "Even here, you're not completely safe. I'm your lawyer so it stands to reason that it's only a matter of time before they end up looking for you here."

"You don't understand, I can't! I'd suffocate. Strangulate. I might even go crazy. You may as well send me to lock-up. There's not much difference. At least there the inmates won't be haranguing over my soul."

"Haven't you been listening?" Germaine tapped her foot impatiently. "Marco's right. It is safer at the convent. These guys are serious. And they've already given you one beating."

"No, several," Father Daniel chimed in.

I glared at him. "She stands corrected," I addressed Germaine. "This isn't fair."

Germaine cleared her throat and switched to a forced, but distinctly softer voice, "They will find you sooner or later."

Father Daniel hoisted his portly body up from the table and added, "Even if they tracked you to the convent, there aren't going to be any men getting in. There is security and well, frankly some of those nuns can become pretty disagreeable. I know I wouldn't want to try it."

Germaine smiled as if she were proud of her little army of black-hooded gnomes.

I sighed in defeat. Like the old Kenny Rogers song, "The Gambler," it was time for me to walk away.

"It's settled," Germaine announced triumphantly. "And I've already cleared it with Mother Superior." Her eyes brimmed with mischief. "And think of it, you've always wanted to dress like a nun. You used to when you were little. You can again."

Things momentarily looked brighter. She was right. I'd always dreamed of wearing a habit, walking around piously, blessing everyone. Piousness without the commitment. A fantasy come true.

Germaine must have noticed the gleam in my eye because she rattled on, "And no one will recognize you in a habit. You can go about your business, and no one will be the wiser."

Sold! "Well, if you think it's best." They knew they had me. I could see it in their collective grins.

I stood up. "Well, we really should be going, Germaine. I suspect the convent locks its doors early. We women of the cloth wouldn't want to be late. And I really need time to get my habit, er, wardrobe ready."

They all groaned, but I ignored them, left the dishes on the picnic table for Marco to deal with, and gathered my things. I left Marco's walking tall. I, Penelope Santucci, was going to give myself, at least my physical body, to the church, to God. Temporarily anyway.

CHAPTER THIRTY-TWO

I tried to organize my thoughts on the drive to the convent. My anxiety level continued to build until I felt like the wicked witch when she looked up and saw Dorothy's house plummeting toward her. Things were coming to a head. I could feel it.

A visit to the Government Center early Monday morning topped my to-do list. Okay, so Marco didn't want me involved, but I hadn't actually promised him that I wouldn't talk to Jack's friend.

Germaine turned up the radio and began humming softly to an old Abba song. I scrunched down in my seat, turned my head toward the window, and watched Minneapolis fade away as St. Paul loomed ahead.

Just before we entered the convent grounds, Germaine piped up. "Pen, what's next?"

I stiffened, expecting a lecture and tried to sound casual. "My plans are fluid."

Germaine looked at me. "Things have gotten out of hand. I'm beginning to agree with you—if we don't find the murderer, and soon, it could be bad for you."

A believer? Was I hearing correctly? I sat up, shifted my position to face her. "You *agree* with me?"

She smiled weakly as she put on her left blinker. "Yeah, I do."

A grin spread across my face, and I lightly punched her shoulder. "You're pretty smart for a girl whose entire wardrobe is battleship gray."

She ignored my jibe and nodded her head slightly. "You're welcome. So, what do we do next?"

"We?"

She made another left turn. "Yes, we. I'm not going to let you go down without giving it everything I've got." Her face firmed up like a warrior, like a determined Joan of Arc, ready to die for her sister. But then a fleeting hesitation marred her saintly determination. "If you could try to keep the criminal aspects to a minimum, I'd appreciate it." She turned her head and smiled. "I just want to help my baby sister."

I looked heavenward. *Thank you, Lord.* "Really? Cross your heart?"

"Cross my heart." She grinned. "Hey, if you go to prison, like you say, I'll be stuck dealing with Ma on my own. Not good for me."

We drove through the convent gates as I explained my plan for the next day. Germaine nodded occasionally, and as we entered the back door of the convent she said, "I'll have to get someone to cover my classes tomorrow, but it shouldn't be a problem. I'll go with you."

I grabbed my sister's hands and screeched, "You're really going to help me?"

We rounded the corner and walked toward the stairs. At the bottom, Germaine paused. "I said so didn't I?" Yes, she had. I was so happy I would have skipped up the stairs to the second floor where Germaine's small three-room apartment was located if my battered body had allowed it.

After we got ready for bed, Germaine called another nun to cover her classes. I made up the sofa bed while I listened to her side of the conversation. Germaine went to the bathroom, and I slid under the covers and looked around.

I'd been in Germaine's small apartment numerous times but had never really looked at it. There were photos of our family framed and sitting on top of the television, a small stereo system played some light jazz.

Bookshelves overflowed with novels, biographies, and a myriad of religious books. Her furniture was mostly cast offs with snazzy slipcovers. It was warm and cozy. Just what I needed. I snuggled down under grandma Santucci's old patchwork quilt and felt safe and secure for the first time since finding Paul's body.

I was just getting drowsy when Germaine emerged from the bathroom. "Pen, I want to show you something."

I started. "Umm!"

Germaine said, "Oh, sorry. I didn't realize you were asleep."

I pushed myself into a sitting position. "It's okay."

She disappeared into her small bedroom, and I heard what sounded like boxes being tossed about. I got up, wandered to the bedroom door, and peered inside. "What are you doing?"

Germaine's muffled voice came from the bottom of the closet. "They're here somewhere."

"What?"

She tossed several more boxes aside. "Wait just a minute, will you?"

I shrugged and leaned casually against the door frame. Germaine backed out of the closet dragging a large white box.

She got to her feet, lifted the box, and tossed it onto the bed. "Here," she said as she lifted the cover.

White tissue was pushed aside and she drew out, piece by piece, a nun's habit. "I knew it was here somewhere. I almost never wear it."

I walked to the side of the bed, reached down, and began gently sifting through the garments. "Wow!"

Germaine laughed. "You crack me up. You always wanted to be a nun, yet I'm the one who entered the order."

I nodded absently, lost in my childhood fantasy. I looked

expectantly at Germaine, "May I?"

Smiling, like a proud older sister, she nodded. With her help I got dressed. I had no idea how complicated getting into a nun's habit could be. When I was finished I walked to the bathroom, struggling to see as much of myself as possible. Grinning from ear-to-ear, I looked to Germaine for approval. It was the closest I would ever come to pious.

Germaine looked me over from head to toe and proclaimed, "It's a bit long, but it'll do."

I strutted from the bathroom and did a proper nun's walk through the small apartment, blessing the TV and the paintings as I gracefully passed by. When I came to a picture of the pope, I curtsied. Germaine followed me, laughing out loud. "You don't curtsy."

"Well, its just a picture, so it's pretty hard to kiss his ring."

It wasn't long before, weak from laughter, Germaine collapsed on the sofa bed.

Her eyes focused on a print hanging on the far wall of the small living room. "There's something I need to clear up with you, Pen."

I straightened the skirt of my habit and responded primly, "Yes, my child?"

But she didn't laugh. "I wasn't exactly honest with you, Marco, and Father Daniel earlier."

She had my attention. "What does that mean?"

"Ah, I might have led everyone to believe that the order, the nuns here in the convent," her arm swept outward, "were okay with you wearing a habit."

I walked toward Germaine. "Now don't tell me these women do not know a civilian is here."

She threw her hands upward. "No, no! I cleared that." As an aside she added, "And it wasn't easy. Some of these women . . . well, let's just say they're not exactly thrilled about harboring a possible murderer."

"Germaine!"

"Okay, okay. Here's the deal: they know you're here, but I didn't clear you wearing the habit."

"So?"

"So, it wouldn't go over well, Pen."

"Then, let's just clear it."

"Not that easy. I mean, technically, well . . . they'd think it sacrilege for someone who isn't a nun to wear it."

I settled on the sofa bed, bunching the skirt around my knees. "Then why did you tell me I could?"

"I think you *should* wear it. You need a good disguise right now. But," she twisted the corner of the quilt, "to be perfectly honest, I added it as an incentive."

It all became clear. I nodded, "So I would agree to stay here. Oh, Germaine, I love it! You're learning to think like me." *Scary thought.*

She frowned.

I ignored her obvious guilt over her newly minted skills of deception. "I've got it! I'll walk out of here in the morning in my street clothes, go to the nearest coffee shop, change and go on my merry way. And then before I return here, I'll reverse the process."

Germaine considered what I'd said. "It'll work."

I put my arm around her shoulders. "Of course it will work. We'll make it work." *Forgive me Father for I not only fudge the truth, but I teach others to eat that fudge.*

We shook out the habit, hung it in the closet, finished our bedtime rituals, and went to bed. I closed my eyes and went straight to sleep, the deep contented sleep of the not-so-innocent but blissfully hopeful that all would turn out okay. After all, my sister was on my side.

★ ★ ★ ★ ★

The next morning I made several phone calls, including one to my office, just to check in. I wasn't expected to return to work yet, but I wanted to keep everyone informed. I also wanted to see who was covering the arraignment calendar. When I went to the clerk's office, I didn't want to run into someone from probation. That is *if* I went. It was ten o'clock and I hadn't heard from Jack, but I'd given him twenty-four hours and his time wasn't up. There were other things I could do while I waited.

I dug through Germaine's closet, found a cloth bag, and filled it with everything I thought I'd need for the day. Germaine had gone to the college administration building to pick up some files and hadn't returned by the time I was ready to leave. Knowing Germaine, she'd probably run into a student and lost track of time.

I made another telephone call, surprised that the information I needed was so easy to get. Pausing in Germaine's miniscule kitchen, I wrote a note telling her that she could reach me on my cell phone, then left. It wasn't until I reached the lobby that I realized I didn't have a vehicle. "How can I be so dumb?"

I turned around and walked to the elevator, and when it arrived I hastily punched the button for Germaine's floor. I opened her door with the key she'd given me, wondering why nuns needed locks on their doors. Did it mean that God's helpers occasionally helped themselves to other people's stuff? Interesting puzzle to ponder.

I grabbed Germaine's car keys from the counter and hurriedly added an explanation to my note about why I was stealing her car. She wouldn't like it, but she'd like where I was going and what I was about to do even less. Couldn't be helped. At least, that's how I saw it.

Retracing my steps, I left the building and walked as fast as I could to the parking lot. My battered body was healing nicely. I unlocked the car door, slid behind the wheel, and wondered if my behavior had "crazy woman" stamped on it. I didn't have much of a plan, and that concerned me because bad things tend to happen when one doesn't have a plan. But then bad things can happen to one when there is a plan. My entire life was proof of that.

So I referred to Murder Investigation 101. If you don't have a plan, wing it. And a prayer wouldn't hurt either. *Amen to that, Sister.*

The botched burglary of Judge Kassner's house hadn't been that long ago, but it felt like a million years. I turned the ignition key, shifted into reverse, looked both ways, and glided out of the parking space. There was a lot to do and learn, and time was not on my side.

CHAPTER THIRTY-THREE

I wound my way through Edina, searching for the unfamiliar address. A canopy of large gnarled oak trees lined the street, hiding avenue signs and building addresses, as if protecting the up-scale suburb from would-be intruders by remaining obscure.

When I slowed to ask a passerby for directions, I glanced to my left and spotted the building up ahead. "Bingo!" I drove halfway up the street and cruised into an empty parking spot. Rock-star parking. Yeah!

Taking a deep breath, I adjusted my sunglasses, hoping to hide my battered eyes, and walked to the entrance, stopping to study the classy sign above the door. It must've cost more than my living room furniture.

I adjusted my jacket, pushed through the day spa's entrance, and stated my business to the impeccable specimen behind the desk. "Stephanie Collins, please."

She smiled at me with perfect, straight, white, definitely capped teeth and asked in a voice oozing sexuality, "Do you have an appointment?"

My telephone call earlier confirmed that Stephanie was at the office, and I had impulsively decided to pay her a visit.

The receptionist's syrupy voice interrupted my thoughts. "I said, do you have an appointment?"

There were several approaches to get past the front desk, but a simple lie should work. In a soft southern drawl I exclaimed, "No, I don't have an appointment." I patted my hair. "I don't need an appointment." I waved my hand in the air. "Why I just now came from the airport and rushed over here to surprise li'l ol' Stephanie."

I leaned over the reception desk, looked from side-to-side, and in a conspiratorial voice said, "I'm her cousin from Dallas. As in Texas." I stood up. "We haven't seen each other in such a long, long time. She's actually not expecting me for several days."

I giggled, covering my mouth with my hand and continued, "I finished my Chicago business early." I touched my glasses lightly. "You know, a little preventative nip and tuck," and decided to fly my li'l ol' self right on up here and surprise her. She just loves surprises." My surgical explanation should take care of any questions she might have about visible bruises.

The receptionist smiled broadly. Gotcha. Now to reel her in, snag her in my net, and let her flop around in the bottom of the boat.

I whispered loudly, "So, if y'all could just point me in the direction of her office, I'll jus' sneak on in and make her day." Oh my! Wouldn't I just do that?

The receptionist hesitated. "I don't know."

She was wavering. Quickly, I began, "As I said, if there is one thing Stephanie likes, it's a surprise. Mostly jewelry, of course." I laughed and the receptionist expelled a small titter of understanding. "But she does like these family surprises, too. Now, let's keep our Stephanie happy. You wouldn't want me to tell her that you interfered with our happy family reunion, would you?" I shook my head mournfully, "Darlin', I don't think Stephie-dear would like that, do you?"

Fear snapped in her eyes as she realized her job description might include latrine duty if she ticked off the boss. That's when I knew I'd clinched the deal. It seems keeping Stephanie happy was important. I'll just bet.

The receptionist stood up and walked around the desk. In a perky voice she asked, "Why don't you come with me?"

Oh, no! A personal escort was not what I had in mind. Too many awful things could happen. Like me being thrown out or having the police summoned.

I reached out and ever so lightly touched her arm. "Ah, Hon, just point me in the right direction. You must have so many other things to do. And I'll be sure to tell Stephanie just how helpful you were."

She rocked back and forth on her heel. "I . . . I guess it's okay."

My smile grew. "Oh sure, it is. Just point the way, Hon."

She tittered again and pointed a perfectly manicured finger, "Just take an immediate right there. Her door is the first one on the left."

I didn't wait for her to change her mind. I swung my hips toward Stephanie's walled world and marched off southern-belle style. As I turned the corner, I called out over my shoulder, "Thanks, Darlin'. I don't care what they say, you northerners are ever so helpful."

Standing outside Stephie-dear's office, I briefly questioned my sanity. The personal price for my freedom seemed to be growing like a child's night time monster lurking under the bed.

I sighed loudly.

I didn't know if Stephanie could help me find Paul's killer, but I couldn't pass up the opportunity to find out, even if it did mean fibbing to her receptionist. What's the worst Stephanie could do? Throw me out of the office on my fleshy (not fat) behind. Worst case, she could scratch my eyes out or, and here's the part that worried me, call the cops.

My stomach did a half-gainer with a full twist. I was ready to turn tail when the door abruptly opened.

There she was, chattering on her cell phone, gesturing wildly with her free hand. When she saw me she gasped and said, "I'll have to call you back." She snapped the phone shut, dropped it into her jacket pocket, and stepped into the hall. Her face screwed up in an unbecoming frown. "And what do you think you're doing here, Missy?"

Missy? What decade is she from?

"I wanted to have a little chat with you." There I sounded as archaic as she did.

She tried to finesse her body around mine but the narrow hall made it impossible. I slid my foot to the left blocking her escape. She reached out with both hands and gave me a push. I'd seen it coming, dug in my heels, and said, "Oh, no you don't, *Missy.*"

I pushed back and unlike me, she hadn't seen it coming. She tripped on her three-inch heels and stumbled backwards into her office. I followed and quickly slammed the door behind me.

In the scuffle we bumped chests. She hit the floor sputtering obscenities. Her short skirt had inched its way up around her hips, her left shoe lay, with a broken heel, about three feet to her right. She began sucking on her right pinky finger. Oops, a broken nail. Now she really would be irritable.

No matter, I was determined to have my say before being thrown out.

I stared at my husband's former lover. In her current state she wasn't exactly attractive. In prison, without benefit of her expensive clothes, weekly facials, and forty dollar manicures, she'd probably be downright bow-wow-ish. Ah, and didn't that do my heart some good?

She reached for her desk and pulled herself up from the floor while screaming vile obscenities.

"Now, now Stephanie. A lady ought not say such things."

Another string of expletives spewed out of her mouth.

Upright now, she pulled her skirt down as she looked for her shoe, found it, and jammed her foot into the pointed toe. Stabbing the air with her finger she demanded, "What?"

The broken heel hadn't been noticed. Yet.

She stumbled again, picked up her foot, gazed at the heel dangling at a rakish angle.

"What the. . . . ?"

"Hey, no need to talk like that."

Still staring at her broken heel she yelled, "And where do you get off telling me what I can or cannot say?"

I wrinkled my nose. "You don't talk like that in front of customers, and I could be one someday."

She laughed, a gurgling sound that almost gagged her. "I don't think so. I'm going to throw you out on your big fat ass and ban you from the premises, permanently!" She paused, then added, "And that means forever."

Duh.

My, my, she was touchy. "Look Stephanie, I'm sorry."

"Humph!"

I held my hands out in supplication. "I know, I know. It might not seem like it, based on the past two minutes, but really, I am sorry. I only came here to ask you a few questions. All this was an accident. I didn't mean to bump into you."

She patted her hair into place, tucking dislodged locks behind her ears, pinning other strands up in back. "I don't have to talk to you and I'm not going to." Her voice turned shrill. "You killed my Paulie. Took him from me. The future father of my children."

That did it. The wench was in denial, delusion and had serious illusions of grandeur. "Cut the crap, Stephanie. *Paulie* dumped you. Everyone knows that."

A deeply injured look replaced rage. "It's not true. Paulie and I were in love." She dragged out the word love so long I thought I'd puke.

I shook my head. "A *reliable* source says you and Paul were history."

She began to speak, and I held up my hand. "Can it. You know the truth, and I know the truth." I'd throw her a bone. "Paul dumped me for you, and you for someone else. It was his style. He was a jerk." My voice softened. "Now I just want to help you."

She snickered. "You want to help me? Yeah, I've got a picture of that."

My voice quavered ever so little as I attempted to look sincere. "Okay, I want you to help me, and in turn I want to help you."

Her eyebrows arched.

I leaned toward her shaking my head from side to side. "When the police learn that Paul dumped you, well, suddenly I don't look quite so good for the murder. Know what I mean?"

She had the audacity to look perplexed. Not the brightest bulb in the building. I'd have to spell it out more clearly. Tell her the ABCs of police procedure. "If Paul dumped you, the police might look at you for his murder. They might think that you had a better motive than I did." I cocked my head and studied her. "You do know what a motive is, don't you?" At this point, I wasn't sure about her IQ, but I had a good idea the Mensa people wouldn't be knocking on her door anytime soon.

She smoothed her skirt with her hands. "Of course I do."

Her words said she understood, but her voice said she didn't have a clue. Where did Paul find this one? Didn't he have better sense than to date a woman with the IQ of a gnat? Apparently not. There must have been something about her that attracted him. But I'd be darned if I could figure out what it was.

I threw her another bone. "The police might think you were angry with him about the break-up, that you flew into a rage, and you know . . ." I paused, "and well, you killed him."

"I did not!"

"Well, do you have an alibi?"

She pouted. "I don't have to talk to you."

"Hey, it's me or the police. Do you have an alibi?"

There was that perplexed look again. The bimbo was as smart as a box of rocks. I drew in a deep breath and exhaled slowly, patiently. "Can you prove to the police that you didn't kill him? Were you with someone else at the time of the murder?"

Stephanie pulled off her broken shoe and stared at the dangling heel. "You do know that this is a Manolo Blahnik, don't you? You broke it."

The tables turned. She was speaking a language I didn't understand. "What?"

She pointed. "My shoe, it's a Manolo Blahnik. You broke it."

What is this woman talking about? "Listen Stephanie, I don't know what you're talking about. I didn't break your Manolo or Canoli or whatever. You broke your shoe. Get over it. Buy another pair."

"They're expensive."

"It's just a shoe, for Pete's sake. I'm talking about alibis and the police, and you're worried about a pair of shoes."

"A five-hundred-dollar pair of shoes."

She dangled the broken shoe between her thumb and first finger. Nah, she couldn't mean . . . I squealed. "Five hundred dollars? For shoes? It's a piece of leather with a strap. I don't believe it."

She smiled wickedly. "Believe it."

"Who pays five hundred dollars for a pair of shoes? All my shoes together didn't cost that much."

She slowly took in my frame, head to toe. "I believe that. Just look at you. You have no style."

Score: Stephanie, one; Pen, zero. "Come on, Stephanie, we're not discussing the price of your shoes."

"Well, someone will have to pay."

"Not me, sister. I don't make that kind of money. And besides, if you don't come up with an alibi, you won't need shoes like that anymore. I think they issue K-mart brand tennis shoes in prison."

She shuddered. I had her attention.

My voice softened. "Now, look. I'd like to help you, I really would. But you're going to have to work with me here. Where were you when Paul was murdered?"

Her gaze left her shoe as she stared at me. She let go of the heel, and it fell to the floor with a thud. The woman was nuts.

She straightened her back, patted her hair, and said, "I have an . . . alibi."

I waited and waited. Finally, "Yes?"

She stuck her nose in the air. "I don't have to talk to you, Penelope. And maybe, instead of attacking me, and ruining my favorite pair of Manolos you should talk to that other woman."

"What are you talking about?"

"The new girlfriend."

Wow! She had known Paul was cheating on her. I could hardly believe my ears. She didn't have to share this with me, but she did. I'd have to coax her a bit. "I know, Stephanie. It's difficult, especially when you cared so much." I leaned toward her, trying to empathize with her for her plight. *Yeah, right.*

It must have worked because her eyes clouded over and she sniffed ever so softly and emitted a tiny hiccup. "I don't know why I'm telling you this."

I held my breath.

A lone tear slithered down her cheek. "I saw them, you know. At the Heartwood Inn restaurant. Paul didn't know I would be there, but I was and I saw him."

I waited. "And?"

She tossed her head, pointy little nose in the air. "They were huddled over salads. She was crying, and he grabbed her wrist."

Who? I wanted to scream, but I didn't want to interrupt her. It wouldn't take much for her to clam up.

More tears gathered at the corner of her eyes. "They were having an argument. At least, that's what it looked like."

My chest heaved with excitement.

Stephanie moved to her desk, pulled out the chair, and fell into it. "I don't like you, Penelope. But I don't want the police suspecting me either."

I nodded my understanding; sympathy covered my face. But she was somewhere else, didn't really know I was in the room anymore.

She continued, a faraway look in her eyes. "I just stood in the doorway of the restaurant watching them. The woman began crying, looked up at Paul, and he just stood up, pointed at her, said something and walked away. Then he did something really weird. He stopped, turned, walked back to the table and paused. I couldn't see his face; his back was to me. But then he leaned over, patted the woman's head, and kissed the top of it."

I felt the room press in on me. Her story sounded crazy. Paul *never* would cause a scene in a public place. Ever.

Stephanie interrupted my thoughts. "When he turned and started walking toward me, I got scared. The look on his face was of pure hate."

"What did you do?"

She looked at me. "I ducked into the hall by the coat check room. I must have stood there for about ten minutes, just to make sure they were both gone."

"Who was the woman?"

Her head jerked. "I have no idea. They were across the room from me, so I didn't see her close up. But I do know one thing. She wasn't any spring chicken. In fact, she seemed a lot older than Paul. But classy and sophisticated by the way she carried herself and the clothes she wore."

Now that was curious. "It wasn't his mom?"

"Of course not," she sniffed. "I know what Astrid looks like. She was across the room but close enough so I could tell it wasn't Astrid." She moaned, "I do know something was going on. They looked so intimate, but at the same time really scary and creepy."

"You're sure you didn't recognize her?"

Stephanie looked bemused. "There was someone who looked a bit like her at Paul's funeral. But that woman had shorter hair and seemed older somehow than the woman in the restaurant. I can't really be sure."

"Would you know her if you saw her again?" I didn't know why I thought this woman would be important. Maybe it was a gut feeling.

"I don't know."

"Did you tell this to the police?"

She glared at me. "They didn't ask."

Figures. She didn't want to tell the police she and Paul had had a falling out.

"Pen, it's time for you to leave. I don't want to talk to you anymore." She sniffed. "I've already said too much. My private life is my business."

It wasn't the time to remind her that her private life was the business of the police when it came to murder.

I moved closer to her. "Just tell me one thing."

"No! I said I didn't want to talk to you anymore." She got up and limped toward me. "Now get out of here."

She gave me a weak push. "Hey!"

"Get out! I don't like you."

I turned toward the door, not really wanting to get into another cat fight with Paul's former girlfriend. The town would be talking about me even more than they already were. I didn't want to be viewed as the jealous wife. And I didn't want the police to hear that story either.

I pulled open the door, gave Stephanie my best look of hopelessness. "Please, Stephanie, would you know her if you saw her?"

"Out!" She pushed the door, and I tripped and did a three point landing on the floor, slumped over and stunned.

As I struggled to my feet, rubbing my head, I heard the door slam. I turned to face the receptionist.

Still rubbing my head, I smiled weakly. "She didn't like the message from her mama."

I hurried from the building, wondering what had possessed me. Then I realized that while I didn't get all the answers I had wanted, I did get some new information.

I got into Germaine's car, looked at my watch, and realized that while I needed to get to the Government Center, I needed to talk to Marco right away. He wouldn't like that I had confronted Stephanie, but he would appreciate the information.

Germaine crossed my mind just as my cell phone rang, which probably meant I was busted.

I dug my phone out of my purse and answered sweetly, "Hi it's Pen. Can't talk now, I'm in traffic, and it could be dangerous."

I heard Germaine's high-pitched voice, "Penelope! Get back here!"

CHAPTER THIRTY-FOUR

Germaine laid into me for running off without her. Traveling around Minneapolis alone didn't meet her safety criteria, especially since two goons were scouring the town for me. In the interest of family harmony, I made a detour back to the convent.

On the way to St. Paul, I called Marco and was relieved when his secretary said he was in a meeting. I left a message. Better a message than a lecture.

"Please, tell Marco he should talk to Stephanie, Paul's girlfriend. She has some interesting information." I gave her the details and then asked, "Did you get all that?" I lowered my voice to a whisper, "And tell Marco not to believe anything Stephanie says about me, okay?"

She promised to relay the message, even the cryptic part. I knew Stephanie would rat me out. And right now, I had enough on my plate—I didn't need another lecture from Marco just because I got into a teensy weensy cat fight with the world's craziest bimbo. Given his prior experience with me he'd probably buy her story over mine, but at least I had a head start on her.

I turned onto Highway 100 south, then took the 394 heading east and cut off on 94 E, toward St. Paul. It was out of my way to pick up Germaine and then head back to Minneapolis, but her wrath wasn't something I wanted to tinker with.

I'd convince Germaine to go with me to the Government

Center to talk to Jack's mystery woman. But first, I'd need to talk to Jack and find out who she was.

I dialed his office since he hadn't called me as he'd promised.

He answered on the second ring. "Hey, Jack."

"What are you doing calling me at work."

"Hello to you too."

He growled—I was getting a lot of that these days.

"You were supposed to call."

"Well, since you've called me, I guess I don't have to."

I signaled a lane change and pulled between a SUV and a BMW. "Don't screw with me, Jack. It doesn't make me happy. If you don't want to talk, I'll find out who she is and I'll tell the police."

"Don't you dare."

"Jack, I'm not calling to convert you, I'm calling to get a name from you."

There was a long pause.

I waited.

"Okay, okay." There was another pause. "Ya know, I really dislike you."

"Yeah, well you're not on my hit parade either. So speak up."

I was bluffing but hoped my voice didn't sound like it.

He hesitated. "Joyce." He sighed like I'd just flushed his pet goldfish. "Joyce Olson."

I knew Joyce. She was a nice woman. Smart, cute, good sense of humor. For the life of me I couldn't figure out what someone like Joyce would see in someone like Jack. *Ick!*

"Thanks, Jack. I gotta run now."

"Wait!"

"Can't, Jack, I really have a lot of people to see, things to do."

As I hung up I heard him yell into the phone, "If you make trouble for Joyce, I'll—"

I didn't need to hear the end of the sentence, I could imagine the gory threats. But I had the name—that was the important thing. I slapped my hand against the steering wheel in celebration, looked over my shoulder, changed lanes again, and continued east.

Somehow, it felt like I was nearing the finish line. I knew breaking the tape at the end wasn't going to be easy or without cost. I could only hope the price wasn't too high.

I'd arranged to meet Germaine in the parking lot near the west entrance of the college campus. She was going to expect an apology, so I needed to think of something worthy of her forgiveness.

The best tactic to take with Germaine was the truth. And since I hadn't used it much during the past couple of weeks, it would certainly be refreshing. Not only for Germaine—but for me too.

I took the Cretin exit and noticed Germaine's gas tank was low, so I pulled into a service station and filled it up.

When I finally drove into the parking lot, Germaine's hands were on her hips and a scowl covered her face. She did not look like the Welcome Wagon lady. I pulled up next to her, barely putting the car in park before she ripped open the door, plopped herself on the seat, and screamed with indignation. No one could do indignation like Germaine; not even Ma. And Ma was really good.

"Who do you think you are, Penelope Santucci? How dare you run off like that! You stole my car!"

My head hung low, I softly said, "I know, Germaine. There's no excuse for what I did and for how I've been behaving." Suddenly a rush of words and emotions gushed, like an overflowing creek bed.

I leaned back in the seat. "I've let this predicament cloud every decision, every thought, and it's caused you and everyone else a lot of suffering." I hung my head again in deep shame.

The first time was heartfelt, the second was for effect because, oh baby, she was hopping mad.

Germaine peered intently as I brushed away the beginning of a tear. "Whew! You know how to take the wind out of a girl's sail."

"Hey, I've been awful."

I peeked just in time to catch the corner of her mouth curling slowly up in a crazy half-smile. Then she shook her head and a tiny bubble that might almost be a giggle floated up from her throat.

Maybe I'd driven her over the edge—toppled her sanity once and for all.

She said, "Just when I get really mad, determined to give you a piece of my mind, leave you in the lurch, you find your conscience. At least, I think, part of that little scene was real."

I edged up in my seat, losing the remorseful sinner slump. "Does that mean you forgive me?"

She reached out and pinched my cheek. "You're my little sister, and you drive me crazy. Lately you've almost driven me to a jail cell. But I love you."

I smiled broadly and exclaimed, "There just might be something to telling the truth." I peered heavenward. "Thank you," I whispered.

She gave me a little push. "You might try it more often. It would probably save you a mountain of trouble." She added, "Now, get out of the driver's seat, and let's go. I want to hear more about what we're doing today." She smiled conspiratorially. "I want to make sure that there is no way we're going to get into any trouble."

I shook my head. "No way I can promise you that."

She nodded her understanding.

We exchanged seats, pulled out of the parking lot, and merged into traffic.

I spent most of the trip to Minneapolis telling her what I'd learned.

Of course when I say I told her the story, that doesn't mean I elected to share *everything*. For example, I didn't think she needed to hear about my little tussle with Stephanie or her broken cannolis. The basic facts were sufficient. Besides, Germaine wasn't angry anymore, and I wanted to keep it that way.

When we were about ten blocks from the Government Center, I told Germaine to find a gas station.

She looked at me, surprised. "You have to go now? You couldn't have gone before we left?"

"No, silly. I want to find a restroom so I can change my clothes."

She cocked her head to the side. "Change your clothes? Oh, the habit."

"Yeah, I don't want to be recognized. I'm supposed to be home, resting, remember?"

She grumbled, "It might be safer for all of us if you were."

I resisted several unsavory urges. "Funny, Germaine. Just find a station."

Germaine drove for a few minutes before she spotted a Holiday station and pulled into the parking lot.

As I got out of the car she quipped, "Sister Penelope, I'll wait here. Don't be long."

The urge to lift my middle finger skyward was overwhelming. I resisted. After all, I was about to become Sister Mary Theresa Penelope—beloved, saintly, bles—what the . . . ? Then I tripped in a pothole.

I recovered my balance, retrieved the restroom key from the manager, and made my way to the back of the station. I locked the door and placed my bag on the sink, careful not to get anything that I couldn't readily identify on Germaine's habit..

When I finished changing clothes, I looked in the grainy wall mirror. "Not bad, not bad at all."

I turned and drew Germaine's shoes out of the bag. They were a tight squeeze, but I could manage them for a little while. I picked up Germaine's rosary to finish accessorizing my outfit. I started to attach it to the loose belt around my waist while admiring its simple beauty. Bending over I tried to figure out how to affix it to my belt. I stepped forward and stumbled. Dratted shoes. I spun around, clutched at the wall for balance, and watched in slow motion as Germaine's rosary slipped from my fingers, finally plopping into the toilet bowl. "Ewww!" My hand instinctively reached down and then just as quickly pulled back.

In horror I peered into the toilet, pondering my dilemma. The bathroom was none too clean and the last thing I wanted to do was reach down and scoop the rosary out of what was possibly the dirtiest, most germ ridden place in all of the Twin Cities. I quickly searched for something that would allow me to fish it out without actually putting my hand inside the toilet bowl. Nothing.

I leaned against the wall and argued with myself. I could just leave it, but then Germaine's rosary, a gift from a nun who was very special to her and currently with God, would be lost. Not a good choice. And very selfish. The only other choice was to . . . I slowly reached into the germ infested pit and in one fell swoop snatched it from the jaws of the sewer system.

I turned the water spigot, squirted soap over the rosary, and scrubbed it and my hands as fast and as thoroughly as I could. When I was done I quickly attached it to my belt, still cringing and imagining all the diseases I might contract.

Closing my bag, I headed out the door and, as inconspicuously as I could, dropped the key on the counter and headed for the car whispering, "I know I'm crazy, God, but help me out here, will you? I need a miracle or two. Amen." I made the sign of the cross as I dipped my head. I'd seen that gesture in a lot of movies.

Just before I got to the car I looked down. I hadn't dried the rosary and as it flapped against the habit, I saw a wet spot grow larger. "Oh, no!"

I covered the spot with my hand vowing to never, ever tell Germaine where her precious rosary had been. I just wanted to live to see another day.

Germaine tried to be courteous when I got back into the car and didn't seem to notice the wet spot. She covered her mouth and coughed modestly, trying to stifle a laugh, no doubt.

I turned to her and said, "Don't think it. Don't say it. Just drive."

She laughed anyway. "Okay, sister."

I closed my eyes and sank back into the car seat.

CHAPTER THIRTY-FIVE

We parked the car and walked through the skyway to the Government Center. The shoes Germaine had lent me were a half size too small and were killing me.

At security-screening I surreptitiously looked around, praying no one would recognize me. The guard wasn't familiar, and I breathed easier. We placed our bags on the belt and walked through the line without setting off any warning bells.

The guard handed me my bag. "Here you go, Sister."

The temptation was too much. "Thank you, my son. And, God bless you." I smiled sweetly.

Germaine nudged me in the back with her elbow as she followed me to the elevator. "Stop snickering," I snapped, glancing around for familiar faces, and, in a calmer voice, added, "My child."

As we entered the elevator, I turned and gasped, "Oh, no!"

"What?" Germaine turned to me.

The two men who had broken into my condo were exiting the elevator directly across from us. The taller man must have recognized us. He nudged his partner and pointed. Our elevator doors closed with the swiftness of your great granny shuffling across a football field.

"Oh, sweet Jesus." I punched the close button again, and then quickly punched it three or four or maybe six times more.

Germaine saw the two goons, and her eyes widened. Jumping up and down like a jack-in-the-box she screamed, "Close the doors! Close the doors!"

I hammered at the CLOSE button as one of the men reached out to wedge his hand inside. Germaine tried to squeeze the doors shut faster—like she was Hercules or something. Fortunately, just then the doors shut tight. I hit the button for the eleventh floor.

"Dear, dear God." Germaine's mumbled prayers were soft and hurried.

"Pray harder, Germaine. Faster!"

It was several seconds before either of us spoke.

My heart raced. "Can you believe that?"

Germaine repeatedly punched her chest as she made the sign of the cross and shrieked, "How could this have happened?"

I leaned wearily into the back wall of the elevator as we whooshed skyward. "I don't know. Well, maybe I do. They're criminals. Maybe they were in court for something else and just happened to be leaving as we arrived."

Germaine's hands were in a vise-lock, one with the other. "Pen, coincidences like that only happen in movies."

My hands flailed. "Do you see any cameras, Germaine? This is not a movie. Ashton Kutcher is not here yelling, 'You've been punked!' This is for real."

I scanned the elevator buttons. No stops so far. It wasn't the end of the work day. People wouldn't completely clear out for a half hour or so. At best, stopping along the way was a crap shoot. I punched a button just as the elevator stopped at our floor.

"What's the matter now?" Germaine paced the small cubicle.

"This elevator didn't stop. If they're watching the board downstairs they know which floor we got off on."

Germaine's face drained and she stumbled against the elevator wall, clutching at her chest. "They're gonna kill us aren't they? We're dead meat."

I put both hands on her shoulders and shook her. "They're not going to kill us. They won't know whether we went to the clerk's office or a courtroom or walked across the bridge to the Administration tower."

Her wide eyes were filled with terror. "You don't know that for sure."

The doors opened. I grabbed her arm, and she followed me off the elevator. "Get a hold of yourself. They have too many choices. They won't find us."

Germaine faced me, her face contorted in rage. "You promised nothing would happen!"

I tugged at her arm again. "Germaine, stop it. Don't draw attention to us."

She shook free and hissed, "Look around, Pen. There isn't anyone here. It's almost the end of the work day. A lot of people have probably left already."

I started for the clerk's office. "We'll talk to Joyce and then clear out of here, pronto."

Germaine's chest was pumping like a treadle sewing machine, but finally she shook her head in defeat.

I was pretty scared too, but it wasn't the time to let her know that. I was almost afraid to let me know. It wouldn't take much to turn around and run like a mad woman for St. Paul and the safety of the convent.

I took a deep breath, then grabbed Germaine's hand. "Come on. Let's get this over with."

She shook free from my grasp but continued to follow me to the Clerk's office where Joyce Olson worked. Before I pulled open the door, Germaine put her hand over mine and asked, "You know this woman, right."

"Yes, I know her."

Germaine took her hand from mine and began wringing hers. "Isn't she going to think you're crazy showing up here in that?"

She pointed at my habit.

I followed her gaze down the length of black cloth all the way to the too-tight shoes. "I didn't think about that."

"You don't think about a lot of things."

I let it pass. She was entitled. "Too late to worry about trivialities."

She muttered something I'd rather ignore as I pulled open the double door and looked in. There wasn't anyone around. Good for us.

I strode in with Germaine trailing about five paces behind me and sauntered to the counter. As I was about to ring the bell, Joyce walked out of the copier room. She stiffened like a fresh corpse when she saw me. I leaned toward Germaine and whispered, "Looks like Jack's already talked to her."

Germaine shrugged. "And you're the last person she wants to see."

"You got that right."

I boldly leaned over the counter and said quietly, "Joyce, we have to talk."

She hesitated. "Jack told me you'd come here. I hoped he was wrong."

She must have been in agony. I'd be as kind as I could. "I know this is hard. And I know I stepped on Jack's toes. Don't blame him. I forced him to tell me about you."

Lips pursed she spat out, "I could lose my job."

"No one is going to lose her job. I just need some information. Can you get it for me?"

Joyce silently stared at a blank spot on the floor.

I waited, and when she didn't respond I said, "I don't want you to go to jail. But you can understand, I don't want to go either. I'll do everything I can to keep your name out of it."

Her eyes traveled slowly from the floor to my face. "Why are you in a nun's habit?"

I straightened my head dress, or whatever it's called. "It's a long story. I'll tell you about it someday. That is if you're still talking to me. But right now, my sister and I," I turned and gestured at Germaine, "are in a really big hurry." There was no way that I was going to freak her out further and tell her there were some bad dudes in the building and they were looking for us to "make their day."

Joyce walked to a desk near the window. Over her shoulder she said, "I guess I knew you'd come."

She leaned over the desk, fished through some papers, picked up a manila file, and walked back to the counter and looked around before she thrust the file at me, looking like a whipped dog. "It's all in here."

Wow! That was easy. Surprised, I peered at Joyce who looked as if she was going to dissolve into tears.

I pulled the file to my chest and breathlessly said, "Oh, Joyce. Thank you! You don't know how much this means to me."

"Your freedom maybe? Now go. You've got what you wanted."

I reached across the desk for her hand, just as she withdrew it. "I'm sorry Joyce."

I looked at Germaine, nodded slightly, and we turned toward the door. I couldn't help myself—I had to see what was in the file. As Germaine opened the door, I opened the file and couldn't believe what I saw.

I stared at the contents, my hands shaking, my head whirling. Why? My mind clicked into overtime, and I remembered something I'd heard before Paul's death. His father talked about his adoption and how it affected him, and the judge said he'd made enemies. Could the two be related? Suddenly little pieces of nothing started falling into place like dominos.

I stood stock still in the doorway, gripping the folder so tight my fingernails dug into the paper. It couldn't be. And yet, it was the only plausible explanation.

Germaine grabbed my arm. "Come on, Pen. We've got to get out of here. There are a couple of bad men looking to break our legs."

I shook her off. "Wait. I'm thinking."

She rocked back on her heels, crossed her arms across her chest and announced, "If you don't come with me right now, I'm leaving you here alone."

Without answering her, I turned and rushed back to the counter.

Joyce stepped back. "I gave you the information, Pen. Please leave."

"I know. But I need one more thing. And it's a big thing."

Joyce looked dejected. "Pen!"

"I need you to make a call."

She covered her eyes with her hands. "No."

"You don't even know who I want you to call."

Joyce pointed at me. "Look, I've always liked you, but I can't do anything more."

I whined. "Just one more thing. Then I'll leave you alone, I promise."

Joyce stood at the counter, and I reached across and grabbed her arm before she could remove it. Another clerk walked out of the office. I withdrew my arm, and Joyce dropped hers to her side.

The clerk didn't seem to have noticed anything strange, and I looked away so she wouldn't recognize me as she waved to Joyce, " 'Night. See you in the morning."

Joyce grunted, "Good night."

Germaine's loud intake of breath exploded into the silent room. I hoped she wouldn't faint or bolt because I didn't have the time to take care of her.

When the door closed I leaned over. "Don't make me choose between my freedom and yours."

Joyce looked beaten. "What do you want me to do?"

"You know most of the clerks, right?" I grabbed a stray pen and paper from the counter and began frantically scribbling. "This is where I want you to call and the information I need. Tell me you know someone there."

She glanced at the paper and then back at me, "I don't understand."

"Just answer me—do you know someone?"

She slowly nodded.

"Then call."

"She won't give me the information. It's sealed."

"But she can get it?"

Joyce reluctantly nodded. "But it's like, breaking the law."

"I understand. Then call and ask. Tell her whatever it takes to get her to give up the information. Tell her it means the difference between life and death."

Joyce's eyes darted from the paper to me.

"My life or death—I'm begging."

Joyce sucked her breath in and walked to the phone.

Germaine stepped toward me and said, "What is all this about, Pen."

"Shhh. I'll know in just a minute."

Germaine leaned into me, "Tell me!"

I turned and looked hard at her. "I can't. Just pray that Joyce's friend hasn't left work yet."

My head snapped toward the sound of Joyce's voice. I couldn't hear what she said she was speaking so low. I leaned as far over the counter as I could, straining to hear bits and pieces.

Occasionally Joyce's voice raised, and it sounded like she was pleading. Then whispers.

Germaine pinched at my elbow. "What is this all about?"

I reached back waving my hand. "Not now!"

She must have realized how serious I was because she took a

step backward.

My attention reverted to Joyce. I distinctly saw her wipe away a tear. Then magically a smile spread across her face. She looked at me and gave me a thumbs-up sign as she hung up the phone.

"I can't believe that worked. Or that I could get the information so fast. This was a sealed file. Says something about the world and computers, if you have the right password." Joyce exclaimed as she wrote the information on a card, walked to the counter, and handed it to me.

Germaine nuzzled up behind me and peered over my shoulder as I read it. I cocked my head to the side, and we stared at each other.

Germaine expelled ragged breaths and shook her head. "Is this true? Are you sure?"

Joyce nodded. "Yes, I'm sure. Hard to believe isn't it?"

This time when I reached across the counter and took her hand, she didn't pull away. "Joyce, I know how dearly this cost you. I am so grateful. I'll never forget this."

Joyce lowered her head. "If you want to thank me don't tell anyone. I just broke the law, and my friend could get into trouble, too."

Giving her hand a squeeze, I assured her, "They can pull out my fingernails. I won't tell."

"Thanks," she mumbled.

Looking from the card in my hand and then back at Joyce I said, "Joyce, there's one more thing."

The blood drained from her face. "No more, Pen, I can't."

I smiled. "All I want is for you to keep this information to yourself."

The look of relief was evident on her face. "Oh, I'm not telling anyone anything."

"Good. Is the judge still in?"

Panic covered Joyce's face. "You're not going in there?"

Without thinking I crossed myself. My nun's habit must have switched me to auto pilot. "I have to. If I'm going to keep your name out of it, it's the only way."

Joyce sniffled and nodded her head. "The judge is in, I think."

"Good. You leave now, and no one will have to know that you were here."

At that moment two judges and their clerks rounded the corner, gave a wave to Joyce as I hid my face to prevent them from seeing me.

Just then, the real nun among us chimed in, "Pen, we have to get out of here. Remember, the bad guys are looking for us."

I glanced up at the clock, hanging high on the wall. "We've been here less than fifteen minutes. If they haven't found us now, they won't. The judge is here. It's now or never."

CHAPTER THIRTY-SIX

As we passed each open doorway, I quickly glanced in, hoping Joyce was right about the staff being gone for the day. I didn't want any observers when I confronted the judge.

I skidded to a stop at the door, paused, drew in a deep breath, and entered the office.

"Judge," I said more calmly than I felt.

Judge Eloise Hunter looked up from her desk, placed her pen on the desktop, and said, "Pen, what are you doing here? And why are you wearing that get-up?"

I'd forgotten. I must look like I was on my way to a Halloween party. "It's a long story," I sputtered.

She looked over my right shoulder. "And I see you brought your sister along. Again."

Germaine waved weakly at the judge. Judge Hunter nodded slightly. "Well, are you going to tell me why you're here?"

I dragged Germaine further into the room and quickly closed the door.

"What's going on here?" Judge Hunter stood.

I clutched the rosary hanging from my waist and fingered the beads. "We need to talk."

She glanced at her watch and shook her head. "I have an appointment soon. I really don't have the—"

I stepped closer to her desk. "Your appointment is going to have to wait."

Behind me, Germaine gasped.

I shot her a *clam-it-up, sister* glare from over my shoulder and turned my attention back to the judge. "Like I said, we have some unfinished business."

Judge Hunter strode from behind her desk and stopped just to its left. She casually placed her hand on the corner and said, "Penelope Santucci, I don't like your tone. Probation officers don't tell me what to do, I tell them."

I shifted my weight from one foot to the other. "Well, this time I'm telling you."

Germaine gasped and said, "Stop it, Pen. There are other ways to do this."

I didn't bother turning around. "Germaine, stay out of this. This is between me and Judge Hunter."

"Pen, if you don't leave now, I'm going to call security," said the judge.

"Go ahead. I think they'll be quite interested in my story. So will the police."

She took several steps back and sat in her chair. Her eyes flashed rage. "How dare you!"

"You heard me. The police. Go ahead and call. I have information that I think they will be interested in. Because I know you killed Paul."

At that point both women gasped. The room fell silent, and I waited, not daring to look at my sister. I was stepping out on a limb, but with the information I'd just received from Joyce, I was positive I had the killer. And if I didn't, well I could kiss my job good-bye. If I was wrong I'd be waiting tables to support myself, but if I was right and didn't follow through with my suspicions, I could find myself being served meals three times a day in prison. It was worth the gamble.

Germaine reached out for me. "Pen, this is crazy."

The judge didn't miss a beat. "Yes, Pen, this is crazy."

Pursing my lips I stepped forward one step and replied, "No,

Judge Hunter. You killed Paul. I'm not sure of the sequence of events, but I know you killed him."

Judge Hunter's weak smile spoke volumes. "Perhaps you'd like to tell us all what you think you know."

I sauntered to a chair in front of her desk and dropped into it. Germaine didn't move a muscle. She continued to stand like a statue just inside the closed office door.

I started twirling the rosary hanging from my waist as I started my story. "I really thought Judge Kassner killed Paul. But I just couldn't find anything that supported my theory."

Out of the corner of my eye, I saw Germaine listing to and fro like a boat rocking on the ocean. She was making me nervous. "Germaine, for pete's sake, sit down." I pointed to the chair next to me. She meekly walked over and sat down.

My attention returned to the judge who hadn't moved in the thirty seconds since she'd last spoken.

I continued, "I've been running around town trying to keep my sorry ass out of jail, looking at anyone and everyone who had a motive to kill Paul. And let me tell you, there are quite a few folks who wanted to do away with my ex."

The judge nodded, and Germaine sat in breathless silence.

"Actually, I overheard you tell Astrid, at Paul's funeral, that Paul had enemies that might want to kill him."

Judge Hunter sat up straight. "I'd had too much to drink. You can't use anything I said—"

I threw out my hand to stop her. "Forget it. I overheard you."

"Besides, a few slurred comments certainly don't mean I killed him."

I shifted my position in the uncomfortable chair. "No, of course not. But after a lot of running around and talking to people, I found out something today."

"And what was that?" Judge Hunter sneered as she crossed her arms over her chest.

My mouth suddenly went dry. I licked my lips and continued, "I knew Paul had fallen in with his criminal clients. He always wanted to be rich, and I think he decided to take some shortcuts. He was taking money from clients who wanted a sure thing in court."

"Interesting, Pen, but that still doesn't connect me to his murder."

I put my hand up again to stop her. "I'm getting to that. Paul needed a judge to fix court cases, and that judge is you."

Her back stiffened, and Germaine's breathing was so loud it could probably be heard in the clerk's office down the hall.

I licked my lips. "He had something on you. Something big. So big that you were willing to sell your court decisions."

"How dare you suggest I would do something criminal. This is completely absurd. I'm going to stop—"

"I dare because it's true. I have a list of court cases that should have been slam-dunks for the county, but they weren't. They all went Paul's way. And you know what?"

Silence filled the room for a few seconds before the judge hissed, "And what is that?"

"All the slam-dunk cases appeared before you."

Judge Hunter turned a little pale, but her voice was strong when she said, "Coincidence."

"I don't think so. Paul was blackmailing you."

She stiffened. "That's preposterous."

"No, it isn't. Let me tell you the abbreviated story. Paul learned that he was adopted."

A small moan escaped from the judge. "Pen, stop all of this. Right now! You have to leave."

I never was good at taking orders from authority figures. I kept going. "It's no secret that you're awaiting a nomination to the Minnesota Supreme Court. You wouldn't want anything to interfere with that. You've worked too long and too hard to lose something as precious as an appointment to the highest bench in Minnesota."

"I won't hear any more of this!" The judge stood suddenly.

Germaine and I flinched. "Unless you want me to call the police myself, you'll hear me out."

She paused, didn't sit in her chair, but on the edge of the desk. It would do in a pinch.

"Now, I don't know the entire story, but the way I see it, when you were a young woman you made a mistake. And that mistake resulted in the birth of a baby."

Germaine started. "Pen!"

"Shush, Germaine." I continued, "And that baby was Paul. You put him up for adoption, but somehow he found out. It wasn't difficult because it only took me a matter of a few minutes to learn you were his birth mother."

The judge's face filled with rage. "You have no right!"

"I do have a right. You killed Paul because he was blackmailing you, and I could go to prison for it."

She turned scarlet and shook like one of Ma's strawberry Jell-O molds. She stumbled back behind her desk and dropped into her chair, holding her head in her hands.

"There's something more there, I just don't know what it is. But there must be something. I don't think having a child without a husband is enough to squash your aspirations to the Supreme Court."

Judge Hunter look at me like I was a bug she wanted to squash. "You have no idea."

She yanked open her desk drawer, drew out a handgun, and pointed it at my chest. "I don't know how you found this all out, but I'm not going to allow you to kill my career."

Germaine screeched like a hen laying an ostrich egg. The terror on her face probably mirrored mine.

Judge Hunter slowly rose from her chair, holding the gun on us.

A gun? Who thought there would be a gun in the Government Center offices. What to do, what to do? I didn't think the time was right to point out that she was the one who killed her career when she murdered Paul.

"Judge Hunter, if you kill us here, there's going to be a very loud noise and a lot of blood. People will find out because the mess alone will be a big clue. Oh, and I doubt if it will help your career any, either."

She skirted her desk, hugged the wall, and shook the gun at us. "I'm not going to kill you here. Get up. We're leaving."

Germaine said, "Huh?"

"Get up!"

"Do you really think you're going to just casually walk out of this office and nobody's going to notice that you're holding a gun on us. And me a nun." I was really working those rosary beads now, "Hail, Mary, Mother, full of grace, or whatever . . ."

"You're not a nun."

Duh!

"Now, get going unless you want to die right here."

"I don't want to die at all!" Germaine was muttering real nun prayers and crossing herself repeatedly.

"I said, get up."

Despite my usual disobedient tendencies, I complied. She was, after all, an authority figure with a gun. "Okay, at least give me the satisfaction of knowing the truth. You killed him, didn't you?"

She continued her slow walk to the door. "Yes, I killed the bastard. He was going to ruin my career. Everything that I worked a lifetime for. Gone. My own son." She laughed a cold, sad laugh. "Move it."

We moved.

Waving the gun, she directed us toward the door.

I needed to stall. Gain some time to think about how we were going to get out of this. Somehow I didn't see God intervening. We were on our own. "But why? I just don't see how having a child would kill your career."

She blew out a curt gust of air. "It wasn't just the kid. He found out about the drugs and theft charges. Everything together, that would have destroyed my career."

She reached for the door handle and just as she pulled it open, two men burst in, knocking Judge Hunter to the ground and the gun from her hand.

Germaine squeaked. And I think she nearly laid an ostrich egg, for real. "We're gonna die!"

The two goons saw the gun fly and made for it at the same time I did.

Unfortunately, when I made my dive for the gun, I tripped over the hem of my habit and went head over heels onto the floor. The skirt twisted around my waist like a crazy rubber band. Thankfully, I'd listened to Ma's ranting about clean underwear and emergencies.

Germaine yelled, "Get the gun, Pen."

I wiggled like a worm across the carpet, but the skirt of my habit didn't make it easy and the rug burns stung like the dickens. One of the thugs took a swan dive, made contact with my ankle, and twisted. "Owww!"

I rolled onto my side and gave him a hard kick in the chest with my other foot. The impact was enough to free my leg. I rolled again, tore off my headdress, wimple, or whatever it's called, and shoved it over his head as he made for my throat. He fumbled with the fabric while I slithered on my stomach toward the gun.

Germaine was involved in her own brawl. She felled the other goon with a sharp chop to his neck, turned, and dove for the gun too. We were within inches of it when Judge Hunter's foot jerked outward and knocked it out of our range. "No!" We both yelled.

The gun tumbled across the floor like a roulette wheel marble with everyone scrambling after it, hoping to be the big winner of the day.

One of the thugs clambered over me trying to reach the gun while the other did a belly flop on top of Judge Hunter. Well at least *she* wasn't going to be shooting anyone soon. Germaine, well, Germaine caught the heel of her shoe in my skirt hem and was trying to untangle herself.

I couldn't shake my attacker, but my belt had come undone and was on the floor next to me. Without thinking I snatched the rosary while he tried to squeeze the life out of me. Instinctively I thrust my elbows out, broke his grip, circled his neck with the chain, and pulled. I hoped God's wrath wouldn't be visited upon me for using the rosary as a garrote.

His face reddened, and I gave the chain another tug. It snapped. Tiny beads sailed around the room, ricocheting off every surface, eventually peppering the floor with Germaine's beloved prayer counter. This was not good.

There wasn't time to think about Germaine's take on the demise of her rosary. The thug I'd tried to strangle with God's necklace threw himself on top of me, pinning me down as he increased the pressure of his fingers on my neck. Yup, he was choking me to death.

My struggle to breathe intensified, and as the room turned to black, I knew I would die in a judge's chambers, in a nun's habit shoved up around my waist, my multi-colored polka dot panties shouting to the world; alas, she is dead but she had a sense of humor. The Trib would have a field day with my demise.

As I lost consciousness I heard a noise coming from outside.

My last thought before dying was, what the heck is going on? Even in death I wanted to be in the know.

CHAPTER THIRTY-SEVEN

I didn't die.

When I came to I was lying prone on the floor with the habit up around my chin. I couldn't have been out for more than a few seconds because the chaos around me continued.

Judge Hunter wasn't moving, and a trickle of blood oozed from her forehead. I hoped she was only unconscious and not dead. Unconscious I could handle; dead was too permanent. The paperweight by her side must have been the culprit.

It was Germaine's predicament that made my heart leap into my throat. The two goons had her cornered and were pummeling her. Her martial arts training kept them at bay, but they were winning.

She kicked at one, and the other snatched her leg and pulled. She flopped to the floor, and both men were on her immediately. The one called Danny had her by the throat.

Everything blurred, and the room started spinning. My sister was being murdered because of me. Everything slowed down as I realized that my desire for freedom was going to cost the person I loved the most, to lose her life. Just because of my impetuousness.

If it was the last thing I ever did, I would not let my sister die because I hadn't thought beyond my personal freedom.

I eyed the gun lying on the floor between me and the thugs. My heart raced, beads of perspiration dripped from my face, my body ached in places I didn't know it could. There wasn't time to think. I heaved myself toward the gun at the same time Danny dove for it. He reached it first and pointed it at Germaine while talking to me. "Don't move, or I'll shoot her."

The blood drained from Germaine's face. Lloyd backed around Judge Hunter's desk. Danny beckoned to Germaine. "Come here."

She began shaking.

I got up slowly.

"Come here. Now!" he ordered.

Germaine took a tiny step toward him.

"Danny, you don't want to do this."

He swung the gun toward me. "Shut up. It's because of you that I have to do this."

The terror on Germaine's face broke my heart. I couldn't let him take her. "Danny, please. Your boss won't like it if you kill me. You don't have his money, and I know where it is."

The noise I'd heard a few seconds earlier grew louder. It was just enough of a distraction that he turned toward the door.

I'd put Germaine in the middle of my problem, and I couldn't let him hurt her or kill her because of it.

I lunged for Danny, gave his arm a twist, throwing it upward. The gun went off and flew from his hand. "Run, Germaine!"

She didn't need coaxing. As she fled for the door, I dove for the gun, snatched it up, rolled, and pointed it at him. "Make my day!" Oh, lord, I'd just been transported into a Clint Eastwood movie.

Germaine fled as two cops, guns drawn, entered, followed by Marco and Jack. I started giggling uncontrollably and collapsed on the floor, the gun clutched tightly in my hands.

"Everyone stay where you are. Drop that gun," the first cop ordered.

Two pairs of hands reached for the sky.

I was still laughing uncontrollably as the room darkened then filled up with light. I'd died and gone where? Heaven? Hell? Either would be a surprise. I hate surprises.

"Pen, let go. Give me the gun."

"What?" I wasn't going to give up the gun. It was my ticket to safety. I pried open my eyes. Germaine and Marco peered down at me.

I tried to speak but nothing came out. I struggled to sit up, but Germaine restrained me. "Give Marco the gun, Pen."

I glanced at where the ugly piece of metal was welded to my hand. "No, I . . ."

Marco, concern etched on his face, carefully peeled my fingers open, pried the gun from my grip, and handed it to the cop standing behind him. "Here, take this."

The officer took it.

I tried to sit up again. "Don't move just yet," Marco ordered.

My head began clearing, and I remembered the fight and the goon who'd tried to kill us. Literally.

I cleared my throat and croaked, "What happened?"

Germaine stroked my forehead and said, "Lie still; the paramedics will be here in a minute."

I tried to sit up again. "No! No medics, no doctors, no hospital."

Marco gently pushed me down. It seems our entire relationship consisted of him trying to control me in some way. I made a mental note to discuss it with him.

Marco said, "Pen, you have to be looked at by medical personnel."

"What happened?" My voice was a scratchy whisper.

Marco firmly said, "Be still."

Germaine had tears in her eyes. "You saved my life, Pen."

I attempted to nod, but it made my head ring. Limply, I held up my hand, attempted to point at Marco and wheezed, "How did you get here?"

Just then someone called Marco's name, but without turning away from me, he mumbled, "Just a minute. I'll answer all your questions, Pen, but right now the police want me."

That got my attention. "The police?"

Germaine leaned closer, "Don't try to talk."

There was a lot of commotion, and I had to know what was going on. "Germaine," I squeaked, disregarding orders as usual and issuing one of my own. "Tell me everything."

"Shhh."

"Are you okay? He was going to kill you. I couldn't let him kill you. It's all my fault."

She began stroking my head again. "No, you saved my life."

I grunted.

"After you held the gun on them, the police came in and took over. You passed out again, probably from the lack of oxygen earlier and shock." Germaine laughed and scooted her body closer to my head. "I think Danny and Lloyd were almost more afraid of you swinging the gun around than they were of the cops."

I wheezed. "Help me sit up. I'm feeling better."

Marco returned and knelt down beside me. "No. You have to stay still until the paramedics look at you."

I began to protest when Marco interrupted, "Pen, just this once, could you please do as you're told. It's just to make sure there's no permanent damage."

I closed my eyes. I could live with that. "Explain how you got here."

Marco told us he'd spotted Germaine and a nun getting into the elevator as he was leaving the Government Center. He also saw two men trying to force their way in. He deduced it was me in the nun's habit and realized we were in trouble. "I ran to the security office, told them to call the police, and ran back to the elevators. But I didn't know where you had gone."

Germaine looked from me to Marco. "How did you find us?"

Marco explained, "I was frantic. I guessed the only reason for the two of you to be in the building and Pen dressed in that get-up . . ." He paused, almost involuntarily, and took a good long look at my twisted up habit—too long a look. Hey, I don't see how he could be thinking what I look like under this big ol' thing, never mind that it was hiked up to the top of my thighs. There was enough fabric to build a tent, even so . . .

My cheeks grew hot and probably turned red. "I—"

"Quiet." Germaine patted my hand. "Let him talk."

Marco nodded and continued, "I knew you must have found out something that led you to the judge you kept talking about. I was about to go to the elevators when Jack walked up. He was on his cell phone."

"Jack?" Germaine asked.

He nodded. "He told me you were here. His friend Joyce was on the phone."

Imagine that! Jack came to my rescue. I still didn't like him, but maybe I'd cut him some slack in the future. After all, he probably saved my life. And that was worth something.

A new level of chaos cut Marco's story short. Two paramedics arrived and began working on me. I figured if I cooperated they'd do what they had to do and then leave me alone. I tried to talk.

The tall blond, probably named Sven, commanded, "Be still, please."

"I want to . . ."

"Be still," he ordered, not too nicely, I should add.

Marco said, "She just wants to know what happened. It'll be easier for all of us if you don't tangle with her."

As Herr Sven placed a blood pressure cuff around my arm he conceded to Marco, "You can talk. She can't."

Marco started in on his story again. "Jack said Joyce left the office, and the two goons who tried to kill you accosted her."

Germaine gasped.

Marco turned his attention to her and said, "They dragged her into the restroom and questioned her. She told Jack that when she wouldn't answer their questions, they hit her and she fell and hit her head on the sink."

Germaine said, "Oh, that poor woman."

My heart dropped. Because of me, Joyce might have been killed. "Is—"

"Shhh!" Herr Sven, The Terminator, pumped the BP cuff so tight blood started to back up in my brain.

Germaine said, "Go on, Marco."

"They hit her again, so she told them you were in Judge Hunter's chambers. Told them how to get there. Then they gave her a shove, and she fell against the wall and hit her head again. She thinks she was knocked out for a few minutes."

Germaine put her hand over her heart and began mumbling her traditional prayers for when trouble makes a visit. I glared at her before I lost sight of her face as the other paramedic leaned between us blocking my sight line and placed a stethoscope over my heart and then took my pulse.

Marco continued, "When she came to, she called Jack. The rest is history."

The paramedic said, "We're going to have you sit up now."

What a relief. This lying on the floor and carrying on a conversation was uncomfortable. The two paramedics got on either side of me and slowly helped me to a sitting position.

The other guy asked, "How are you feeling? Are you dizzy at all?"

Dizzy? The world was spinning, and I was at the center. But I'd die before I'd tell them. "No," I answered, holding my head as still as possible. They helped me to the chair, and I sank into it, resting my elbow on the arm and my head on my hand.

Germaine tugged on Sven's sleeve, "I'm her sister. Is she okay?"

He glanced at Germaine like she was a foreigner and shrugged, "Yeah, but she's going to hurt for awhile. And talking is going to be difficult."

Duh! I thought. My voice sounded like I'd been smoking cigars for forty years.

Concern filled Germaine's eyes. "Should she go to the hospital?"

How could she do that to me? "No!" I squeaked.

"I just want to do what's best for you."

Sven closed his bag. "No. She should just take it easy for a few days. If her throat continues to be sore, she should see her doctor."

With that pronouncement the medics packed up their bags and left, but the cops filled in where they left off.

Their leader, Detective Masters, stood fuming in the center of the room.

So, Detective, we finally meet again, at the scene of my would-be death. I'll bet he wishes Danny had been successful. The way I felt, I wished he'd been successful.

Masters asked Marco, "Can she talk?"

No! I've had a near death experience and he wants to talk. I don't ever want to talk to the cops again. Especially him.

Marco came to my rescue. "You can talk to her tomorrow."

My knight without a white horse.

Master's sputtered, "We have to take care of this now."

Marco took a step toward Masters, planted his feet firmly on the very floor I'd almost met my maker on. "Detective Masters. These women have had a traumatic afternoon. The questioning will wait. You've got the basics, and it's enough for now. You've got the judge and the thugs. They can give you the information about their boss. If they talk. The rest can wait."

"But . . ."

A second man placed his hand on Masters' arm and said, "It can wait."

Masters face reddened, and he turned and marched from the room. I could just picture Booger as a child. He lost, so he was going to take his bat and ball and go home.

Then it hit me. Judge Hunter? Alive *and* arrested? I was a free woman? No stripes! No bad food, no Big Bertha! If I could have yelled I would have.

Instead I motioned Marco to come closer. He kneeled down in front of me. "Take it easy. You need to rest your voice."

I hacked a couple of times and then whispered, "I'm free? They arrested the judge?"

Germaine joined Marco on the floor in front of me. It looked like communion. I was tempted to make the sign of the cross and bless them both. "Yes. I told the police that Judge Hunter confessed. And that you got the gun and held it on Lloyd and Danny after they'd beat the hell out of us."

Both Marco and I whipped our heads around and stared at Germaine. Her hands fanned the air, "Well, three people tried to snuff us out. I think I'm allowed one small curse word."

Marco chuckled, but when I laughed it sounded more like a dying rooster.

Marco stood and said to Germaine, "Let's get our girl home and into bed."

I couldn't wait.

Marco drove us to my condo. Germaine planned to pick her car up the next day. Marco let me know he'd pick me up in the afternoon and take me to the police station where I would talk to the detectives, whereupon, hopefully, Judge Hunter would start her life of bed and board compliments of the State of Minnesota. A far cry from sitting on the Supreme Court of Minnesota.

I meekly waved goodbye to the best attorney in the world and let my bossy older sister minister to the cut above my head. She was probably dumping holy water into it, but I didn't care.

Life was good.

While Germaine saw to my wound, I noticed my answering machine blinking. Without thinking I reached over and hit play.

"Penelope Santucci, this is your mother! Where are you? Your father and I have been worr—"

Before she could finish, I hit delete. I still didn't want my mother.

EPILOGUE

I slowly trudged up the stone steps of St. Alphonse, making sure I didn't stumble and fall. My battered body couldn't take as much as a slip at this point.

I heaved open the big wooden doors and peered into the semidarkness. It didn't look any different today than it had when I was a child. Some things never change.

A woman walked out of the small confessional, so I picked up my pace. I didn't want anyone getting ahead of me. I grabbed the door handle before an elderly man who'd probably been waiting a good bit could reach it. Tough. I was on a mission, and even if he was eighty years old, I was the one who looked like I might expire at any moment, and the way my head felt, I just might.

I opened the door, sat down gingerly so as to not bruise anything else. When I tried to speak the temporary damage done to my vocal cords made me sound like the godfather.

I cleared my throat and rasped, "Forgive me, Father, for I have sinned. It's been two weeks since my last confession." I didn't bother to add the words "and four days and two hours." It wouldn't make a difference. I still wasn't a Catholic.

"May the Lord be on your lips and on your mind and in your heart."

The long pause that followed obviously meant it was my turn to spill the beans. "I have a whole lot of sinning to cover, Father."

"Just start where you'd like, my child."

"Well, it's been a tough couple of weeks." I coughed and tried to find some part of my old voice.

"Continue."

"Well, I haven't kept the Sabbath in years. I've committed several burglaries and involved a priest and a nun in my distorted journey to prove my innocence in a murder. And—"

"Penelope, is that you?"

Like I always say, nothing's lost on this old fox.

"Yes, Father Daniel."

"What are you doing here?"

Good question. This was where I needed to be, wanted to be. Tears of relief and gratitude spilled from my eyes.. "It's over Father. They have Paul's murderer. I found the murderer."

"Oh, Pen." I could tell he was shaking his head. "How?"

I grinned. "Elementary, my Dear Father Daniel. I had people who believed in me and helped me, even when in peril themselves. When I finally found the one piece of information I needed, I just knew it was the butler in the dining room with the candlestick."

The old priest laughed heartily and slapped shut the screen. I heard the door on the other side of the compartment close.

There was a sharp rap on the confessional door, and I slowly sat upright. "I'm coming."

I dragged myself to a standing position, threw my shoulders back, plastered a broad smile on my face, yanked open the confessional door, and said happily, "Hello, Father Daniel. Long time, no see," and fell into the old priests arms.

He hugged me and said, "There's still the matter of the money, Pen."

God's warrior wasn't going to let it go. I suspected he'd already found a good cause for it.

ABOUT THE AUTHOR

Andrea Sisco and her husband, Bob Pike, travel extensively. They reside in Minnesota during the summer months and Arizona during the winter.

Andrea has had an eclectic career as a probation officer, television host, flight attendant, book reviewer, and adoption activist.

The charge that the character of Penelope Santucci is autobiographical is only partially true. It is true, however, that her husband consented to his murder, but only if it took place on the pages of a book. She has kept her promise.

Andrea is the co-founder of www.armchairinterviews.com, a Web site that reviews books and interviews authors. *A Deadly Habit* is her first mystery. She is currently coauthoring a Young Adult Fantasy series. Her Web site is www.andreasisco.com.